RESIDENT EVIL: RETRIBUTION

THE OFFICIAL MOVIE NOVELIZATION

RESIDENT EVIL: RETRIBUTION

SCREENPLAY BY PAUL W. S. ANDERSON
BASED ON CAPCOM'S VIDEOGAME RESIDENT EVIL
NOVELIZATION BY JOHN SHIRLEY

TITAN BOOKS

RESIDENT EVIL: RETRIBUTION
Print edition ISBN: 9781781163153
E-book edition ISBN: 9781781163160

Published by Titan Books
A division of Titan Publishing Group Ltd
144 Southwark Street, London SE1 0UP

First edition September 2012
1 3 5 7 9 10 8 6 4 2

Resident Evil: Retribution © 2012 Constantin Film International
GmbH and Davis Films/Impact Pictures (RE5) Inc.

Motion Picture Artwork © 2012 Columbia TriStar Marketing
Group, Inc. All Rights Reserved.

A CIP catalogue record for this title is available
from the British Library.

Printed and bound in Great Britain by CPI Group Ltd.

Did you enjoy this book? We love to hear from our readers.
Please email us at readerfeedback@titanemail.com or write to
us at Reader Feedback at the above address.

To receive advance information, news, competitions, and
exclusive offers online, please sign up for the Titan newsletter
on our website: **www.titanbooks.com**

DEDICATED TO FANS OF RESIDENT EVIL,
IN ALL ITS MANIFESTATIONS

RESIDENT EVIL: RETRIBUTION

AUTHOR'S NOTE

This novel is based on Mr. Paul W.S. Anderson's script for *Resident Evil: Retribution*, which I had a lot of fun reading and adapting. Everything in the screenplay is dramatized in the novelization. All the dialogue in the script is found in the novel, too. Other dialogue, of course, has been invented for the novel. A novel requires legroom, and stretching out, and there are scenes and characters and even a subplot not found in the film—but they are all *inspired* by the screenplay; by settings, ideas, events and character types found in the screenplay. And the film's continuity is very much the overriding structure of this novelization.

So far as I'm aware, nothing in the novel contradicts the film.

And now... we have a dark journey to undertake together...

PROLOGUE

THE LONG, DARK JOURNEY

1

What has gone before.

The mansion, in the Arklay Mountains...

She wakes in the void—in a psychological void, with her memory a blank. She only knows she is naked, lying on the floor of a shower.

And she is alone.

She finds clothing, puts it on, and explores the dimly lit mansion—where no one seems to live. She feels as if she should *know* this place... but remembers nothing. It is as if she sees everything from *outside* of herself. Even her name is remote.

She sees a picture of herself and a man, framed on a table. *Is this my husband?*

Continuing to search, suddenly, she finds someone. Or he finds her. He's investigating the Umbrella Corporation, she learns, while pretending to work for it....

Then the soldiers burst in, faces seeming inhuman in gas masks. They're with the Corporation, they announce—the world's most powerful and advanced

1 3

pharmaceutical multinational. They take her at gunpoint, and she begins to learn the truth. She had been an important security operative for Umbrella, but something strange and ugly has gone down—a mass murder in the *Hive*.

Something to which Alice may be relevant.

Whoever she may be.

The Hive is some distance away; a vast, underground facility located far below the nearest large town, Raccoon City. Almost an insectoid creation, in its design, it's like a giant wasp nest in the ground but made of steel and plastic and fiberglass and watched over with security cameras. The monarch of this hive is the Red Queen: a computer with total control.

A high-tech underground rail links the mansion to the Hive, and it's on this train that Alice meets Spence. As dazed as she is, he's at once familiar and unfamiliar to her.

They reach the Hive, where an automatic laser defense system activates, operated by the Hive's artificial intelligence, its central computer. Without warning it slices and dices most of the commandos— one of them ends up *cubed*. It occurs too quickly for them even to scream. Death, easy and instantaneous.

Death is the new master of the Hive.

It was the Red Queen who released the gas that suppressed Alice's memories, to eliminate a potential threat without killing her. *Never destroy a valuable asset—one that might be used again.* But confined with a precious few survivors—Matt, Spence, and Rain—Alice slowly begins to know her past... her own part in bringing about the horror.

Someone has deliberately released the Umbrella Corporation's experimental *T-virus* into the air vents. The Red Queen sealed off the Hive, and used its control over the underground facility's systems to kill those who would become infected. But it couldn't stop the virus from spreading amongst the survivors...

The T-virus kills—and then it resurrects. *The dead have risen* in the Hive; the dead walk again.

Zombies? But old-school zombies are low-grade horrors compared to these Undead. These creatures are unspeakably vicious, at times capable of moving quickly, of forming deadly mandibles, of configuring into overgrown living-dead variants. The lab-developed T-virus has created the new Undead, hungry for human flesh—and capable of being genetically modified into something even worse.

The Red Queen reveals this, and more.

With her few surviving companions, Alice escapes and shuts down the Red Queen. In doing so, they unknowingly release the Undead into the Hive's echoing corridors. A sickly young woman has become a rapacious monster, and one of the team, Rain, is bitten by her—and infected with the T-virus. Alice admired Rain for her courage, her individuality. But the virus eats its way into her brain, and all that's left is for that brain to be destroyed.

A bullet to the brain, a hatchet, a knife: destroy the brain, cut the brainstem, it's the only way to stop the

Undead. Shooting them in the heart doesn't work. It's not easy to kill what has already died.

There *is* a cure for the virus, they learn, if it can be administered soon enough. Alice and Matt find it... And Spence, the man who'd once been Alice's lover, steals the cure. It's worth billions, and Spence was the one who released the virus in the Hive—to create panic, cover his tracks, and destroy those who would stop him.

But there are other black experiments in the Hive, including a virus-borne variant—a crawling, powerful monster with swollen brain tissue where its eyes should be, and a tongue that is a weapon in itself. Released by the Red Queen to finish her dirty work, *the Licker* lurks, stalks, and strikes.

And that's what takes revenge on Spence. After he leaves the rest to die, the Licker corners him, "tears him a new one"... and then it comes after Alice and her friends.

They escape, tricking the creature into destruction, only to run headlong into Umbrella operatives. Matt is taken away for something called the Nemesis Project. And Alice? Her they strap to a table, in another facility. For another experiment entirely.

But there is still the Hive, swarming with the Undead. Another Umbrella biohazard is sent into these stumbling, ravenous creatures, only to be overwhelmed—trampled and ripped, recruited... to become more of the Undead. And the team left the door open.

The Undead are released into Raccoon City, where with tooth and claw, they reproduce through an orgy of sheer violence.

Somehow Alice wakes in the lab, emerging from her sedative-laden sleep. Someone has awakened her, given her a chance. She finds a way out of the locked laboratory, makes her way to the street...

Where she finds a world ravaged by the apocalypse.

2

Raccoon City seems empty but for the Undead. Alice sees nothing but wreckage and fire everywhere. But she knows there must be other survivors out there.

She finds a shotgun in a police car, loads it and strikes off, determined to locate them.

Alice never once falters, for she knows what she is capable of doing. A lab experiment has given her incredible physical powers, agility, to enhance her already impressive skills.

Yet she is captured by Umbrella, and faced with a monster called Nemesis, a hideous super soldier both repellent, and pitiful. To her horror she recognizes what was once her fellow survivor and closest companion. This monster is Matt. He lives just long enough to help her escape.

Horror follows upon horror: cities disfigured, a demented world roamed by the ceaselessly hungry Undead; ruins where flocks of crows feed upon the carcasses and mutate into flying horrors, where only a few survivors huddle in endless terror, behind locked doors. All seems hopeless.

Until one day, a radio transmission calls out to survivors, telling them that something called Arcadia is free from infection. *Arcadia offers food and water.*

Make your way to Arcadia...

Alice discovers some of these survivors, led by the heroic Claire Redfield, and tells them about Arcadia. But the Umbrella Corporation is watching, like a malignant sky god, from its own spy satellite. Umbrella's researchers try to modify the Undead, to make them controllable slaves, and it tests them as controlled violence sent against Alice and her new friends.

Only a handful survive—including the inspiring Claire, the woman who leads this small cadre of humans across the American Southwest, in search of a haven.

But they're running out of food, and supplies.

Alice helps them steal an Umbrella chopper so they can fly to Alaska, and Arcadia. But she stays behind—to get at the full truth about the Umbrella Corporation.

With the Earth in the throes of apocalypse, there is no cash except as trash—or as ammunition, since Alice uses coins instead of conventional shot in her shotgun shells. The Umbrella Corporation now deals in another kind of acquisition, the kind that Genghis Khan coveted: goods, property, and people. Umbrella's troopers simply *take* whatever the corporate overlords need. It acquires goods, and instead of employees, it has mind-controlled slaves.

Not so different from the old days of corporate culture, at that.

Alice's journey lays open more dark revelations—including an army of *herself*, for hundreds of adult-sized copies of Alice have been created. She liberates the clones and—with them—makes her way to Tokyo, where the worldwide plague has spiraled madly out of control. There Alice penetrates a huge Umbrella facility run by the man named Wesker. Scores of "Alices," each of them fast, powerful, and heavily armed, slaughter Umbrella's henchmen, showing no mercy.

But Wesker himself is transformed into something more than human. He's fast, too fast... and he injects her with a serum that suppresses her powers.

Suddenly... she is just a human being again. And the facility is destroyed, along with the clones.

3

Alice finds Claire in Alaska, and then locates a few others, including Claire's brother Chris, sequestered in a besieged Los Angeles prison. They fight their way to Arcadia—which turns out to be a ship.

Arcadia is something else, as well—it's a trap. The Umbrella Corporation needs healthy specimens for its experiments. So a friendly radio transmission lures them from around the world, to the gigantic cargo ship.

ARCADIA...

There, Alice and friends free the human cargo from suspended animation, take control of the ship, and manage to destroy Wesker. The world is still thronged with the living dead, but for the moment, the *Arcadia* is free.

Until the black ops commandos of the Umbrella Corporation approach, flying in a flock of black choppers, descending like rapacious, unliving crows...

MY NAME IS ALICE...

I worked for the Umbrella Corporation, in a secret high-tech facility called the Hive. It was a laboratory, developing experimental viral weaponry. There was an incident, a virus escaped, and everybody died. Trouble was... they didn't stay dead.

This was the start of an apocalypse that would sweep the entire world.

A last handful of survivors sought safety on a ship called Arcadia. We thought it was a safe haven.

We thought it was free from infection. But we were wrong.

Once again, the Umbrella Corporation had deceived us. And once again, my friends and I found ourselves fighting for our lives.

My name is Alice. And this is my story...

...the story of how I died.

1

It was a sunny, tranquil day at sea on the tanker *Arcadia*, off the coast of California. A *lovely* day, really. Occasionally a bit of fog caressed the white caps of the blue waves, and then drifted away. Could have been quite restful, a day like this, if the *Arcadia* were a yacht, in the days before the world started dying; before humanity started eating itself alive.

Alice was standing near the aft on the steady metal deck of the *Arcadia*, reveling in the cool breeze. She watched as a group of figures—freed experimental subjects, all dressed in white—milled about on the deck of the enormous, retrofitted tanker ship, trying to reorient themselves to this new reality.

She could imagine what they were thinking—all but hear their voices in her head.

"*I heard the radio transmission—that there was safety in* Arcadia—*no infection, no Undead to attack me—that there was food and shelter. Finally I found the ship.*

"*The men in black commando togs grabbed me,*

*slapped the mechanical scarab onto me, and then...
nothing. Nothing else till I woke in the high-tech hold
of the ship, in a tube... like an insect on display in a
bottle.*

*"The woman—Alice—led me out into the open air...
But what now? The Undead are still out there.*

"What happens now?"

What now, indeed.

They had taken this ship—for the time being. She
and Chris and Claire had killed Albert Wesker—and
Wesker had been the most powerful individual in
Umbrella, as far as she knew, now that Lord Spencer
was gone. Maybe Wesker's death would keep them
safe for a while, throw the enemy into disarray.

If Wesker is really dead...

How could she doubt it? She'd riddled his body
with bullet holes. She'd left his corpse limp, bleeding
out on the deck of a hold, far below. No, he was dead.

He had to be.

The breeze sighed in the superstructure of the
converted tanker. Test subjects murmured to one
another, milling and talking, gazing at the horizon.
The waves whispered against the hull of the big ship.
In the distance, on the shore, she could make out
some of the Los Angeles skyline—or what remained
of it. Downtown Santa Monica was charred, smoking,
many of the buildings just skeletons of girders. But it
wasn't deserted. There were still throngs of Undead
plague victims, crowding the streets, savaging
anything that moved—except, oddly, one another.
They craved fresher meat than that.

First thing to do, Alice figured, would be to get up
to the *Arcadia*'s bridge and work out how to safely

pilot the ship. Maybe it was so computerized it could almost pilot itself. If it was fueled up, it could take them anywhere in the world.

Like—where?

An island, she was thinking. Catalina, maybe, an island twenty-two miles off the coast of Los Angeles. Catalina itself was less than twenty-three miles long, eight wide. There would be Undead there, sure, but not that many. She could take a team out, methodically sweep the Undead from the island. Exterminate them... like they were insects.

Except that the Undead used to be *people*. Men, women, grandmothers and grandfathers, children—even children were Undead. Alice often wondered, could there be a spark of humanity left in the Undead who roamed the streets, moaning and growling, dripping bloody saliva?

She'd never seen the slightest hint of it. The Undead seemed more mindless than rabid wolves. Probably all vestiges of human feeling—perhaps even the *soul*—departed the victim's body when they died. And once reanimated, they were soulless things, caricatures of human beings.

Still, that spark had glimmered in what was left of Matt, though he'd been transformed into a different kind of monster. Turned into a hideous super soldier by Umbrella researchers using a variant of the T-virus.

If there was anything human left in the Undead, it was helpless, she supposed. That tiny speck of inward humanity had been hijacked by the virus; at best, it was forever along for the ride. And it must suffer terribly in there, trapped inside a monster.

So if she exterminated them, she was doing them a favor.

Keep telling yourself that, Alice.

Catalina. Once she cleaned up the island, they might be safe from the Undead for a long time. The zombies weren't known to swim...

It was *some* kind of plan, anyway. So she decided to find Chris Redfield, ask him if he knew how to pilot this ship.

Alice glanced over her shoulder at the people she'd set free... and sighed. She felt responsible for them, now. Somehow, she kept falling into that role. She'd tried to avoid it, wandering in the deserts of the Southwest—and then she'd got drawn in again.

Life had been so much easier when all she had to worry about was security at one of the world's most powerful corporations. She was exquisitely trained in martial arts, in the use of every weapon. She'd been a person of confidence and strength.

And then she'd seen what the Umbrella Corporation was doing, in the Hive. Her conscience had forced her to turn against Umbrella; against all that she had been. Maybe this new burden of responsibility was the karma, biting her on the ass for her time with Umbrella.

Still, she was still young and strong. Men found her beautiful. If she got everyone on the ship to safety, maybe she could settle down, even find a mate among the survivors. Chris seemed attracted to her. And he was a ruggedly good-looking guy. Impressive, if a bit grim. But... could she live like a normal human being, ever again? With a lover, a child—a family?

She had to believe there was a chance. Somewhere, someday, the dark journey had to come to an end.

"What's that?" Claire said, as she walked up to Alice. She pointed at the sky.

With a stab of dread, Alice looked up.

"It's trouble," Alice said, dully. A fleet of flying vehicles was blotting the sky, bearing down on the *Arcadia*.

Of course. There was no end to the nightmare. Every time there seemed to be light at the end of the tunnel, it turned out to be a guttering, forgotten candle... a tiny flame that sputtered, and went out in a wisp of smoke.

Alice recognized the silhouettes against the northern sky.

"V-22s," she said, her voice hoarse. Why couldn't she have time to breathe, to think—just one real chance to *help* these people? "Umbrella's version of V-22s, anyway," she added, almost casually. "Based on the Marine Corps' Ospreys—they're helicopters and planes in one."

"Oh, no..." Claire breathed. As she did, Alice checked to make certain her shotguns were secure in the holsters on her back, then began to move.

Umbrella's V-22s were more advanced than the Corps' Ospreys. The black choppers could tilt their rotors forward to fly like planes, or tilt them upward to hover, and were even more armored than Ospreys. There were auto-cannons mounted in the snouts.

And there was a whole aerial fleet of them coming her way, so many that they quickly darkened the sky. They were probably packed with Umbrella troopers, too.

Alice reached the survivors and started to shout.

"Move!" she said. "Head for cover!"

Had Wesker sent for those troopers, before he'd died?

Good chance he had, and the Corporation had responded instantly. Like any multinational, they wouldn't want to surrender all the tech, the test data, and the experimental subjects on this ship.

She had to get them to safety.

But V-22s were fast. Seeing them head-on was deceptive, and before she knew it, the big black choppers came hurtling in, rotors roaring, gunners firing as they came. Shells burst on the decks, instantaneous blossoms of fire and shrapnel. Alice ran, shouting at the others to get back, get under cover, but the vast deck was like a football field, open and flat and broad, and there was no cover.

They'd tumbled from tranquility into chaos, in the space of a few heartbeats.

She scanned the area, looked for Chris, and Claire—and saw several of the white-garbed people they'd rescued, caught in a detonation and tossed into the air by shell blasts that made the deck ring like a sledgehammer on a giant bell.

She groaned at that, cursed in frustration, her stomach churning—then heard the drumming of the choppers steadying, felt the wind of their rotors as they hovered over the deck, and she skidded to a stop, near the rail.

Turning, she saw Umbrella troopers rappelling down from the V-22s. They were all in black, armored, faces covered in gas masks, weapons strapped to their backs—black to the white of the survivors she'd freed.

Not freed for long.

The first three troopers to hit the deck quickly unstrapped capture guns, non-lethal weapons looking like small bazookas, that fired compressed nets at their targets. The net capsules opened and engulfed a number of the survivors, as if in gigantic spider webs.

Alice looked up again, and saw a familiar face. Jill Valentine rappelled down, her face unmasked, her dark blond hair fluttering in the wind. She fired with a submachine gun as she came. Bullets strafed up the deck in Alice's direction, whining off the metal, and she threw herself aside, the rounds narrowly missing her.

She came to her feet tugging the automatic pistol from her waistband, and returned fire. But she missed Jill—was it intentional? This was the woman who'd once fought beside her.

Alice thought she caught a glimpse of one of the mechanical scarabs, on Jill's bosom.

Then she emptied the clip, tossed the pistol aside, and lost sight of Jill behind a cloud of smoke. She smelled engine exhaust, felt the rotor wind, and a shadow fell over her. Craning her neck, she realized she was being targeted by a V-22 that was tilting down to fire at her. She drew her sawed-off shotguns from the holsters. Pulling the triggers, she felt the weapons buck, and the silver quarters she'd packed into the shotgun rounds smashed through the windshield of the V-22. They blew the pilot's head off.

But the V-22 was a little too close. Alice turned to run as, pilotless, the big chopper nosed down and crashed into the deck.

Cannon shells were packed into the front end of the V-22, and there was a fuel line not that far behind the shells. The impact of the chopper on the deck detonated a half-ton of explosives, ripping the V-22 apart from within, so that fifty-pound chunks of jagged metal, like fragments from a giant hand grenade, ricocheted across the deck. Flame gouted, consuming the remainder of the chopper, the blast tearing the rotors off so they spun through the air and sliced through another V-22.

And Alice just wasn't fast enough. The shockwave from the explosion slapped her with punishing force, so that she thought her back might break. She was lifted off her feet and flipped bodily over the railing. Suddenly she was spinning end over end, down toward the sea, gasping—the shockwave had knocked the wind out of her.

Sky and sea changed places; sea and sky spun round again, and then, before she could take a breath, she was flung headlong into the face of a big, pretty, blue wave, while blazing debris hissed into the water all around her. The water closed over her as chunks of the V-22 rained down close by, helicopter parts plunging into the sea trailing streamers of bubbles.

The fuel sprayed by the spinning, falling fuel tank coated the waves, blazing up as it was struck by fiery debris.

Instantly Alice was sinking, seawater burning her lungs. She was in shock, stunned, maybe paralyzed—she didn't know. She just knew that the thudding pulse she heard, her own pulse sounding in her ears, was slowing... slowing....

Above she could see the wrinkled, translucent surface burning, water seething as fuel burned off it. Darkness from below rose up to swallow her, as blue and orange flames consumed the rest of the world, overhead...

She was detached, fascinated by the sight, that ceiling of flames, even as her pulse became irregular, skipping a beat. She wasn't sure, but she thought she might have blurrily glimpsed a sling, dipping toward her, lowered from a hovering V-22

Were those arms, grabbing for her, to pull her to the sling?

She hoped not.

She'd rather die than be their prisoner. Their slave…

Delirium swept over her, and she seemed to see the mechanical scarab—the one that she'd taken off of Claire. Something between jewelry and insect, the scarab was as big as her hand, climbing up her like a living thing, looking to sink its needle fangs into her; to numb her with the drug that had taken control of so many others…

No. It wasn't really there. Just the cold wet darkness.

Her thoughts sank away, too. There was just one thought left.

I've failed.

She had failed to protect all those people who counted on her; all those dazed people she'd brought to the upper deck of the *Arcadia*, where they were shot or captured. She'd failed them.

It was too much to bear, that final, aching thought. Much easier to let her pulse slow, slow…

So much easier to just drift downward, downward…

My name is Alice. And this is my story…
…the story of how I died.

* * *

Alice woke. In a bedroom.

She was lying in a comfortable, rumpled double bed, in an ordinary middle-class American bedroom.

Someone was looking at her. She turned her head, and saw a handsome man smiling down at her—dark, Semitic, his hair as rumpled as the bedclothes—as he pulled on his boxer shorts. He gazed at her at her with a kind of wry familiarity, an intimacy. Like a husband.

He couldn't be her husband... she *had* no husband.

But he had a wedding ring on—she looked at her own finger—one that matched hers.

Then it came to her—his name was... Todd. That was it.

Todd.

Looking at him, thinking that she'd known him by a different name, once, long ago... But that name fled from her. He was simply her husband, Todd. Nice that her husband was such a sexy guy.

Hadn't she been on a ship, shooting at someone? She remembered an explosion. She'd been picked up by a shockwave, tossed like a discarded doll.

She'd drowned, hadn't she?

No. That hadn't been real. It couldn't have been. She could still smell her husband's sweat, his aftershave on her, other smells from last night, when they'd made love. She felt a little sore, between her legs. He was a vigorous guy...

This was what was real. This was... much better.

The other was just a dream. A bad dream.

Forget it, Alice.

"Come on," Todd said, chuckling, pulling on his pants. "We're late. Alarm didn't go off. Becky isn't up yet. Mrs. Henderson's going to be pissed. You know how they get at school when we drop her off late."

But the sea. The Arcadia. *Those people needed her. They all needed her...*

"Baby!" Todd stopped dressing, staring at her, a concerned look on his face.

Alice felt tired and disoriented. She should get up, she knew that, but...

"Baby?" He looked at her, lips pursed.

She cleared her throat, and sat up, still a bit dizzy. *The sea. The waves burning overhead...*

Todd leaned toward her a little. "Baby—are you okay?"

"Yeah," she said. "I'll get..." *Becky.* "... I'll get Becky up."

"You look tired. You didn't sleep well?"

"I'm fine."

He didn't seem convinced. Neither was she, for that matter.

"You sure?" he asked.

"Yeah."

He stared at her, the way husbands stare at their wives.

"I'm okay—really," she insisted.

"Well, in that case..." He whipped the bedclothes off her. "Get that cute ass out of bed."

Alice smiled wanly, and did as he asked. She felt stiff. Her lungs seemed to hurt, when she took a deep breath.

Reaction to that bad dream...

She caught sight of herself in the bedroom mirror. Wait—that wasn't right, was it? When did she get blond hair?

She shook herself. No wonder Todd was staring at her.

Sometimes dreams linger and confuse you.

Yeah, that's what it was...

2

Alice put on a robe, and went down the hall to wake...
Becky.

The seascape in the hallway was familiar to her; the scuffed hardwood floor was familiar; the smells were familiar. This was their home, hers and Todd's, their one-story, old, suburban, ranch-style house.

So why was she so disoriented?

She went into Becky's room, paused, and smiled, looking at the sleeping girl, seven years old, sprawled on her small bed with its flower crested headboard.

What a sweet face she had. She looked so peaceful, so adorable, Alice was reluctant to wake her. It felt good just to watch her sleep.

But she sighed and leaned over, gently shook Becky's shoulder. Her daughter opened her eyes, and blinked. So like her mother's, those eyes. The child didn't say anything—she didn't speak much, she'd only learned to do it by feel, and when she spoke her voice lacked pitch control. She had autosomal recessive deafness, an inherited birth defect that left

33

her missing critical structures in the inner ear.

Both Alice and Todd could hear, so the defect was assumed to be the result of a recessive gene in one of them. Someday, if they planned to have another child, there would be a test to see whose genetics were the problem. Perhaps they'd resort to donated semen or an egg, for a second child. But Becky needed their full attention right now.

Alice kissed her good morning, and laid out her clothing.

Alice took a quick shower, dressed, and went to the kitchen. She was humming to herself, feeling a little better as she made fresh orange juice in the juicer. The coffee had just finished perking, the rich smell filling the room.

Alice poured the orange juice, put the glass in front of Becky and signed.

"You want eggs?" They signed to talk, using ASL.

Becky stuck out her lower lip and signed back.

"Pancakes?"

"Cereal?" Alice asked her. The girl needed something more substantial than pancakes.

"Pancakes," Becky signed insistently. Alice pretended to think it over, as if she were engaged in a serious diplomatic negotiation. Finally she signed back.

"Cereal—then pancakes?"

Becky smiled.

"Deal."

Todd came in, looking shaved and combed, pulling the jacket of his dark suit on over his crisp white shirt.

She looked at him appreciatively. The man cleaned up good. Handsome and kind—and sexy. She was lucky to have him.

He poured himself a cup of coffee, filling the cup a little too much.

"We're going to be late... again."

Alice glanced at him as he swigged the coffee—and she saw two drops of coffee fall on his crisp white shirt.

"Shit!" Todd said.

Tom laughed as Becky and Alice both said, "Watch it!" Becky had read his lips.

Alice bent to examine the stain.

"There's another shirt in your closet. I picked up the dry cleaning yesterday."

Todd grinned. "You're my angel."

"Don't you forget it."

He leaned toward her. Alice smiled.

"Easy, tiger... we're running late. Remember?"

Todd walked toward the living room, headed for the bedroom and that clean shirt. He was thinking that Alice probably didn't want a weekend away from Becky, his parents babysitting or not. His mother didn't know much about signing and seemed exasperated, at times, with Becky's attempts at speaking.

He stopped, looking down the front hallway. Why was the front door open? And wide open, too...

He was about to call out, ask Alice if she'd left the door open—and that's when the guy with blood on his face leapt at him, charging from the bathroom. The man snarled, fingers bent into claws as he came. He wore a bloodied, torn suit, as if he'd been on his way to work when this madness swept over him.

Todd reeled back, yelling incoherently, and then the guy—a complete stranger—bit his forearm. Hard. Tearing through fabric, through skin, sinking his teeth into Todd's flesh. Blood splashed across his crisp white shirt. Todd wrenched his arm away, then struck the stranger, making him stagger back a step.

But he wasn't going to run away—Todd could see it in his milky-white eyes. He was going to finish what he started.

Who or what *was* this guy?

Alice and Becky ran into the hall gawking, Becky started making a high-pitched noise of fright, deep in her throat, seeing her father fight with the madman.

"Todd!" Alice shouted.

Alice knew, somehow, as she scooped up Becky in her arms, what the attacker was. Not a madman—nothing so simple. Not some drug-addled housebreaker, either. No.

This strange assailant was... *undead*?

How did she know that? She wasn't sure...

Todd flung the Undead off him, so that the man stumbled back, crashing through a glass table in the front hall. Broken glass flew and tinkled. But the Undead was up on its feet almost instantly.

"Get Becky away!" Todd shouted, crouching to block his family from the creature.

Unsure of what to do, how to help Todd and protect Becky both, Alice stepped back—and heard a riotous smashing of glass behind her. She turned, looked through the archway into the kitchen, and saw another one, half lunged through the broken glass of the upper half of the kitchen screen door. He was caught in the window's remains, the jagged edges in the frame ripping at his stomach, but didn't seem to notice or care.

He clawed toward Alice and Becky, growling hungrily, heedlessly ripping his belly more as he tried to slither into the room.

She looked for Todd—and didn't see him.

A third Undead came roaring through the front door—and straight at Alice.

Still carrying Becky, she ran down the hall, moving full tilt, and Becky somehow felt light in her arms. Adrenaline was singing through her veins, but it was as if she was running in slow motion, the hallway sliding slowly, slowly past her as she headed for the laundry room. She glanced over her shoulder, saw the Undead, a chunky white man in a blood-splashed green golf shirt, pursuing her from the living room

He seemed to move in slow motion, too.

Time sped up to normal as she darted into the laundry room. She lowered Becky with one arm, while with the other hand she slammed the door in her pursuer's face. There was no lock on the door.

She jammed her shoulder hard against it and immediately felt the pushback, the Undead trying to force the door open, growling, the living dead man whining in frustration on the other side like a vicious dog on a short chain.

"Mommy!" Becky screeched, waving her frantically signing fingers in front of her mother's face. "What's happening? Where's Daddy?"

Alice couldn't hold the door much longer. The creature was slowly pushing it open, its slavering, bloody, snarling face pressing into view. She gave it one more shove, with all her strength, momentarily pushing the creature back—then she let go.

Before the Undead could move, Alice pulled over a heavy shelving unit that stood beside the entrance. The cabinet fell on its side, blocking the door, spilling boxes of Tide and conditioner but jamming the way—at least for the moment.

There was a gap, still—and several Undead reached through to wildly claw the air, ravenously trying to get at Alice and Becky. And she knew what they wanted. Some half-forgotten nightmare whispered to her, from the deep recesses of her mind.

They want to eat you. They want to eat Becky—they want to strip the flesh from her body and gobble it down while she still lives...

Alice looked desperately around and saw only one tiny window. She grabbed a small stepladder leaning near the dryer, carried it past the silently sobbing Becky, to the wall under the window. She opened the ladder, climbed up, knocked the mesh screen away.

Behind her she heard a scraping sound as the door was being pushed further open, the cabinet raking the floor.

And she realized that the window was too small, even for Becky.

Alice jumped down from the stepladder—and Becky ran up to her, pointing at the door, where the Undead were pushing the heavy cabinet further out of the way, inch by inch. There was nowhere to go, nothing with which to fight with. Scanning the room, she saw only a washing machine, a dryer, and dirty clothes in a hamper. The concrete floor was solid.

So Alice looked up, because that's all that was left—and remembered the crawlspace.

3

Bringing the stepladder over, she climbed it and signed to Becky to bring her a mop. The little girl, her face pale and drawn, a caricature of raw anxiety, grabbed the mop and did as she was told. Balancing on tiptoes atop the stepladder Alice grabbed the mop handle and slammed it hard into the ceiling. The plasterboard material was thin, feebly nailed in place, and the mop handle broke through almost immediately.

The Undead were scrabbling, snarling at the door, worming over the cabinet, getting in one another's way—but they were almost through, and they were more than ready to feed...

Alice cleared enough room to tear at the plasterboard with her bare hands, her strength madly increased as she fought to protect her little girl. Dropping the mop, she clawed frantically, pulled chunks out of the way. Insulation slopped down, fiberglass and dust slithering over her shoulders. She pulled herself up, enough to force her head through. Shafts of light streamed up around her, illuminating swirling motes of disturbed dust.

Down below, the howling built to a triumphant fever pitch as the creatures crawled over the cabinet. The first one tripped and fell into the room.

Alice lowered herself back onto the stepladder and jumped down, signing to Becky—even as an Undead, sprawled on the floor, struggling to its feet, took a swipe at her.

"Grab a hold!" Alice signed. "Climb!"

Becky scrambled up the stepladder, and Alice lifted her, gritting her teeth, shouting, "Climb!" though her daughter couldn't hear it.

Becky reached through the ceiling hole, grabbed the rafters, and Alice pushed her up, lifting her rump and the bottom of her feet. Becky vanished through the hole in the ceiling and Alice jumped up, grabbed a rafter, pulled herself up, feeling muscles beginning to tear with the effort.

She lifted herself up off the stepladder, and kicked it down flat. The Undead were slow-witted, little more than sheer reflex, and clumsy in most things. They probably wouldn't be intelligent enough to set the ladder up again.

How do I know that?

And then teeth snapped at her kicking feet. She lashed out, felt her shoe connect with a wet, gape-mouthed face. She heard the thing stagger back from her, blundering into the others that were coming into the room.

Alice pulled herself up further. Becky was kneeling near her on a rafter, trying to tug her mother up, her small hands of no real help. Alice's legs flailed. She lost her grip, her fingers slick with sweat, and almost fell back through the hole—and felt an Undead clawing at her ankles, reaching its filthy, blood-caked hands to grab at her thighs, rake at her crotch...

Spurred by a rush of fear she pulled herself up higher, almost halfway through the hole.

She felt hands grasping and teeth gnawing at the shoe of her right foot, not yet breaking through—and she kicked out viciously, connecting with what felt like a jaw. The grip was gone and she heard the Undead stumble back into the washing machine.

She could hear more Undead swarming into the laundry room—and knew she wouldn't be able to fight off all of them. They'd pull her down if she didn't get through—*now, right now.*

With a Herculean effort she pulled herself up, shouting wordlessly with the strain, scratching her stomach and hips in several places. Something clutched at her heel—then she dragged her feet into the attic and crawled up onto a walkway of two unvarnished planks, beside Becky.

Alice rolled, panting, onto her back, mouth dry, coughing up dust. Becky made her jump a little as she leaned over into her mother's line of sight, her childish face taut, mouth quivering with sobs.

Sitting up, trying not to focus on the sound of the frustrated, furious creatures scrabbling about beneath them she looked around, scanning for anything that could help them.

There, at the other end of the planks—an old cardboard box of sporting equipment. A half-deflated basketball, a worn-out baseball glove, and a worn baseball bat.

Alice gathered herself in a crouch and crept quickly

over to the box, then plucked out the baseball bat.

Becky was sitting on the planks, hugging herself, rocking in place, staring into space, making tiny little whimpering sounds in her throat.

They couldn't stay up here. Sooner or later the Undead would find a way up. And they'd be trapped.

To one side was a hatch, set into a kind of shallow wooden box. That should go down into the main hallway, she thought. Laid over the rafters was a retracting aluminum ladder.

Carrying the bat, Alice crept over to the hatch, carefully lifted it up, and looked down. She saw nothing but the floor below. She lowered her head enough to peer down the hallway—it was empty, as far as she could tell.

She'd have to go down there and scout it out. They needed a way out of the house. Her heartbeat—which had just begun to calm down—resumed its feverish pounding, just at the thought.

She thought about getting to a phone, to call for help—but her cell phone wasn't charged, and Todd's was on him. They didn't have a landline.

Just get out of the house.

Moving as quietly as possible, she set the bat aside and took hold of the ladder. She tilted it up, and lowered it, slowly, on its hinges, down through the hatch to the hardwood floor.

Alice looked at Becky, smiled reassuringly, and signed.

Wait a moment.

Then, picking up the baseball bat again, she began to descend the ladder, moving with exquisite care. She went as quietly as she could, but every step made the ladder squeak. If the Undead heard it...

She peered down the hall. There was nothing there but the painting, knocked askew on the wall, and the little side table with a flower vase on it just to the left of the ladder. There were no Undead in sight, but she could hear their frustrated scrabbling and growling in the laundry room.

Hefting the bat, Alice heard a noise up above and looked up through the trap door. Becky was crouching up there, in the attic, shaking visibly, eyes wide, staring down at her.

"I don't see them," Alice signed to her. "Come down. We'll find a safer spot..."

Becky shook her head, the motion almost a convulsive twitch of terror, and signed a reply.

"No! No!"

"They might come up there," Alice signaled. "We have to get to somewhere safer. Come on."

Becky's mouth quivered, but after a long hesitation she began to descend the ladder, Alice wincing at the squeaking of her daughter's feet on the rungs.

When the girl got to the bottom Alice took Becky's clammy-cold hand in hers. If they could move quietly enough, they just might get away.

Down in the laundry room, one of the Undead snarled at another, causing Alice to turn sharply that way. Her bat tapped a vase that sat on a small side table. The vase rocked, then fell toward the floor.

No! If that vase smashed on the floor, the Undead would be upon them in moments. They might outrun the creatures, but there was no telling how many more might be nearby.

Alice let go of Becky and grabbed at the vase,

surprised at the speed of her own reflexes as she caught it an inch from the impact. Water slopped out, a few flowers falling, but she'd kept it from hitting the floor. Gingerly she placed the vase carefully on the side table—

And an Undead burst from the laundry room door at the other end of the hall. It spotted them immediately, began shambling toward them. It was the same one who'd attacked Todd.

The only blessing is that it didn't alert the others— not yet.

But Becky shrieked in wordless fear—unable to hear her own scream—and Alice scooped the girl up in her arms, still carrying the baseball bat as well. Toting the child, she raced down the corridor to her bedroom.

The bedroom—where she and Todd had awakened just a short time ago. Her husband smiling at her. A nightmare fading...

Somehow, she was trapped in yet another nightmare. But this one was horribly real.

And where was Todd?

Alice let Becky slip to the bedroom floor, turned, slammed the door in the Undead's face, and instantly locked it. That gave them a moment to—

A splintering crash and the Undead's bloody fist smashed through the flimsy wood. It clutched at her.

"The window!" Alice signed to Becky, and pointed. "Quick!"

The girl ran to the window and struggled with the latch, fingers fumbling at it. Alice hurried after her, hearing the crunch of the lock beginning to give way as the Undead thumped itself against the only barrier that stood between the creature and its meal.

Baseball bat in her right hand, Alice unlocked the latch with her left, forced the window open, and glanced out. Seeing no Undead in the backyard, she helped Becky climb out.

Hearing the crack of the door breaking open, the rapacious snarl of the zombie, Alice turned, gripping the bat with both hands, completing the turn by swinging the bat hard into the charging creature's forehead. The bat shuddered with the impact and she felt bone give way. The Undead was knocked off its feet, all the energy of a mother defending her child knocking it back through the air. It fell flat on its back on the bedroom floor and lay there, twitching, blood pooling in the crater she'd made on its forehead, purple tongue flapping in its mouth.

Hit them in the head, that takes them down.

She dropped the bat out the window and climbed through, dropping to the grassy backyard where Becky was crouching, whimpering, small hands balled into little white-knuckled fists.

"Stay close to me!" Alice signed. Her heart was hammering, though no stalkers were in sight. The fear, the spurting adrenaline, her thundering pulse— it was all just the backdrop of life, now. It went on and on, like a maddening car alarm that wouldn't shut off.

She took Becky's hand, and scooped up the baseball bat. They ran to the wooden side gate that led to the front of the house. She could hear sirens, a whole lot of sirens. Maybe the police would be out in the street, or the National Guard—someone who could help them. Maybe Todd would be out there. And maybe he'd be alright.

Maybe...

She kicked open the unlatched gate and they went through, stopping at the front corner of the house, where they stopped to stare at the street.

The quiet, sunny suburban neighborhood had been transformed into a war zone. At least half the houses on the street were afire, huffing smoke and flames. She heard the crack of gunshots, and screams. Two cars, unoccupied and abandoned, were locked in a smoking death grip of twisted metal at the corner. A cop car raced by on the cross street, sirens warbling.

Alice opened her mouth to shout to them—but they were already gone.

She saw an older woman she knew, Mrs. Grady, running barefoot across the street a few houses down. They'd exchanged recipes, and June Grady had given her a cutting for some flowers in the backyard. Now Mrs. Grady was running for her life. And the Undead who pursued her... wasn't that her husband Raymond? He was tottering monomaniacally after her—and yet he'd been in a wheelchair for years, unable to walk.

The Undead Raymond leapt and tackled his wife, and she went down screaming as he gnashed at the back of her neck.

Becky made that frightened, unconscious whimper again as she watched Raymond Grady tearing into June with his teeth. Alice covered the child's eyes with a hand, pressed her close.

She saw others, at the end of the block, running from the Undead: an old man running from an old woman; a woman running from her twelve-year-old daughter; the Reverend Granger, naked from the waist

47

down, chasing another man, his choir director. The Reverend's arms were extended, fingers clutching...

And there seemed to be simply nowhere to go from here.

4

Alice heard a gurgling snarl coming from the backyard. The Undead had climbed out the window. There was no going back, and there was no staying here—either way they would find her. And Becky.

Strange—how all this wasn't *entirely* strange. There was a distant resonance of familiarity, almost *déjà vu* quality about it all. She knew, somehow, that the bite spread some kind of infection—it killed, and then it resurrected, but what it raised up was soulless, ravening, and existed only to feed on human flesh. It was a kind of inverted, diabolic mockery of the resurrection of Christ.

The opposite of a savior, arisen...

But how did she know all that? She shook her head, trying to clear it, wasn't sure of anything—except that she had to find somewhere, someplace that was safe—where she could protect her daughter.

Alice took a deep breath—then, head swimming, she took Becky firmly by the hand, and, half dragging her, led the way to the street. She had a vague notion of finding an empty house, one not already overrun, something she could barricade.

Just get to that house, across the street. It's not burning, it looks quiet. Ignore the screams. Don't look...

From her left a car horn blared, jarringly close, and Alice turned to see a Prius bearing down on her, a young dark-haired woman behind the steering wheel—the car's wheels screeched as the woman slammed on her brakes, and Alice was frozen, overwhelmed, clutching Becky to her...

The car skidded to a stop, the bumper two inches from Alice's left hip.

A young Latino woman leaned out the window.

"What the hell are you doing, lady!" she shouted. An odd question, given all that was happening.

"I'm sorry, I..." Alice looked down the street, where four Undead held a shrieking woman down, feeding on her—eating her alive. Becky was weeping silently now, face pressed against her mother.

"What's going *on*?" Alice muttered.

"Get in!" the woman in the Prius yelled.

Alice glanced back at her house.

"My husband—he's still inside." He might be. Or he might be shambling along the street, snarling, face bloody...

"*Get in the car!*" the woman shouted again.

She stared—didn't she know this woman? The young Latino woman was dressed casually, with a light tan jacket. Her face seemed terribly familiar. The name *Rain* came into Alice's mind.

But from where?

Alice led Becky to the back door of the car, wondering if a vehicle would be safer than an empty house.

And then a horde of Undead, scores of them, came shambling around the corner behind the Prius, like some hideous gore-spattered parody of marathon runners. Their mouths were all open—growling, howling, squawking, spitting up blood, gasping with psychotic hunger.

The woman in the car looked over her shoulder.

"Told you..."

The horde was close—there was no time to argue. Alice opened the car door, bundled Becky through it and jumped in beside her.

The horde reached the back of the Prius, and an Undead who'd once been a young man jumped onto the car as the young woman accelerated down the street. She drove right over a body, and Alice watched in a side mirror as the bump of going over the corpse shook the Undead off the back. It fell into the street with a crunching *thud* that would probably have killed a human being.

But not the living dead. It just lurched to its feet and came after them, its neck broken, its head wagging with each step.

"Rain" floored the accelerator.

"Buckle up," she muttered.

Alice saw to it that Becky was buckled in, then she put on her own seat belt, feeling absurd worrying about seat belts when the neighbors had turned into murderous zombies.

They passed a group of Undead wandering blindly down the street, mouths agape, eyes milky white. One of them, a woman, still clutched her purse. But her lips were dripping red foam.

"What is all this?" Alice wondered, aloud. Was it

the end of the world? Prophesied Judgment Day? Had the Trump of Doom sounded while she'd slept?

"Your guess is as good as mine," came the reply. "One minute I'm coming back from my morning class, the next—"

"Why are these people—" Alice shook her head in numb incomprehension— "*doing* this?"

"Those things are not people. Not anymore."

"I'm scared, Mommy," Becky signed. She didn't know the sign for *terrified*, and Alice wasn't sure there was one. They needed one now.

"It's going to be okay," Alice signed back. It was easier to lie when no one could hear your voice. She put an arm around the girl as the Prius raced through an intersection—

And was T-boned by a massive garbage truck—a mountain of metal that seemed to come out of nowhere.

The world spun sickeningly as the car flipped over and rolled. Alice clasped Becky protectively close as the windshield shattered. Metal crumpled, the side windows cracked and broken glass spun about like hail in a whirlwind. Alice lost her grip on the baseball bat and it vanished in the chaos.

Becky made an "*Eeeeee!*" sound in her throat as the car rolled—and then fell silent as the car skidded on its rooftop, trailing sparks, finally coming to a halt upside down, smoke billowing up around them.

Fire. We could be burned alive in here...

Hands shaking, Alice unclasped Becky's seat belt and eased her down to the overturned car roof. She undid her own seat belt and wriggled down beside her. She felt battered, bruised, yet intact, but Becky was hyperventilating, staring, apparently in shock.

"Are you hurt?" Alice signed.

Becky didn't respond. Alice shook her, gently, and locked eyes with her. But the child's gaze wandered away, her eyes going in and of focus. Alice signed again.

"Baby... look at me! Can you move?"

Still no reply. Becky's fingers were silent.

"I'm going to get out so I can pull you free," Alice signed.

Becky just stared.

Alice coughed as smoke swirled more thickly around them, and crawled out through the bent, wrenched-open door, getting to her knees, immediately turning to pull her daughter out, hands gripping her upper arms, trying to not to drag her through broken glass.

She got Becky clear, all the time looking for the Undead. She saw some in the distance, past the steaming truck. She couldn't see the driver of the totaled vehicle—just a splash of blood running down the inside of the crack-webbed windshield.

Becky sat up, hugging herself, rocking, and put her thumb in her mouth, sucking it like a baby.

Alice knelt by the front of the car, looked in to see Rain—or whoever she was—hanging upside down from her seat belt, her jacket making it difficult to see. She didn't appear to be breathing—most likely she was dead. Her hair and arms dangled down limply... a little blood dripped down from a gash on her head.

If she *was* dead, or dying, would she resurrect as Undead? Alice wasn't sure, but she wasn't going to risk Becky by sticking around and finding out.

Glancing around, as if through a haze, Alice saw that they were on the edge of a housing estate she'd passed by many times on the way to the supermarket. The sign over the gate read SUNDOWN MEADOWS. One of the big, split-level homes was burning out of control, almost entirely consumed by a single great red-and-blue flame. But there was no sign of fire trucks.

The next house's roof was caved in by something that she had to stare at for a moment to recognize—it was the crashed, warped wreckage of a news helicopter, embedded in the top of the garage. Its rotor blades were still lazily turning, swirling the gray smoke that rose from its engine.

Alice looked at her daughter—Becky was still in a state of shock.

Movement down the block caught her eye. A cluster of Undead, gathered at the next corner, was turning their way.

Time to get a move on. But it was hard to know which way to turn. It seemed as if nowhere was really safe. Suddenly Alice felt sick to her stomach; felt pins and needles in her feet and hands.

Is it a concussion from the wreck? But she didn't have time for that. "Come on," she signed to Becky, and scooped her daughter up, felt Becky's legs reflexively clasp her around the waist as she carried her toward the upscale housing project—one large home, directly across from them, seemed intact, might be untouched. Perhaps the people had fled, had gotten away. Maybe there were no Undead inside—because there was no one there to eat.

Arms and back aching, Alice forced herself to run. They crossed the street and she climbed the porch stairs of the big house. The door was slightly ajar, as if someone had left in a hurry. She kicked it open the rest of the way with one foot and carried Becky inside, set her on her feet.

The house seemed empty.

Becky began coming out her fugue. She looked vaguely around, and then signed, with jerky movements of her hands.

"What... are we... going... to do?"

"We're going to be safe," Alice signed. *Lying with my fingers*, she thought. "Someone will come and help us."

"What about Daddy?"

Alice licked her lips, assumed a neutral expression.

"Daddy's going to be okay. We'll see him soon." She couldn't face telling Becky what she suspected, not right now. Later, if they lived, there'd be time to grieve for Todd.

She went to the door and looked out at the intersection, the still smoking car wreck, and the woman she thought of as "Rain"... who was *moving*. Rain was struggling, still hanging upside down in the smoking car but clearly alive after all, trying to get out of her seat belt.

I should go and help her...

But then Alice saw the pack of Undead scurrying toward the overturned vehicle. She couldn't get there and help the woman before the Undead reached her. Suppressing a sob, and feeling a hot stab of shame, Alice closed and locked the door before she would have to see the Undead overwhelm the young woman who'd just tried to help.

Alice took a long breath and turned away from the door.

Focus on right now.
On survival.
On Becky.

"Upstairs," she signed. They climbed the carpeted stairs. When they branched, she turned left, up stairs with a wooden banister, leading them to the second floor.

There Alice looked in each room they came to. Extensive, perfectly matching furnishings—showing the hand of an interior decorator. No sign of human beings, though. In a bedroom was a dresser with most of its drawers pulled out, as if someone had packed as fast as they could.

At the end of the hallway Alice found a nursery, unoccupied, a rumpled blanket in an empty crib. Becky seemed attracted to the little room, and walked into it as if in a trance. Alice followed her in, looking around. It was a nursery for a baby girl, judging from the decorations, the pink curtains.

They closed the door behind them, thinking that the Undead who'd gone after Rain might've seen them go into the house. They had to hide, and soon. Somewhere Becky might feel safe.

Then Alice froze, listening. She'd heard a thump from the front of the house—and another. The sound of someone breaking down a door.

Downstairs.

She went to the louver doors of the closet, and slid them open, turned to Becky and signed.

"Inside—quick!"

Becky walked into the closet, still moving like a ghost, and Alice slipped in beside her, closing the doors. A little light angled through the tiny slat between the two halves, but otherwise they were in a darkness that smelled of old clothes, carpeting and dust. A few items of toddler clothing, perhaps left over from another child, were hung on plastic hangers overhead. On the floor was a folded pink comforter.

Alice and Becky sat down, and Alice leaned back against the wall, clasping her daughter to her. At least she didn't have to tell her not to speak.

They waited. She could feel Becky's heart racing, under her hands.

A shudder seemed to go through the house—then silence, for ten distinct heartbeats.

The quiet was broken by shuffling footsteps, the sound of someone making a slobbering growl.

A piece of furniture overturning, the crash of glass breaking.

They were coming.

Alice fought with herself to remain motionless, *perfectly* still. Maybe the Undead wouldn't find them; maybe the creatures would simply give up and go away. But then she heard one of them fumbling at the doorknob to the nursery. Pulling the door open.

Through the slats in the louver doors, Alice saw a shadow darken the room—and an Undead walked stiffly in, its movements lizardlike. It had once been a young man, a burly, broad-shouldered college student, still wearing the blue-and-white team jacket with a football insignia. The lower half of its face was finger-painted with blood, and its hair was slicked back with red gore.

Becky whimpered.

Alice put her hand over the girl's mouth.

The Undead looked around, sniffing the air. Angrily,

it upended a table of toys, scattering them across the floor. A toy monkey rolled, and came to a stop on its back, clashing its cymbals together.

The Undead shook itself, as if it had a bad chill, and turned toward the door. It was going away.

Alice felt a long shudder of relief.

Then the creature stopped on the threshold. Turned its head—and opened its mouth, wide. Wider... and wider still, till it split its face unnaturally. Something was forcing its way out of its mouth, as if being born—something like mandibles, each one about seven inches long. Four in all, shaped almost like large barbed stems of coral, dripping with blood and sputum.

The mandibles waved about as if they were sense organs... as well as weapons.

She knew, somehow, that they were both.

Becky made an unconscious squeaking sound—and her eyes widened as she saw the Undead's mandibles waving, seeking, snuffling at the air. The thing turned around, searching for them, sensing, now, that they were close at hand.

Alice signed to Becky.

"Whatever happens, you stay here." Becky looked at up at her, open mouthed, staring, rigid with fear.

Hands trembling, Alice forced herself to sign.

"I'll come back for you. I promise."

She reached for the blanket, began to cover Becky with it.

"I love you, Mommy," Becky signed.

Eyes hot with tears, Alice responded.

"I love you, too."

5

Alice pulled the comforter over Becky, aware of the Undead standing just outside the closet door. She felt it looming; she could smell the reek of it.

She got slowly to her feet as the Undead pawed at the door—took a breath, and threw the doors open, the edge of one catching the creature on its down-tilted head, making it stagger back, lose its footing.

The thing crashed against the crib, smashing it, entangling in its blankets and hinged fragments. It thrashed for just a couple of moments, long enough for Alice to slam the closet doors shut.

As long as it didn't see her...

When she turned, the Undead was freeing itself, getting to its feet, mandibles gnashing furiously. Alice raced toward the door, the living dead man stumbling and lurching along behind her, raking the back of her right shoulder with its grasping, clawlike fingernails.

She went through the door, tried to slam it in the Undead's face, but it slapped the door aside and came after her. So she ran. She was partway to the stairs when it lunged, grabbed her around the waist, and knocked her to the floor. Alice turned, writhing around in its grasp, hating to look at it but forced to face it so she could push it away. The thing was clawing its way up her body, the mandibles waving.

She bent her leg, bringing her knee up hard and sharp, into its throat—the mandibles retracted a little and the creature shook its head, seemed confused, its grip on her legs loosening. She scuttled backward, kicking at its hands, and got to her feet. It was up almost as quickly, clawing at her, pushing its head forward, trying to get its snapping mandibles within reach...

She smelled the corruption of its dead, decaying innards, the rot it gasped into her face...

Alice teetered on the edge of the top step. The Undead sprang at her, and she recoiled, losing her footing. They both went over, down the stairs. Alice tumbled one way, almost somersaulting down the carpeted steps. The Undead crashed through the wooden banister.

Groaning and winded at the bottom of the stairs, Alice forced herself to stand. No bones seemed broken—but *everything* ached. She looked for the Undead—and saw that it had impaled itself on the splintered support of a railing, the spike going through its belly and out its back. Rotting black blood seethed up around the wound. The creature struggled, its mandibles helplessly grabbing at air—but it wasn't going anywhere.

Alice turned—and found herself staring into the red-rimmed, glazed eyes of what had once been her husband.

It was Todd—or what remained of Todd. His white shirt was soaked in blood. His face was the color the shirt had been when she'd gotten it from the dry cleaner's. Dead white.

"Todd..." The sound of his name escaped from her throat in a whimper.

The Undead Todd stared... For a moment she thought, perhaps, the thing remembered her. She thought it might turn away, and let her go.

And then it struck, grabbing her shoulders in a painful grip, its mouth opened—wider, too wide—ripping open so the mandibles could extrude, sharp as fangs, extending to rip into her face.

All the fight drained from her, and she felt the mandibles crunching through the bone of her skull. Darkness rose up, like the shadows from the depths of the sea, to swallow her alive...

Alice opened her eyes.

She was cold. She felt the chilly air on her bare legs. She was lying on a hard floor—a floor that seemed to glow.

She sat up, moving with a crinkling sound. She was wearing a patient's garment of thin paper cloth, and nothing else. Her head throbbed.

She was sitting in a high-ceilinged cell, on a plexiglass surface. She had no shoes, no underwear. Light streamed up from below. The plexiglass formed a distinctive eight-sided shape—one she knew very well. It was the outline of the Umbrella Corporation logo.

Becky.

The memory was already fading.

What had it been?

A memory, a fantasy—a dream?

She shook her head. It had seemed too real for any of that. But it couldn't have been real. She had no husband. She had no daughter. And she didn't have blond hair.

She saw herself, a muted reflection in one of the glassy panels. She was a brunette.

Alice sighed, and looked around the almost featureless chamber. The octagonal ceiling was at least forty feet above. The walls were glassy, streaming with light, and there was a window, about thirty feet up—well out of reach, now that Wesker had muted her powers.

Flush with the wall across from her was a steel door. At least she assumed it was a door—though it had no hinges, no handle.

She stood up and looked around.

No way out.

6

Alice moved over to the door-shaped rectangle in the wall, felt its edges, looked for a way to open it. A hidden panel, something—anything.

Nothing.

Abruptly, the cell lights switched off, plunging her into darkness. The air was charged with imminence—and after a moment, the smoked window, high in the wall over the door, lit up with a powerful light. In the window, now, was a familiar silhouette. Alice thought she recognized that shape.

Jill Valentine?

Her voice emanated from a speaker overhead.

"Project Alice, who do you work for?" A pause, and then Jill continued, "Project Alice, why did you turn against Umbrella?"

"Jill?" Alice called. "Is that you?"

"Project Alice," Jill repeated insistently, "*Who do you work for?*"

Alice ignored the question. She wasn't in the mood for any "art of interrogation" psychodramas.

"Where are Chris and Claire? Where are the others from the ship?" she demanded.

And then Alice was punished. She was stabbed by sound.

Squealing, hyper loud, painfully shrill feedback filled the room. It was beyond deafening, echoing back and forth between the walls as if it were hitting her face, over and over. Alice clapped her hands to cover her ears, but the shrieking noise only increased in pitch, in volume, passing unbearable and reaching what had to be near-lethal intensity.

She hunkered down, putting her head between her knees, trying to block out the sound, wondering if she would come out of this with her hearing permanently damaged. It couldn't get any worse than this, she thought desperately.

It got worse.

Louder, higher pitched yet...

She writhed on the floor in agony, and then lost consciousness.

Alice woke, finding that she had been moved, somehow, onto a cot. Her ears were still ringing from the sonic assault. Her stomach was roiling with nausea.

The lights were brightly streaming up from the floor. The clinical glow seemed to say, *"We are watching you, Alice. This is the light of pure observation."*

The lights suddenly switched off. And even in darkness she felt eyes...

And then the light in the window. Jill Valentine's silhouette overhead.

"Project Alice, who do you work for?"

"Jill... what *happened* to you?" Alice asked hoarsely.

"Project Alice, why did you turn against Umbrella?" Jill's cold, impersonal voice reverberated around the octagonal chamber. "Why... why... did you turn..."

"Jill—answer me! Why are you doing this?"

And the punishment began again. The high-pitched feedback assaulted her so loud she could feel it rattling the bones of her head, vibrating in her chest, shivering her teeth. She fell to her knees, clapping her hands over her ears.

Like Becky—she screamed... and couldn't hear it.

Alice fell to her side, and the assault on her ears, her whole being, got worse... and worse... until...

Alice woke on the cot, ears ringing, stomach twisting in her belly. She lay there, pretending to be alive.

They weren't fooled. The lights switched off.

No, Alice thought, sitting up. *NO*.

Jill Valentine appeared in the window above.

"Project Alice—who do you work for?"

There she is, right on schedule, Alice thought. She stood up, trying to marshal her dignity, her defiance.

She just stared up at the light. Words didn't help. She knew her face spoke for her. Her eyes said it all.

I defy you.

But inside, she squirmed in fear, waiting for the assault, the scream that screamed for her...

And it came like an invisible bolt, a crack of lightning in the form of sound, an electrocution that never ended—shrilling, screaming, shrieking—till it filled all time and space.

Blood ran from Alice's nose. Blood trickled from her ears.

She tried to remain standing but found herself on her knees, keeling over, writhing at the pain in her head, pitching into darkness.

Alice woke on the cot, ears ringing.

She lay there in rigid dread. Could she bear it one more time? She was dehydrated, hungry, her belly churning, her head throbbing...

She sat up.

The lights dimmed—and went out.

No.

But the light up above didn't go on. No silhouette appeared in the window.

No Jill Valentine.

Not yet.

A light, just one spotlight, illuminated a steel drawer that came sliding out from the wall. Alice stood up, feeling weak and wobbly, and walked over to the illuminated drawer. In it she found a black Umbrella Corporation combat outfit, neatly folded, as well as a pair of boots. Her size. She picked up the battle suit. Under the outfit was a bottle of liquid. On the bottle was a label: HYDRATION AND NUTRITION.

It might be poison—or it might be a drug. But she was parched, and weak. She'd been, what, days? Yes, days without a drink, or food. She had to take a chance. She opened the bottle, and drank deeply, feeling enormously better after just a few swigs. The liquid was a little thick, a little sweet, and it tasted of vitamins. She waited to see if it would make her sick.

It didn't. It restored her.

She drank the rest, dropped the bottle in the drawer, then pulled on the black outfit. It fit perfectly, of course. But there were no shoes—she was left barefoot.

A slight click sounded behind her. She turned her head to see the door opening, just a little.

She spun on her heels—and waited. No one came through the door. It was as if the unlocked portal was an invitation.

An invitation to escape—or into a trap? Into something even worse?

If someone was helping her escape, why were they doing it? What was their agenda?

She had no options. She had to find out...

So she took a deep breath, and walked to the door, slipped out into the corridor.

Alice looked to the right, and saw only a seemingly endless, white corridor. She looked left—and found the same view. Made of milky glass lit from behind, the corridor walls seemed almost alive, as if, once more, the light streaming from the walls was aware of her, watching her.

She heard nothing except for a hint, a faint hum that might be air filtration. She could hear her own breathing, it was so quiet.

She'd half expected someone out here, to meet her, to explain why they'd released her. But there was no one. And yet they had to be there... behind those glowing walls.

Jill Valentine sat on her barracks bunk, near a squad of other, subordinate Umbrella troopers; they all wore the leather masks and breathing apparatus of lower-echelon troops. They sat calmly, waiting for activation. Near them leaned their weapons—combat rifles, loaded and ready in case of need.

They all had the metal and glass scarabs on their chests. The scarab was the comforting node of Umbrella's control; the source of the peace Jill felt, when she was in "neutral" like this; the source of the reward of hot stimulation she felt when it was time to act.

She felt that stimulation now, as a soft alarm bell sounded, and the room's lights pulsed in warning. The scarab she wore over her bosom began to glow.

Against the milky-white walls stood various types of equipment, including a bank of surveillance monitors.

The scarab glowed, the alarm sounded, and Jill obediently stood up, marching smartly to the surveillance computer. The other troopers stood, as well, their scarabs pulsing with life. They snatched up their weapons and waited for her orders.

Jill touched the corner of the monitor, activating the "scan for irregularities" surveillance system. The system immediately provided an image of Alice, seen from a high angle, walking quickly down the long, seemingly empty corridor. She was wearing a black Umbrella combat suit. That was wrong, Jill knew. She should not have had access to it. She wasn't far from her interrogation cell—how had she acquired the outfit?

The HUD style interface that projected images on the edge of Jill's retina lit up with scrolling letters:

ESCAPED FUGITIVE
APPREHEND OR DESTROY

Jill received her orders.

"She got out!" she snapped. "Scramble the security team!"

Striding down that endless corridor, looking for an exit, Alice was encouraged by what appeared to be the corridor's end, at last, not too far up ahead.

She hadn't seen anyone else yet. The only sound was her breathing, her steps on the floor. Until...

Something else. A faint noise.

The sound got louder—it was distant, but getting closer, until it sounded like a giant's footsteps. *THOOM, THOOM, THOOM, THOOM.* And it was coming from behind.

She turned and saw a laser grid, accompanying the booming sound, filling the corridor section by section.

THOOM.

Another section filled with the lethal beams.

THOOM.

Another section, and it seemed to Alice that she could hear the sizzle of the beams, coming ever closer. She turned and ran, knew instinctively that she didn't want to be caught by even one of the beams in the grid...

Even though she had her back to them, she could feel them, hot on her heels.

Suddenly she reached the end of the corridor—and the door. She sprinted, jerked the door open just as the grid caught up with her, and she ran into...

* * *

Tokyo. At night.

Specifically, Shibuya Scramble. She was in the Times Square of Tokyo, where numerous major streets intersected, neon lights burned like hot emotions against the night, and JumboTrons flashed with endless advertisements.

Alice had been here, shopping, before the coming of the Undead, and it was just as she remembered it... except for one thing. There were no people. No cars, no traffic. The only movements were on the gigantic JumboTron screens, digitally capturing laughing faces, happy faces, coy faces, sexy faces... giant two-dimensional people beaming down on the otherwise lifeless intersection.

But the Scramble wasn't quite empty, because Alice was there, walking into the empty street—and marveling.

At least the Undead should be here. The electricity probably shouldn't be on—not now. Not most of it. The buildings should be damaged, some of them burned, wrecked by the apocalyptic coming of the Undead.

But they weren't—everything here was pristine, as if waiting for the crowd to come back.

Maybe there was a drug in that drink after all.

But she didn't *feel* drugged. She touched the roof of a parked car. It was cold metal, very real indeed. Her bare feet felt the rough, cold concrete beneath them.

Walk/Don't Walk signs flashed for vanished pedestrians. The traffic lights changed, as if hopeful that they might attract traffic.

Alice glanced behind her at the featureless building

from which she'd come. The door was closed. There was no information there.

Then she walked to the center of the deserted Shibuya Scramble and stood there, alone, shivering in the chilly night, dwarfed by the city that was Tokyo. It was as if she were the last woman on Earth. She didn't believe she was alone in the world—not for a moment—but she almost wished it were true. A world vacant of people might be better than a world overrun by the Undead.

The lights flashed, the signs blinked, the spotless buildings gleamed. She'd seen Tokyo destroyed. This... could not... be here.

On the edge of the Scramble was a small Tokyo police cruiser, parked against the curb. Alice walked over to the cop car, and tried the door. Locked.

Not for long.

Off to one side was a bicycle rack, with a dozen lonely-looking bicycles neatly stored. There was an empty slot, and lying across the metal of the slot was a bicycle chain with a large metal lock still attached. She picked it up, swung it experimentally. Not much of a weapon, but better than nothing—almost like a chain mace.

She went back to the cruiser and swung the chain, hard, smashing the lock into the side window on the driver's side of the vehicle, shattering it. She pulled some excess glass out of the way, then reached through, unlocked the door, and opened it. Sliding into the seat, she did a quick search and found a .45 automatic stuck between the cushions; a nice Glock with a good heft to it. She could feel by the weight that it was fully loaded. She located a spare magazine on the floor, and stuck that in a pocket.

There was a police jacket in the back. She pulled it on and got out of the car, the gun in one hand, bicycle chain in the other.

Something chill struck her cheek. She touched it—water. She looked up and more struck her face. It was raining.

Suddenly the doors to every department store burst open, all at once, as if choreographed—and the Scramble began to fill up with busy people, who seemed serenely intent on their own personal missions. They were just the sort of people Alice had once seen, here in Tokyo. Dour salarymen in suits and young women in fashion finery and strolling girls in more conservative secretarial wear and teen girls with earphones, looking J-pop, and young men with spiky hair...

Cars swung around the corner, and suddenly there was traffic. Within seconds the streets were choked with pedestrians and vehicles, cars and cabs and trucks.

The rain was coming down more heavily, tapping on car roofs. Umbrellas sprouted throughout the crowd. Alice noticed that the rain seemed oddly warm—anyway, "room temperature."

"Who did this?"

It was a cop. The angry uniformed officer pointed at his car, and the broken glass of his window. He didn't seem to notice Alice.

A teen girl—in a mix of J-pop and kawaii styles—was walking by, frowning as if contemplating some inner conundrum. She was soaking from the rain, one of the few people who, like Alice, was without an umbrella. Something about her was fascinating. The girl's eyes seemed unfocussed and distant.

She stopped at the center of the Scramble, in a crosswalk, and stood there, arms hanging at her sides. A businessman walked by, and glanced at the J-pop girl—who suddenly lunged at the salaryman, knocking him to the ground.

Then she was tearing at his throat with her teeth, so that blood sprayed... to be washed away in the heavy rain.

7

The crowd panicked.

They ran helter-skelter away from her, dropping their packages, bags, and umbrellas in terror.

The businessman was already transforming into the Undead. He came to his feet—his eyes had gone milky white. He stared at a confused kogal—a young woman dressed like a sexy Japanese schoolgirl—who hadn't seen what the others were running from.

Without warning he lunged at her, bit deeply into her shoulder, ripping through fabric and skin with his teeth.

Women in the crowd screamed; men ran.

The panic quickly reached a fever pitch, and the sickness of the Undead spread with remarkable alacrity. Now the kogal spread it, leaping onto a man's back and biting him; and the J-pop girl birthed another Undead, and that one made another...

Alice backed away, gun in one hand, chain in the other—and suddenly the fleeing crowd parted around her, leaving her exposed. She was the only one not actually running.

The Undead, as one, instantly turned toward her.

The J-pop girl raised her arm, pointed, and unleashed an unearthly howl. Majini tentacles exploded from her mouth, whipping frenetically. The salaryman and the kogal flanked her and lumbered toward Alice.

Other Undead, awakening from a momentary death, transformed with radical speed, getting to their feet and turning their milky eyes toward her. There were too many to fight with a gun and a chain.

A strange creaking, evolving into a rumbling, came from behind Alice. She turned, prepared to run, and saw a 109 Department Store building. It was beginning to split open, the front halves of the big structure parting like giant doors. Blinding white light shafted out from within—where nothing else was visible.

There was nowhere else to go. Once more, she accepted the unspoken invitation, and fled into the light.

Pursued by the crowd of Undead, Alice sprinted into the building, blinking, eyes adjusting to the burst of luminescence—it was like the corridor of milky, glowing glass she had left behind, but taller and wider.

She didn't run into the building alone—the Undead were close behind her. She heard their clumsy but relentless feet, their gasping and burbling and the clacking of their jaws.

A corridor appeared out of the glare, but before she was halfway down its length, she heard an Undead pelting up behind her; lunging, pushing her off balance. Alice stumbled against a wall, then had to turn and face her adversary.

The Undead J-pop girl was out in front of the
crowd of Alice's pursuers. Having only just died, her
young body was just as strong as in life—and far
more relentless. There was no time to get a bead on
her head. Alice spun, swinging the chain, her motion
making it difficult for the creature to grab her. The
chain's lock connected solidly with the girl's face,
breaking bone. The jaw sagged down, coming to rest
askew.

But she kept coming, oblivious to pain, clawing
at Alice with long, brightly painted fingernails—
fingernails with glitter on them. Her broken jaw
wagged back and forth.

Alice shot her in the forehead, stepped out of the
way as she fell, swung the chain around the neck of
the salaryman, yanked it hard to pull him off balance
so he fell on his face. She fired past him at the kogal,
the round tearing off a chunk of her skull but not
nailing her brain. The kogal leapt at her—Alice
dodged, and the girl sprawled atop the salaryman,
knocking him down.

Four more Undead—two men and two women—
came next. Behind them, about thirty paces back,
surged a horde of the things, too many to count.

Alice fired at the closer group, blowing a heavyset
blowsy housewife's head apart. The creature went
down, and right in the path of three that were following
her. They tripped over her, as Alice had hoped, ending
in a confused tangle of limbs and snapping jaws.

Something grabbed Alice's ankle, and she looked
down to see the kogal gnashing at her leg. At that
moment she was grateful for the boots. The salaryman

was like a crushed beetle, limbs wriggling, trying to stand. Alice kicked the Undead girl in the face, stepped back, and fired, aiming carefully so that the .45 slug smashed through her forehead, penetrating and angling down into the salaryman's spine.

There was the sound of clomping feet, bubbling snarls, and she turned to see the three Undead she'd tripped up, double-time marching toward her, side by side. Alice fired three times, from right to left, woman-man-man. The tall woman took one right between the eyes, spun around, and fell; the chubby little man at her side took one in the mouth, and fell backward; the third one, a big man, bald, perhaps a sumo wrestler, merely lost an ear.

And kept coming.

Alice sidestepped and jerked hard on the chain that was still wrapped around the salaryman's neck, pulling it taut between her and the paralyzed creature, snapping his neck and creating a tripwire of steel links. The sumo stumbled over the links and went down with an impact that shook the floor. She shot him in the back of the head, then spun and emptied her gun at the onrushing horde, knocking several more of them down.

She pulled the chain free—and ran, just paces ahead of the horde. There were too many of them to fight. She sprinted full out, and up ahead saw an opening in the wall.

Not a good time to look a gift horse in the mouth, she mused.

The horde dropped back a little, but still followed relentlessly. If she slipped and fell, they'd be on her. But she reached the opening and darted through. As soon as she did, twin doors slid shut from both sides, slamming together at the center. Immediately she could feel a lock clicking into place.

The Undead pounded on the door, but the door held...

That was the good part. The bad part was that she found herself in complete and utter darkness.

Jill Valentine led her team of troopers down the corridor to the interrogation room. The lights were strobing on and off at random, all along the hallways. She carried a flashlight, played it on the partly open door to the chamber Alice had escaped.

But how?

Jill opened the door wider and looked inside. The room was empty except for the cot and the paper gown Alice had discarded. A drawer was open, extending from the wall—yet it shouldn't have been openable. Nor should the door—not from the inside.

She went to the drawer. There was nothing in it but an empty plastic bottle. So they'd even given her something to revitalize her.

The monitor had shown Alice wearing a black Umbrella combat outfit—one that fit her remarkably well. Who had loaded it into the drawer? Jill went back to the door, and examined it. She saw no marks, no sign that anything had been used to pry it open, or even to get to the locking mechanism. Someone had to have helped her get out. Someone on the inside.

The strobing irritated Jill.

"Get these lights back online," she said to her second.

"Yes, ma'am," he replied, his voice muffled by the

mask. The trooper jogged off to locate the building generator, in search of an override switch.

"And contact Control!" she called after him. "Find out what the hell's going on."

But she had a strong feeling they knew no more than she did.

The relentless hammering continued, unabated.

Get a clue, Alice thought, as she put a fresh magazine in the Glock. *That door's not designed so you can break it with your fists.* Now—where was she? She turned, trying to make out something in the darkness—but to no avail. It was total.

Until it *wasn't*.

Across the ceiling, lights flickered on.

Expecting to see someone throwing a switch, she readied the automatic pistol, and tensed. But there was no one else to be seen. The room was large, echoingly empty, with a milky glass floor. There was a big red and white logo in the center of that floor— seen from above, it would appear as the shape of an umbrella. The brand was repeated, though smaller, on three of the walls. The fourth was occupied by a floor-to-ceiling window.

She walked over to it and tried to peer out. No good. It was pitch dark out there.

As she moved back across the room, wondering if she'd entered still another trap, the toe of her boot pressed the very center of the umbrella logo in the floor. Something clicked in response. The lights dimmed, and panels in the floor opened up. From them, monitors and a line of high-tech workstations began to rise slowly up out of the floor, humming as they came.

Now that's interesting...

There were a dozen of them, all around the edge of the room—and at each one was an Umbrella trooper, sitting facing away from her. Alice pointed her Glock at the nearest one—who fell from his chair as soon as his station clicked into place.

But she hadn't fired.

She stepped closer, looked at him—and saw that the eyepiece of his mask had been penetrated. Blood traced the cracks in the eyepiece. He'd been shot.

They had all been shot—they were all dead.

Then something else was rising from the floor—a rack of guns.

"Pay dirt!" Alice exclaimed.

As soon as it clicked into place she began to pick and choose. She chose an assault rifle as her primary shooter. Then she filled her pockets with extra clips, and strapped on some throwing knives for good measure. Before she was done, she had strapped on as many weapons as she could carry and still move effectively.

Without warning, the monitors on the workstations lit up, all showing the same image—Jill Valentine, glaring into the camera. The sound of her voice filled the room.

"Control, come in! Control, this is Security Chief Valentine! We have an escaped fugitive! I need her location! Control, respond."

Alice watched the monitor fixedly—but as she did, she was aware of something else.

Someone slipping up behind her. Very quietly.

But...

She spun, snatching a pistol from the hand of a beautiful young Asian woman with short-cropped hair. The newcomer wore a tight red dress slit to the hip, and red spectacles.

The instant Alice grabbed her gun the woman whirled about and—with a precise martial arts strike—kicked the gun from her hand. The pistol spun through the air and in an instant was caught again by the woman in red. She smiled coldly as she pointed it at her target.

But Alice was already in motion. Slipping in under her attacker's defensive stance, she drew a knife and pressed it to the woman's throat...

The result was a standoff. The Asian woman in red was pointing a pistol at Alice, and Alice—all in black—had a knife against the woman's jugular. Gazes locked and weapons gripped tightly in their hands, they glared at each other, neither making a move.

Alice kept it simple.

"Don't," she said, eliciting a reply.

"My name is..."

"Ada Wong," Alice interrupted. "Operative for the Umbrella Corporation and one of Albert Wesker's top agents." Contempt twisted her lips. "I know exactly who—and what—you are." She pressed her blade, fractionally, and a small drop of Ada's blood trickled down her neck.

Ada didn't even blink. Nor did she pull the trigger.

"The real question," Alice said, "is why I shouldn't just cancel your contract right now."

"I don't work for Umbrella anymore."

Alice shrugged, just slightly.

"I don't care. She angled her blade, readying it for

a quick slash... Then she heard a chillingly familiar male voice. An impossible voice. The voice of a ghost.

"You can kill her if you like. But then you'll never get out of this place."

Glancing past Ada, Alice saw the face of Albert Wesker, framed in the monitors. He was wearing shades, as per usual, dressed in black, and grinning with wicked wideness.

"Wesker..." Alice shook her head in wonder. His duplicated faces flashed across the row of monitors.

"How nice to see you again," he responded pleasantly.

"I killed you!"

Wesker shrugged apologetically.

"A clone." He smiled. "You didn't really think I'd put myself in harm's way, did you?"

Alice looked again at Ada... at the gun in Ada's hand.

"Now," Wesker said, "be a good girl and put down the knife."

"I let you out of that cell," Ada said. "I led you here. You wouldn't have made it this far without me."

"Why would you want to help me?" Alice asked.

"I have my reasons. Let's just say, for the moment, your interests and mine are in alignment."

Alice shook her head.

"I'm not going anywhere until I know where we are, and exactly what's going on here."

Wesker sighed.

"You are in the prime Umbrella Testing Facility." He chuckled and added, "The belly of the beast."

Alice lowered her knife. Ada lowered the gun and stepped back. But each woman kept a wary eye on the other.

"Explain Tokyo," Alice demanded flatly. "I saw it destroyed."

Wesker adjusted his shades.

"What you just saw was a detailed re-creation. Nothing more. It goes on for a few city blocks—that's all."

"I was outside..."

"Were you?" Ada asked. "Saw the night sky, did you?"

"It was night," Alice insisted.

"Stars? The moon?" Alice didn't reply, and Ada added dryly, "I thought not."

Around the room, a series of monitors flickered, then showed downtown views of Berlin, Tokyo, New York, London, and several other cities she didn't quite recognize.

"The testing floor," Wesker said, "is a mile across. Three hundred feet high. The ceiling is black. It's *usually* night in there. But isn't that when the monster comes out, anyway?"

Alice still wasn't convinced.

"It was raining..."

"Sprinkler system," Wexler replied, sounding almost bored. "Fitted to the ceiling for climate control. They can even make it snow, if they want to."

It all began to sink in.

How many mock cities were there, here in this facility? And why?

"Why build such a place?" she asked.

"Simple," Wesker said. "The Umbrella Corporation

derived its primary income from the sale of viral weaponry. Something that's impossible to test in the real world. So Umbrella re-created the center of New York, simulated an outbreak, then showed the results to the Russians—and sold them the virus. Then they simulated an outbreak in Moscow... and sold it to the Americans. An outbreak in Tokyo..."

"They sell it to the Chinese."

"An outbreak in China..." Ada added.

Alice nodded.

"They sell to the Japanese."

"Everyone had to have it," Wesker said proudly. "The Umbrella Corporation built a new arms race. Only this time it was biological, rather than nuclear. Highly profitable..."

Alice glanced around the control room, a chill tightening her skin as she imagined it. She stared at the doomed cityscapes displayed on the monitors. She hadn't known about this, back when she was Security Chief of Umbrella. The corporation was notorious for keeping its most secret projects on a "need to know" basis.

Most likely they'd realized she was having doubts about the corporation's T-virus research.

"And this," Wesker went on, with a flourish of his hand, "is where it all happened. Umbrella's greatest investment—their greatest creation. Like I said, the belly of the beast."

Alice sheathed her knife, drew a pistol and turned it toward the floor to ceiling window.

"So why don't we just get the hell out of here?" she said to Ada.

The Asian woman glanced at her watch, and

calmly held up her hand.

"Sunup is in less than a minute. Why don't you just see for yourself?" She nodded toward the window. Alice looked, but still saw nothing but darkness.

Then the first rays of sunlight penetrated the gloom outside. There was something oddly diffuse about the sunlight, as if it were filtered through some translucent medium. It illuminated icy blue mountains—only the mountains were *inverted*. The sunlight intensified, filtering through the icy blue peaks.

Through the...

"Ice!" Alice gasped. She was seeing the crystalline-blue mountains of floating ice floes. The light spread, and underneath the ice floes lay the great, angular sprawl of the facility, built right into the seabed.

The corporation had built their facility under the Arctic ice pack. As more and more light penetrated the waters, a gigantic concrete and steel bunker became visible. On it was emblazoned the hammer and sickle of the old USSR...

8

Alice gazed for a long moment at the frigid vista coming into view through the filter of ice and seawater, just beyond the wall-window. She shivered. That water would be brutally cold—death wouldn't be instant, but it would be quick.

They weren't getting out of here that way...

The glowing ice floes and inverted peaks were fascinating, even beautiful. Shafts of light reticulated, dancing across the murky seabed. A walrus swam past the window, the great beast looking surprisingly graceful. In the distance, she could see the dark undulating mass of a whale.

That hammer and sickle symbol, though faded with time, was still striking in its crimson starkness.

She turned back to Ada and the monitors—where Wesker waited for her reaction.

"Where exactly *are* we?" Alice asked.

"The Straits of Kamchatka," he replied smoothly. "Northern Russia. The old Soviet Union built submarine pens here, back in the nineteen-eighties.

After the Cold War ended, the Umbrella Corporation expanded them—and built the testing floor."

So that was it. After she'd lost consciousness off the coast of Los Angeles, they'd brought her here, to an old Soviet base. But where, she wondered, was Wesker? Was he here in this sprawling facility? Or perhaps in some high-tech den under Tokyo? If she found him, and killed him *again*—would it turn out to be yet another Wesker clone?

How many *were* there?

"How do we get out?" Alice asked, looking at Ada.

"We cross the test floor," she replied, her tone uncannily matter-of-fact, "through the submarine pens, then take an elevator to the surface."

"Just like that?"

"No, not really." Ada smiled.

"I didn't think so."

"But don't worry... we are going to have a little help."

"We," she said. Alice shook her head doubtfully. She had no idea what this woman's agenda was—still didn't know why Ada had helped her escape from the interrogation. And who was this "help" she was talking about? Might they end up being just as much Alice's enemy as the Umbrella troopers?

Sure, I won't worry, Alice thought. *Hell, why should I? Just because this facility is overrun with troopers and well stocked with the Undead?*

"Don't worry."

Yeah, right.

* * *

Two vehicles churned across the snowfield atop a wind-raked ridge. The rectangular tractor-tread vehicles, called Sprytes—bigger than Humvees, and armored—ground their way steadily through the unforgiving expanse of Arctic snow and ice. The Kamchatka Peninsula. A tern flew overhead. Other than that, the only movement was spurts of snow-laden wind.

At last the ungainly vehicles rolled to a halt near the edge of a steep ridge.

Luther West, a tall, good-looking black man with a short-trimmed beard, tugged the fur collar of his military camouflage coat more tightly around him as he climbed out. The wind wasn't strong, but it was so cold that it felt like being hit in the face with a fist of ice. His breath plumed in the air.

"Damn, it's cold!" he said. "You know I'm from *California*, don't you?"

Luther was addressing Leon Kennedy—a rugged man, mid-thirties, whose stern expression suggested that he had no interest in Luther's protestations.

"Barry—let's take a look," Leon called out.

Barry Burton climbed down from the second vehicle. A professional soldier, with an unlit cigar clamped in his mouth—he was trying to quit but couldn't quite give it up—he wore a customized .44 Magnum Colt Anaconda on his hip. He brushed roughly past Luther.

"Did it just get colder around her?" Luther asked, trying to make a joke of their attitude.

No response to that, either.

How had he gotten involved with these guys? They'd shared many of the same trials, coming from the prison he and Alice and Chris and the others had used as a fortress against the Undead. He wasn't a professional gun-toter, but he'd become a pretty good shot. His pro-basketball skills had helped quite a bit.

Could be they thought he was a media whore—resented that for some reason. But none of that mattered now. There weren't any basketball teams—no TV commercials, no endorsement deals, and sure as hell no superstars. There was little television or internet to speak of, anymore. Instead, there was a burning world overrun by the Undead. And in Hell, everyone was equally damned.

They were joined by Sergei, their Russian technical specialist. Barry led the way to the edge of the cliff where the four men stood, side by side. Far below, at the foot of the ridge, Luther spotted a string of weathered, rust-streaked concrete-and-iron bunkers, part of the last century's Soviet military installation. Barry grunted, peering at the bunkers through digital binoculars. Luther could hear the chip-enhanced device humming as he adjusted them.

Beyond the rugged ground at the foot of the cliff lay the rocky beach, and the pack ice of the Kamchatka Strait. It was colder here—where they were exposed to the wind off the sea—and Luther had to work at it to keep his teeth from chattering. But he wasn't about to complain again.

In the distance, he saw the gray hulks of abandoned battleships, and one large carrier, all locked in the ice—part of the old, mothballed Soviet fleet. They seemed like gravestones—forlorn, decaying monuments to another era.

Leon pointed at the three huge vents by the water's edge.

"There they are."

Sergei grunted.

"Intake vents for the submarine pens," he observed.

Barry swept his binoculars over the abandoned facility one last time.

"Looks abandoned."

"That's what they want you to think," Leon observed.

Luther was ready to get moving.

"So what are we waiting for?" he asked. Leon shot him a cutting look. Barry, Leon, and Sergei were a tight unit, used to each other's rhythms. Luther was odd man out, no matter what he did.

Leon sighed.

"Let's get something clear right now," he said in an irritatingly condescending tone of voice. "You're here as an advisor—nothing more. You know this woman, and that's your value to me.

"Understand?" he concluded.

And what's your value to me? Luther thought. But he didn't say it. He had his own agenda, and he didn't want to gum it up with arguments. These guys would reunite him with Alice—and maybe the others...

So he just returned Leon's glare.

"I'll take that as a yes," Leon growled.

It's a yes for now, Luther thought.

He turned and walked back to the ice crawlers.

Jill Valentine felt herself drawn back to the empty interrogation cell. It was almost as if she hoped to find the prisoner here again.

She remembered interrogating Alice, remembered

slamming her with the sonic torture. She'd had a strange feeling, then—almost as if she were prolonging the process. Interrogation was the only kind of prisoner contact that Jill was allowed. Yet sometimes she'd felt as if there was something she wanted to say, something she wanted to do. But she wasn't sure what it was. Perhaps tell Alice that she felt sympathy for her.

Maybe tell her, "I can't control this."

But all that had come out of Jill's mouth had been the pre planned questions. Every time she got close to that vagrant, taunting feeling, a pulse from the scarab muted it, drove it away. Keeping her on task as security chief.

Which was exactly what she needed to be, right now—back on task. There was no place for emotion, for questioning, for intuition, in the life she lived. She was part of Umbrella—part of the great effort, the grand design. That was all that mattered.

So Jill found herself looking down at the scarab-shaped mechanism on her chest. Her intimate connection with the corporate masters.

She reached up to touch it... and suddenly drew her hand back.

No. That's not allowed.

Two masked Umbrella troopers from her squad strode up, and Jill, standing in the open doorway, felt as if she had to say something.

"The lock's intact," she noted, peering intently at the doorframe.

"How did she get out?" a female trooper asked.

"She's obviously getting help from the inside," Jill snapped impatiently. "We have a traitor in this facility."

"Central computer seems to be offline, Ma'am," the

other trooper reported. "We have limited surveillance and communications."

"What about Control?" Jill demanded.

"Still can't raise them."

"Well try harder!" she said. "That was my prisoner—I want her *back*!"

Suddenly a HUD style display appeared, projected directly onto Jill's eyes by the scarab. Scrolling text filled her vision.

FACILITY COMPROMISED
INITIATE LOCKDOWN

At the same moment a masked female trooper pointed her thermal tracking device at the corridor floor outside of the cell. Jill could see the screen—and on it, the outline of Alice's feet.

"We have residual thermal readings... Looks like she's at least twenty minutes ahead of us."

"Good for you, trooper," Jill responded. "At least *someone* is showing some initiative. What's your designation?" Without waiting for a reply she looked at the nametag. "Carlyle. Okay, Carlyle, stick close to me. We're going to track down an escapee... and initiate a lockdown."

The Sprytes ground along the rise above the stony beach, then came to a halt in front of the bunkers. Luther got out of his vehicle, and was instantly shivering.

He followed as Barry exited and moved cautiously over to the structures. They looked formidable, up close—hulking edifices of concrete and iron, the metal bleeding rust like bloody tears down the face. Weeping for the USSR.

Leon strode up beside them, with Tony—the last man on the team.

"Barry, Tony, take care of the vents," Leon said, motioning to the three large concrete structures that stood near the water. "Sergei—you know what to do."

The wind from the sea pushed at the back of Luther's parka as he turned, following Tony and Barry, walking more slowly than they managed. He could hear gigantic fans, ponderously turning in the vents, slowly sucking great volumes of air down into the Umbrella facility hidden far below.

Tony was a scowling American Latino who hadn't shaved in a long while. It looked like there were a couple of fading gang tattoos on his neck. Luther envied the goggles he wore against the wind as he moved his power tools into place at the base of the first tower. Barry hunched down beside him, opening a pack of explosives as Luther walked up to stand near them, trying not to get in the way.

Hope to God they know what they're doing with those plastic explosives, Luther thought. *This would be a helluva place to be blown to pieces.*

Sergei, carrying a laptop, flipped up a rusted metal hatch—which turned out to be camouflage for a state-of-the-art computer port. He plugged in his laptop, holding it up with one hand, typing with the other.

"Running a bypass," he called out.

It's like these guys have been breaking into secret facilities all their adult lives, Luther thought, chuckling. *Maybe they have.*

* * *

Moments later, Leon stepped up to Sergei, handing him a note with a string of numbers written on it. The precious data fluttered dangerously in the rising wind.

"These are the access codes Ada gave us," he explained.

"You trust her?" Sergei asked, typing the codes in.

Leon smiled thinly.

"Just the numbers."

Watching them wire the explosives to the bases of the vent towers, Luther wondered why they were necessary, if they were going in via an entrance other than the bunkers. Surely they weren't there to blow open an entrance.

Maybe its part of the escape plan. It looked to Luther as if Barry set the timer for two hours.

Two hours? he thought—though he didn't say anything. *That can't be right, considering what we're here to do.* Perhaps he'd read it wrong.

On the other hand, maybe the bombs would bring the whole place down on his head, long before he got out.

"Don't suppose you want to tell me what these are for?" Luther said, nodding toward the explosives.

Barry finished pushing a wire into the block, then turned to stare quizzically at him.

Luther shrugged apologetically—not feeling it, though.

"I know, I know... I'm just an advisor." He grinned.

The faintest flicker of a smile showed at the corners of Barry's mouth.

"Listen, don't get Leon wrong," he said, keeping his voice low. "It's not that he doesn't like you. He just doesn't know you."

Luther nodded.

"And what about you?"

"Me?" Barry considered for a moment. "I just don't like you." He stood up, and walked away from the towers, moving toward the bunkers, leaving Luther to wonder if he'd been joking or not.

Giving up, he sighed and followed Barry over to the bunkers, where they joined Tony. Through a warped, yellowed window in a discolored steel door he could just make out rusted Soviet-era equipment that lay inside. There were hulking machines, some with huge pulleys, and he couldn't tell what any of it was for.

Sergei unplugged his laptop, and he looked pleased.

"We're in!" he announced.

Meaning what? Luther wondered. The door was still shut, and looked rusted into place. *How are we getting in?*

The answer came a moment later, when the snow that had drifted between two of the concrete bunkers began to move from below. Before his eyes the ground was opening up, as huge panels yawned wide to reveal a deep, silo-shaped shaft extending straight down into the ground, hundreds of yards into the shadows. There were four open-air elevator platforms attached to the shaft's walls.

Luther sighed—quietly enough that the others wouldn't hear.

"Elevators... I hate elevators." He stared down the

shaft. It was relatively new; the platforms weren't rusty. "The Soviets didn't build this," he said.

"Umbrella built it," Barry replied. "The old Soviet shell is just more masking."

"Come on," Leon said. He led the way onto the nearest elevator platform—it was large, enough so to carry supplies, even vehicles. Luther stepped gingerly onto it, wondering what had happened to the concept of *walls*.

The rest of the team studied the bottom of the platform, and he heard a series of clicks as they attached something to the metal. Then they joined him on the platform, standing close to the curved wall. Luther could feel warm air rising from below. Leon pressed a button on a control pedestal.

The elevator shuddered, causing every muscle in Luther's body to tense. It grumbled mechanically, and began to move slowly downward. He patted the machine gun pistol he had under his coat. He had a strong feeling he'd be using it.

Hope I brought enough ammo.

As they sank into the shaft, the bright Arctic sky— lit by the midnight sun—receded until it was a distant circle of light, far above. And still they descended.

"Synchronize watches," Leon said. "Two hours exactly in three, two, one..."

Two hours till the explosives went off.

One hour, fifty-nine minutes, fifty seconds. Forty-nine seconds... Forty eight seconds...

"Why don't we just trigger the explosives remotely?" Luther asked. *When we're safely out of the damn place.*

"Can't risk them jamming the signal," Leon

countered as he checked that his combat rifle was loaded.

Luther shook his head. These guys were professional badasses, working for people he didn't know—and they liked to play with timed explosives.

What the hell have I got myself into?

He sure would like to see Alice again, though. Now *there* was a woman. "Amazing" didn't even begin to cover it. So he glanced at his watch again.

"And what if we take longer than two hours?"

"Then," Barry said, a little too matter-of-factly, "I hope you're good at holding your breath."

Just then they reached the bottom of the silo, where the elevator entered a much smaller vertical tube, hardly big enough for the platform. An echoing darkness closed over them.

"Into the rabbit hole," Leon said.

9

In the Umbrella control room, Wesker's image had disappeared from the screens. Ada Wong checked her watch. Standing nearby, Alice could see the reading.

01.58.01 – 01:58:00 – 01:57:59 – Something that was going to happen in two hours. Something critical...

"They're in," Ada said. Then she was staring straight ahead, as if at nothing. Suddenly Alice realized that her spectacle lenses were a heads-up display. If she looked carefully she could see minutely projected data on the edges. There was a wire-frame 3D map of some kind. Probably the facility layout, and perhaps their escape route.

Ada nodded to herself and looked at her companion.

"The strike team will eliminate Umbrella resistance, then rendezvous with us and escort us out."

"How considerate," Alice said, glancing at the window; the crystalline shine of the blue-green floes; the inverted mountains of icebergs.

"They have a friend of yours with them," Ada said. "Luther West."

Alice felt a pleasant shock go through her on hearing that name.

"He's alive!"

Ada nodded.

"We picked him up in Los Angeles. He saw them capture you at the *Arcadia*... that's how we knew Umbrella had you."

"How'd you find him?"

"Pretty easy to pick out the humans from the Undead, from the air. We talked to him. He was on the shore, saw the V-22s hammer the *Arcadia*. And he knew that's where you'd gone. Saw you with binoculars when they pulled you from the water. Your interests and ours converge, now—and we figured he would give us a sense of how to deal with you.

"He insisted on coming along in exchange, so..." She shrugged.

"And you tracked the V-22s to here?"

"Yes. To—Umbrella Prime."

Alice considered demanding to know the full scope of her agenda—and Wesker's—but they'd probably just mislead her, if she did that. If she remained patient, however, they might reveal more than they intended...

"So, do we wait right here for your extraction team?"

Ada glanced at her watch.

"We wait till time to move out, and rendezvous with them. We can't wait long..."

Auto pistol in hand, Jill strode across the life-size model of Tokyo's Shibuya Scramble, leading her squad toward the enormous false front of the "109

Department Store." The cars had gone, but she knew there were living dead out here, left over from the unauthorized scenario that someone had run earlier.

"Heat readings are stronger," Carlyle said, looking at the small screen of the infrared tracker. "We're getting close. Looks like they're in the control center."

Jill grunted. This was not good. It would explain the lack of response from Control, though.

She glanced at the readings—the shape of the footprints had changed.

"She's put on some boots, if that's her..."

There was a faint false drizzle, coming down from the water works in the ceiling. Peering around, Jill puzzled at the way they maintained these urban representations. The people they used, artificial though they might be, were unwitting pawns, oblivious as to what was destined to happen to them. What did the corporation tell them, she wondered, right before it all went down?

"This is just an acting job. Pretend you're going about your life, that's all..."

But that wasn't her department. She was in security, intel, and enforcement. Umbrella worked in mysterious ways, and Jill wasn't to question it. The scarab assured her of that.

"Heads up!" trooper Carlyle shouted. "Undead moving in!"

Jill sighed as she swung her auto pistol into position. Maybe they should've taken the long way, so they didn't have to deal with this. But the squad were heavily armed—and the Undead were pretty much idiots. Dangerous idiots, but idiots.

She didn't have to waste ammo on the skinny black

man who came rushing at them—Carlyle shot him through the head and he went down. Blood splashed from the fallen creature's shattered skull, spattering Jill's boots.

She'd just polished them that morning.

Instead she tracked her pistol over to an Undead who'd been a grandmotherly-looking elderly Japanese lady in traditional Asian garb—eyes glazed milky white, the Undead grandma was howling wordlessly as she charged, her face contorted like a kabuki demon.

Jill's first burst caught the woman in the teeth—but too low. Though the creature staggered back a little, she soon recovered and came at Jill again. Annoyed, she squeezed off a quick burst, blowing the Undead's brains out. It flopped at her feet.

She stepped over the mess, continuing to lead the squad across the open Scramble, tracking for another target—but the rest of her team was taking care of business.

"Grenade out!" Carlyle shouted. Jill tossed the explosive toward the rear of the oncoming group, blowing six of them to kingdom come. The others dispatched their targets skillfully, their long practice at headshots taking out the Undead almost as efficiently as a lawnmower would cut down weeds.

There were a few more of the creatures staggering around, but they were stumbling over the corpses of the fallen, and the squad had reached the 109.

The entrance was still open wide, and they headed inside...

* * *

"Look at this!" Alice said, pointing.

On a computer monitor, a surveillance camera showed Jill Valentine and her squad, moving along the corridor that led to the control room.

"They're headed this way," Ada said. She had locked the door and scrambled the unlock code—but there were other ways to get through it.

Framed in the monitor, Jill stared up at the security camera, right into the lens, as if guessing that Alice was watching her. She could see the high-tech scarab on Jill's chest. So that was it—that was why she was working for Umbrella. Why she'd interrogated Alice...

They had her mind-controlled.

A squad trooper stepped up to the door. Taking a power tool off her belt, she began cutting at the metal. Sparks flew, and when Alice and Ada glanced at their side of the barrier, smoke appeared. Their pursuers were cutting their way through.

Alice looked at Ada questioningly.

Ada glanced at the countdown timer on her wrist, and nodded.

"Let's move!" Alice declared.

Ada walked over to the workstations where corpses of trooper techs still drooped in their seats. She grabbed two by their collars, pulled them out of their seats, pushed the bodies aside and signaled to Alice with a jerk of her head.

Following the motion, Alice stepped next to one of the empty the workstation chairs. She watched as Ada tapped the controls, making her own unit sink through the floor.

The hole in the door was larger now, burning, expanding... which meant it was time to fight or go.

No reason to risk the fight—yet—and Alice really didn't want to kill Jill. Her friend had no control over herself, no real choice, as long as that device clung to her chest...

So Alice duplicated Ada's input on the controls, and her workstation panel sank into a square shaft, descending into the floor. In a matter of seconds she was in an entirely different room.

The cutting tool severed the final metal rod of the locking mechanism, and the steel door opened. Two troopers entered ahead of their commander, as per protocol.

"Rooms clear!" one shouted.

"Secured!" the other echoed.

Gun in hand, Jill Valentine walked into the Control Room. All but two of the workstations were there, and all of its occupants were dead—corpses slumping at the consoles. One of the troopers slid her helmet off.

"No sign of them," the trooper, Rain, said.

"Then check surveillance," Jill ordered.

"On it," a second trooper replied. He took off his helmet, revealing African-American features, and checked the dead Umbrella troopers slain at their workstations. "Single shot. Assassination style." Whoever had shot them, Jill reflected, must have caught them by surprise—and must have been damned good at shooting quickly and accurately.

The black trooper rewound the surveillance footage, stopping when it showed Alice and Ada Wong in the control room.

"She was here. And she had help."

He rewound the footage further, to show troopers manning their control stations. Ada Wong entered, unnoticed by them all. With rapid-fire precision she killed them, one bullet through each mask's goggles, with no emotion showing on her face at all. It was over in seconds.

As the tape moved forward again, it showed Alice and Ada's confrontation, and the appearance of Wesker on the screens. Jill's scarab saw what she saw—it communicated with a central computer, and projected an HUD display onto her eyesight.

ADA WONG.
CLASSIFIED: RENEGADE.

ALBERT WESKER.
CLASSIFIED: RENEGADE.

"Ada Wong," Jill said. "That's our traitor. When Wesker went rogue, she must've joined him."

"That's not all," said the trooper with Rain's face. She pointed to another screen. On it, Leon and his team clearly visible. "Intruders! Just leaving the submarine pens. They're headed for the test floor."

"They're here to help our prisoner," Jill said. "Trooper—"

"Yes ma'am?"

"Arrange a little welcome party for our guests."

"Very good, ma'am.

As they moved to obey, Jill peered intently at the two gaping holes in the floor, where the two missing workstations had been.

* * *

The lower control room boasted low ceilings, walls made out of reinforced metal, and no windows. There were slots for the workstations, and additional equipment hummed on one wall.

Alice crouched at the workstation, not daring to move. But it had grown too quiet up above...

Just as she darted away, a burst of bullets smashed into the console—they'd have nailed her head if she hadn't moved. Pieces of monitor, bits of wire, and spark-inflected smoke burst from the computer. She looked up and saw a trooper's mask peering down from the slot in the ceiling, and she fired a burst from her assault rifle. The masked face jerked back—Alice wasn't sure if she'd hit her target or not.

Then she heard a familiar voice calling down from above.

"Alice—surrender and we'll promise you won't be—"

But then the ceiling panel closed, cutting off the speaker. In the dim light, Alice saw Ada pulling away from a switch.

"Where now?" Alice asked as she picked pieces of shattered monitor glass from her right cheek.

Ada headed toward the back of the room.

"Right through here... *fast*," Ada said, scooping up a tool of some sort. "Before they blow that ceiling panel open. We don't want to go in the lower corridor, she'll have troops moving into place out there."

Alice followed her to a corner where Ada used the tool to unscrew bolts on a metal trap door. Once the bolts were released, the door swung back automatically, and the two of them descended, climbing down a steel ladder into a diffused red light...

* * *

A huge vaulted stone chamber carved out of the living rock was one of the facility's few reminders of its Soviet origins. The drafty chamber was dominated by Cyrillic lettering painted high on the walls—which no member of Umbrella Squad Seventeen could read, though they all stared up at it as they entered.

The squad entered rapidly, double-timing into the room, kicking up small clouds of dust, guns at the ready. Their captain followed them in.

"Orders from Commander Valentine," he said. "The facility is to be placed under complete lock down!"

A communications specialist stepped up.

"Sir! We have unauthorized movement of Elevator 2!"

"Contact topside," the captain snapped back. "Find out who it is."

"I've already tried, sir," came the reply. "There's no reply from the surface."

The captain frowned. Someone had sabotaged the transmitters. He gestured toward key spots around the chamber.

"Defensive formation!"

The Umbrella troops responded instantly, and several of them knelt in a ring around the narrow tube that came from the elevator shaft, pointing their weapons. Their fingers tightened on the triggers, a hair's breadth from firing.

"Mark your targets," the captain advised. "Fire at will."

The giant elevator platform neared the bottom, hardly visible in the murk, and the space was pierced by the red rapiers of targeting lasers. But there appeared to be no one on the elevator.

"It's empty, sir..."

Suddenly there was a series of explosions as a group of Jumping Jack mines detonated from the bottom of the platform, spraying deadly fragments in every direction, ripping through the troops. Each detonation was accompanied by a deafening burst of sound.

Then, as the platform reached the bottom of the shaft, the intruders appeared. They'd been lying flat, hiding on the floor at the back of the platform, visible only at the last second when they jumped up, weapons in hand. The captain thought he could see them grinning in the gloom.

One of the intruders flung something at the troopers. It detonated a second later, just as the captain realized it was a Jumping Jack mine. The storm of spiked ball bearings tore through him and his men...

He was knocked onto his back, and when he tried to move—it was no good. One of the spiked balls had pierced his gut and smashed into his spine.

There was a firefight with the few survivors of his squad, but it was brief. As silence descended, he heard two of the intruders talking. But the words seemed to make no sense to him, in the sucking vacuum of pain and chaos and darkness.

"Submarine pens are up ahead," one of the men said.

"Barry, you and I take point..."

"We're down to an hour and forty-five seconds!" another man said.

"I can read my counter, Luther, no need for you to..."

The Umbrella captain didn't hear any more, except the rising wave of white noise in his ears, which must be, he supposed, the sound made by Death as it arrived.

10

The narrow utility shaft, bathed in soft, red emergency lighting, descended about fifty feet to a room containing bulky aluminum heating and air conditioning units.

Ada and Alice dropped from the ladder to the concrete floor, and looked around. Ducts rose to the ceiling like the arms of giant robotic octopi; hulking silver machines flickered with indicator lights.

"I hope you're not lost," Alice said.

Ada shook her head. She glanced at her countdown watch.

"Not lost—just... behind schedule. We need to get to the secondary meet-up—fast." She led the way across the warm chamber, through a smell of industrial cleansers and the faint tang of leaking natural gas, to a stairway that wound up the farther wall. "Up this, and past a utility room, along a corridor, and then out into Times Square."

Five minutes later they were there.

Anyway, it used to be Times Square, Alice thought.

No... it used to look like *Times Square.*

"New York," she murmured. Now it looked like a forgotten war zone. Bodies were scattered about the streets and sidewalks. Some of them were trying to crawl. The cars were burning, many overturned; one was rammed through a store window. Refuse from overturned trash cans blew past Alice and Ada on artificial winds.

Overhead was the darkness of the "night sky"—a distant black ceiling without a star to be seen. Some of the Times Square neon signs still burned and blinked; pretty dancers did choreographed kicks on a huge screen; streams of lights chased around the frames of billboards. Stock market quotes—from a stock market that no longer existed in the real world— flowed past along an electronic sign.

"This way," Ada said. "We need to cross two more test environments to get out."

Alice followed her, still looking around.

"Why would Umbrella still be running these tests?"

"To start with, all they wanted to do was to sell the biohazard. But now they want to study it—learn how to contain it. Control it."

Control it. Alice shook her head. She'd seen them try that, in Las Vegas. Clumsily conditioned Undead had been let loose, supposed to operate as soldiers. The difference between them and the other Undead had been negligible.

What was Umbrella up to, now? It had destroyed civilization. Perhaps now it wanted to create a warped *caricature* of civilization. Maybe it wanted to use the T-virus to create an alternate humanity. New levels of class distinction, perhaps. At the bottom rung would be the controlled Undead. At the top, mutated, virus-warped superhumans.

And in between, everyone else.

That was Alice's guess, although it really didn't make sense to her. But then again, who said Umbrella's plans had to make any sense? Maybe whoever was in charge of it now was as psychotic as the world they had created.

Suddenly she saw light, flashing from directly overhead. She craned her neck and watched as giant banks of lights, mounted in the distant ceiling, began to switch on. Night was turning quickly into day.

"What's going on?" she asked.

"It's the end of the scenario," Ada explained, as she stepped over a moaning woman. "They rarely last more than an hour."

Alice looked up again, her sense of reality stressed to the breaking point. "Times Square" gained a giant, floodlit roof over it, as if it had been a construct in some existential theater.

She chuckled, and shook her head.

"Come on," Ada said.

"They can't be far behind," Alice responded. "They must've seen us come out into the square on surveillance cameras..." She hefted the combat rifle, adding, "Maybe we should set up an ambush."

"No time for that."

"But what if we—"

Then something grabbed Alice's right ankle. Instinctively, she jerked her leg free—just in time to avoid a bite from the snapping jaws of an Undead. It was a bulbous man in a street cleaner's coveralls, with a bruise-colored round face and blood-caked beard.

He got to his hands and knees, and in that position—
growling and making other doglike noises—he looked
like some demented amalgam of man and canine.

He came towards Alice on his hands and knees
surprisingly fast, growling, licking his lips, his milky
eyes staring unblinkingly up at her. She shot him
through those staring eyes, careful to aim so the
bullets continued directly into the brain.

The Undead street cleaner fell flat with a final
whining cry, twitching for a moment, then going still.

Circling around him, Alice followed her companion.
Ada, striding along up ahead, hadn't even glanced
back.

Alice hoped she didn't have to kill Ada, before this
was over. She sort of liked the woman, somehow. She
respected someone with the kind of capability and
tough determination that Ada had. But she wondered
at her choice of allies.

Albert Wesker...

Am I allied with Wesker, now, too?

Her jaw set tightly at the thought.

No. But let him think so... for the moment.

Lying flat under a car, Dori watched Alice stride by.

Is that really her, or just one of the Alice clones?

Somehow, Dori knew. Maybe it was the confidence,
the style that seemed to speak of long experience. The
trained intelligence that glimmered in her eyes. It was
her. The legendary *Alice Abernathy.*

Dori was tempted to crawl out into view and talk
to her, right then and there. But Alice might shoot
her, thinking her an Undead, before she could utter a

sound. Dori looked like a healthy fifteen-year-old girl, but she was pretty dirty and had blood on her face. She'd been standing too near an Undead that was hit by an out of control car.

And besides—JudyTech had told her not to.

"Speak to no one but me unless asked a question. Then only answer the way I've taught you." Dori remembered when JudyTech first told her about Alice. It was the fourth overlay session in the clone crèche. JudyTech always waited till the other bio-techs and the monitor bots were off in another part of the facility, before waking Dori for the overlay.

The normal procedure for an overlay was different—usually the techs approached the clone tank without waking the clone who was floating inside. They'd activate the program for planting artificial memories and basic skills—such as walking—into the clone. The bio-interface transmitted the overlay to the electrodes, which translated it into neuronal encoding. In turn, that was printed into the brain via specially engineered proteins.

Dori knew all that—it was something none of the other clones knew—but she only knew it because JudyTech had told her. Judy had used an old voice-conditioning system long considered obsolete. Dori's language overlays had allowed her to understand what JudyTech said.

She hadn't understood everything, though, until JudyTech had released her from the tank as part of the prep for the testing floors. JudyTech had waited for her chance, then secretly separated Dori from the other clones, taking her to a room that wasn't used by the facility anymore. It was in a sub-basement where there had been Undead contamination, but the contamination was long gone, and JudyTech had fixed up the room to look like a girl's bedroom.

She'd provided simple computer games for Dori to play, and pictures of the world, and a full education. JudyTech had explained that she was one of the few non-clone humans left on the staff, and she'd always wanted a child, and she hadn't had one—and she'd decided that Dori would be her daughter. She was bothered by the way Umbrella used clones, too, and felt they should be given a chance for better lives, especially now with the world so underpopulated. She and Dori would escape, she explained, to get away from Umbrella, to some place that was safe from the Undead.

She'd told Dori about Alice Abernathy, who was a legend. JudyTech had hacked into Umbrella's files to find out all about Alice. And JudyTech told Dori about the Undead, about the testing floors. She'd showed her films of what happened there. She'd told her about the scarabs, too.

Bio-techs and other top scientific personnel didn't have scarabs. They were the ones who *designed* scarabs and put them on other people. But even people like JudyTech could be fitted with mind-control devices, so JudyTech was very careful to cover her tracks.

All of that scared Dori. She hadn't had any real feelings, floating in the tank—she was too sedated in there. But here, away from her sedation, she felt fear, and anger, and worry... and she felt love. She and JudyTech were *bonded*—that's what JudyTech called it.

"The way the world is now," JudyTech told her, "is so lonely. All the survivors are suspicious of one another. No one really trusts anyone else. Most families have been destroyed. So what we have, you and I, is precious and rare..."

Every day, after her twelve-hour shift, JudyTech would come to the hidden bedroom, and she'd train Dori physically and mentally. Dori had athletic skill overlays, copied from Alice, but the overlays had to be activated by training. Because of the overlays, an hour's training gave Dori as much as an ordinary person would get in a month.

But yesterday Dori had gotten restless. And she'd slipped out of the hidden bedroom to explore... She hadn't yet been issued "street clothes," so she'd put on her clone-prep jumpsuit, and she'd gone up some ladders to the lab floors. She'd had an urge to try to talk to other clones, and when she was noticed by bio-techs, she pretended to be sedated like the other clones. She got in the line with them, and the techs issued her clothes, which she had to put on.

Before she knew it, she was herded with the others into an access corridor and out to Times Square. Nearby a woman had turned, then a young boy, and the Undead virus started spreading. But Dori had been ready for that. She'd taken cover—just gotten a little bloody when she'd looked out from under the car, just as an Undead got squished by a taxi.

She considered going after Alice, and that other woman, but... no. If they took her with them, that would be deserting JudyTech. She could never do that. JudyTech was the only reason she had any kind of hope at all.

I'm not just a clone, she thought fiercely. *And I'm going to prove it to the world...*

So Dori stayed where she was for another twenty minutes or so, then she crawled out, looked around, and set out to find her mother.

Luther and the other four men followed a long concrete corridor that led from the bottom of the elevator shaft to the submarine pens. As they approached their destination Leon gestured for them to hang back, and they found cover, peering into the gigantic, dimly lit chamber from the doorway as he slipped out and ran from cover to cover

Leon's breath was steaming in the cold room; sometimes that was all Luther could see of him.

There were six docking bays, and two of them were occupied by large Soviet vessels. A couple of masked Umbrella troopers were setting up a machine gun post atop one of the submarine conning towers. Leon appeared behind the troopers, moving with a stealth that didn't seem humanly possible. Using a silenced pistol, he shot them both in the back of the head— the two shots so rapid they almost blended into one— dispatching them silently.

He looked around, then signaled for the team to emerge. When they came out into the colossal room that contained the submarines, Luther paused, and whistled in awe.

The chamber was dull, dusty—overhead lights illuminated the soaring reinforced-concrete walls— the cement surfaces were stained with rust that bled from iron studs. The two huge submarines were rebuilt Soviet vessels now painted with the red and black colors of the Umbrella Corporation. They were as big as high-rises lying on their sides, and they seemed motionless. But they were floating, he knew; countless tons of steel and glass, fluids and weaponry, suspended in seawater.

Did they have nuclear weapons on them, he wondered? It seemed unlikely, at this point. But who knew what *else* they might contain. Might be a real handy thing to have, a sub like that. Just let the Undead try to get at you in there.

Then Luther shook his head sadly. That was the first thought that came to a man, now, when he walked into a new place. *If I can't eat it or have sex with it... then how does it help me survive? How does it protect me from the Undead?*

The others were double-timing across the pens to catch up with Leon. Luther easily kept pace—running was something he was good at. He spoke up as they reached the shadow of the first big submarine.

"That's some hardware..." he began.

"Typhoon class," Sergei said blandly. "Biggest nuclear subs the Soviets ever built. Umbrella used them to transport bio-weapons all over the globe. Secretly of course."

"How come you know so much about Umbrella?"

"I used to work for them," Sergei replied. "For a boy from Murmansk, it was a good job." He added thoughtfully, "Now I like to consider it a youthful indiscretion."

Luther snorted.

"You used to work for the bad guys—but *I'm* the one nobody trusts?" He shook his head, but let it drop.

Sergei shrugged as Leon rejoined them, looking at his countdown watch.

RESIDENT EVIL:RETRIBUTION

"Let's pick up the pace!" Leon said. "We have less than ninety minutes!"

An empty street in New York City...

Except it wasn't. Alice and Ada walked down the middle of the empty avenue, making their way around a series of abandoned vehicles.

"When do I see Luther?" Alice asked, trying to sound as if she were only mildly interested in the answer.

"The strike team will rendezvous with us in the next environment," Ada said. "But until then, we're on our own."

"Of course," Alice murmured. She'd been mostly on her own since the day she'd awakened in the mansion, out in the country, near Raccoon City.

She wondered if there were anyone left alive there— *really* alive.

Don't think about it, she told herself. It just led her to agonize about her part in the spread of the T-virus. She'd protected Umbrella, as their head of security, while they were developing the biowarfare pathogen in the Hive. She hadn't known what they'd been up to, at least for much of the time—but still, was her ignorance just an excuse?

She'd failed to stop Spence from releasing the T-virus in the Hive; she'd failed to keep it from getting out of the Hive into Raccoon City. And she'd failed to stop it spreading through the world.

Stupid to blame yourself. But she couldn't help it. She never spoke about her feelings. Rationally, she knew it wasn't really her fault. But still—she felt the weight of it all.

There weren't that many people left alive who were capable of doing anything about it. Those few who remained had the fate of the human race in their hands. They had to take responsibility. There was no one else to do it. No excuse for standing on the sidelines...

There *was* a cure for the T-virus. It worked if it was injected into people early enough in the viral incubation process. But Alice had none of the formula—not at the moment. But if she could get that formula, could get it out to protect people from the T-virus, then it might make up for her past sins—for serving Umbrella.

She wondered if there was a supply of it somewhere in this facility. It seemed likely, but there was no time to find it—Ada's countdown watch kept ticking ominously toward zero.

Before she realized it, the woman in red had moved on ahead, outpacing Alice. Some sort of movement attracted her eye, and she found herself staring at an abandoned NYPD police car, off to the left. Alice hesitated, wondering if she should simply toss a grenade into the cruiser. But making unnecessary noise might bring the troopers down on them. So she walked up to the car.

It was hard to see through the blood-splashed windows—

The back door of the cruiser flew open and a slavering Undead launched itself out at her, catching her unprepared, knocking her assault rifle from her hands. The rifle's breach cracked on the street.

The creature's hands closed around her throat, and its momentum knocked her onto the cold asphalt.

She struggled to keep its jaws away from her face. It had once been a woman, but she couldn't pick out any details. Its face was mostly a shaking blur up this close. The Undead stank, though, so badly that Alice gagged, the stench worsening when it opened its mouth wide, close to her face, preparing to rip into her lips with its festering jaws.

It was choking her, so that black specks darkened her vision, like a mass of disturbed flies. Alice grunted with effort, gripping the Undead's wrists, prying them off her throat, forcing it back out of biting range. She gasped for breath, then used all the strength in her upper body to fling the thing off of her. It rolled over to her left.

Alice jumped to her feet, drew her automatic pistol—and froze, staring in shock.

The Undead was someone she knew. Or someone she'd known, once.

It was Rain Ocampo, wearing the tattered remains of an elegant party dress. Rain—who'd fought beside her in the Hive. Alice had shot Rain when the T-virus transformed her into an Undead. She'd blown her brains out.

This couldn't be her.

But it apparently was. It was the Rain she'd killed—and the Rain who'd appeared in a slightly different form, too, in the strange dream she'd had of Todd and Becky and the coming of the Undead. Before she'd awakened in the real nightmare, the interrogation cell of the Umbrella Corporation's undersea Arctic facility...

Clambering to her feet, Rain bared her broken teeth, let out a howl, and lunged. Acting on reflex,

Alice fired a burst from the auto pistol, five bullets shattering Rain's forehead. The creature took two shaky steps backward, and fell into the open doorway of the police car.

Seems like I have to kill Rain every so often, Alice thought dazedly. *Twice now.*

Ada came stalking up to her, frowning—she had the look of an exasperated teacher.

"What happened?" she demanded.

Alice looked down at Rain's body. The oozing, black, coagulated blood slid in big dollops like thick molasses from the shattered skull.

"I know her," she explained. "Her name was Rain. Rain Ocampo. But—how could she be *here?*" Alice shook her head in disbelief. "She died years ago..."

"You sure of that?"

"I should be. I killed her." Strictly speaking, the T-virus had killed her. But Alice had killed her... more thoroughly.

"Not her," Ada said, looking ruefully at the corpse. "Just someone that looked like her. How do you think Umbrella populates these test scenarios? Hundreds of people are killed each time they run a simulation. It's pretty hard to find volunteers."

"Clones..."

"That's right," Ada said. "Umbrella has fifty standard models. They take them out of the deep freeze, and imprint them with basic memories. Just enough to ensure a correct emotional response to the threat of the biohazard." She looked at Rain's dead face. "One time she's a tourist in Beijing, the next, a businesswoman in New York. The next..."

"A soldier working for Umbrella," Alice interrupted.

"All those Umbrella troops. They're all clones?"

"Of course," came the reply. "What could be better? The perfect soldiers—limitless in number, no questions asked, and loyalty guaranteed." With that, Ada turned away and started off again, toward the egress. After a moment, Alice followed, and as she did, memories sparked in her mind—of the clones she'd encountered, lying butchered in a ditch, outside an Umbrella base.

Clones of... Alice.

Alice corpses. It had made her sick to look at them.

Striding along behind, Alice remembered—all of it.

She'd broken into the facility, and found a whole laboratory devoted to developing Alice clones. Someone at Umbrella had been obsessed with Alice. Dr. Sam Isaacs had been convinced there was something special in her genes, something they could use to develop a purer form of the T-virus—both as a cure, and a method for creating the intelligent Undead. He created countless Alice clones, and became infected with a version of the T-virus. One which transformed him into a fusion of monster—and superhuman.

Isaacs had kept Alice trapped, until one of her clones killed him, slicing and dicing him in a laser-trap. So Alice had killed him—and then again, it wasn't Alice at all.

The clones themselves were all killed when Wesker blew up the Tokyo facility. All of those other versions of herself—snuffed out. All those dead "Alices" lying discarded in that desert ditch, awaiting a mass burial.

And now *these* clones—killed routinely as part of someone's little war game, their own little biowarfare "reality show." Or trained to live and die as conditioned "troopers." Such was Umbrella's contempt for human suffering—it used them up like cattle.

Cattle?

It wouldn't surprise her, if this continued, if they made clones for protein. For food...

Before the T-virus had destroyed most of civilization, there had been talk of corporate cultures. Corporations were, after all, the defining paradigm of the modern world, back in those days. A corporate culture affected thousands, even millions of people. Some were relatively benevolent. But others were sick. Pathological.

Umbrella's corporate culture was *beyond* sick. It took ruthlessness to new, unspeakable extremes. Umbrella behaved like a technocratic serial killer.

At that moment, Alice realized it wouldn't be enough to get the cure for the T-virus. No, not while Umbrella still was around. The corporation was going to have to be destroyed. Eradicated.

The serial killer would have to be executed.

11

In the control room, the dead bodies had been dragged out of the way, stacked neatly against a back wall for the maintenance bots to remove. No ceremony was needed—there were always more where those came from.

Jill tapped furiously at the keyboard, shifting through different surveillance camera views. She paused at the shot of a false building front, several blocks high, on the Moscow test floor. A messy complex of high-tech scaffolding, with cables and buttresses, held it all together.

No sight of the intruders here. Just a sense of the theatrical falseness of the test floors.

She shifted security cameras, choosing a view of Moscow's "Red Square." The square was apparently deserted; even the Undead were absent. Yet it seemed populated by ghosts, somehow—perhaps because the shell of the Arctic facility had been built by the Soviets. She could almost imagine the USSR's military parades, its tanks and stiffly marching lines of soldiers in crimson and dun. She wondered what the real Red Square looked like, now. Most likely it was in ruins, with much-chewed skeletons littering the ground, Undead roaming, groaning to themselves in hunger...

On the screen, however, the façade of Red Square's glory still stood unblemished: reproductions of the heroic paintings by Surikov and Yuon, the rebuilt Kazan Cathedral, St. Basil's with its onion domes, the Kitai Gorod merchant's quarter, the radiating streets, the palatial official residence of the president, the monument to Minin and Posharsky

The ghostliness actually came from the mists, she realized—cold wraiths of fog that trailed over the ground, sometimes seeming to form human figures before disintegrating into wisps.

Wait...

There. Entering the test floor, through "Resurrection Gate," walking across the big open space of the square. Five men, heavily armed, were moving into camera range. Jill adjusted the surveillance equipment to take her closer, and ramped up the sound till she could hear them talking.

The tall black man was checking his watch.

"One hour left," he said.

"In a hurry to meet your lady friend?" another responded.

"Don't worry, we meet her in the next environment..." said a third, his eyes wide as he peered around the square. His accent revealed Russian heritage.

Jill nodded to herself.

"I guess we know where to find our prisoner now," she muttered to herself. Then she turned to a subordinate. "Trooper, where's that welcome party?" She smiled icily. "Let's not keep our guests waiting."

The African-American trooper clone looked up from the console.

"Beginning now," he said. The screen in front of him flashed:

MOSCOW SCENARIO 12B ACTIVATED.

"Welcome wagon has been arranged," the trooper added.

"Good," Jill murmured.

The trooper's screen, previewing scenario 12B, showed a variety of monstrous creatures: T-virus variants, mutated test subjects, including the Las Plagas Undead... and Lickers.

Seeing the Lickers, Jill shuddered.

"I hate those things," she muttered. She turned to the other troopers. "Now let's move out. We have a fugitive to run down. And a traitor to kill."

It was night in Red Square.

No—it was merely shadowy in the mock-up of Red Square. But it felt real to Luther.

"Can't believe how real all this looks."

"That's the point," Sergei said. But his words rang hollow—the usual cockiness wasn't there. He seemed spooked by this reproduction of a hallowed place from his home country.

"Always wanted to visit Moscow..." he intoned. Then he tensed.

They heard vehicles approaching, engines gunning,

JOHN SHIRLEY

wheels screeching on streets.

Leon signaled a halt, scanning in the direction of the sound.

"Defensive positions!"

At the other side of the square, six motorcycles skidded to a halt. Luther stared at the riders. They weren't quite human—he could see that from here. But they didn't look Undead, either. For one thing, while their skin looked cold and dead, they didn't have the extreme decay. And their eyes glowed fiery red. And another thing—they could ride motorcycles. No Undead had it that much together.

So what the hell are they?

Whatever they were—they weren't friendly. They were all armed, and one of them even had a chainsaw, which it started with a guttural roar. It scraped the blade along the surface of the square, yielding a shower of sparks. And it grinned hideously...

"What the hell are those things?" Barry echoed.

"I don't know about you," Sergei said, "but they aren't giving me a warm and fuzzy feeling inside."

Leon put a fresh clip in his assault rifle.

"They're infected by the Las Plagas virus. Depending on the strength of the infection, the subject retains motor skills, some degree of intelligence." He shrugged. "It can also develop unnatural strength and speed."

Barry snorted.

"Always with the good news."

We'd better take them out quickly, and get the hell out of here, Luther thought to himself. He opened his mouth to speak...

When more vehicles pulled into the square—

flatbed trucks and pick-ups mounted with heavy machine guns and rocket launchers. The plague soldiers, as Luther thought of them, were dressed in tattered Russian military uniforms. And every set of eyes glowed hellish red.

"Aaaaand it gets better," Barry remarked dryly.

A plague soldier on a flatbed truck racked back the slide of a machine gun. To Luther, it looked like a small cannon.

"Fall back!" Leon yelled. "Everyone fall back!"

They ran for cover.

Alice and Ada strolled down the middle of a deserted New York street. Bodegas, brownstones, and shops crowded each side of the street. Cars were parked in neat rows. Dimly visible in the distance, two figures were coming toward them.

Alice reached for her holstered auto pistol.

Ada put a hand on her arm.

"They're okay." She waved—and instantly one of the figures waved back. Something about it seemed strange.

As they drew closer, Alice realized that they were approaching a giant mirror. It cut across the street, reflecting the cars and buildings—and the two women. Ada gestured toward the mirror.

"The edges of the test environments are all like this," she said. "Gives the illusion of depth." They moved close to the glass, and Ada waved her hand over it. Suddenly an illuminated keypad appeared on the reflective wall.

"Most scenarios," Ada continued, "are run at the

center of an environment. The test subjects may glimpse this from a distance, but rarely get a chance to reach the edges." She tapped the keyboard, keying in a number, and a mirrored door appeared in the glass. "After you..."

Alice stepped forward.

"Through the looking glass."

They stepped through the door and found themselves facing a large steel wall. Ada went to a set of stairs and started to climb.

"This way."

As they approached the top of the stairs, Alice paused, looked up—and saw a blue sky.

"It's day!"

"It's a sky dome," Ada said, shaking her head without stopping. "Just paint." Sure enough, looking closer, Alice could see the edges of the painting. "Doesn't hold up too well if you stare at it for long," Ada added. Alice hurried to catch up with her.

"How did people believe it?"

"When they were running a simulation, no one was looking at the clouds."

They reached the top of the stairs and passed through a door, into another set... an iconic suburban neighborhood. It was familiar to Alice. But she wasn't sure why. Some faded memory of a dream...

In front of them was a four-car pile-up—at the foot of a sign announcing the gateway to the SUNDOWN MEADOWS gated housing project. One home was a blackened ruin, and the wreckage of a helicopter poked out of a nearby garage. In the middle of the intersection was a crashed Prius, upside down like an overturned turtle.

RESIDENT EVIL:RETRIBUTION

Alice found the sight disturbing, but she wasn't sure why.

Ada looked around, frowning.

"This is our rendezvous point." She looked at her countdown watch, causing Alice to peer over her shoulder. Less than fifty minutes remained.

"Where are they?" Ada murmured.

Alice caught a flicker of movement from the corner of her eye. She turned, saw a curtain dropping at the upstairs window of a large house.

"The house behind us—there's someone moving," she said quietly. "Upstairs window." Ada turned and looked, but the movement didn't repeat.

"Maybe," Alice whispered, "that's where your friends are. Maybe they're keeping their heads down. It'd make sense. The troopers can't be far off."

Ada frowned dubiously, but she led the way across the street, to the big house. They hesitated on the porch, weapons in hand. Alice reached out and turned the knob, pushed the door inward.

The anteroom was a mess. There was a wreckage of hall furniture and broken banisters—and the body of an Undead, once a man, impaled on what remained of the staircase.

Then Alice saw something else in the debris—it was her.

"What is it?" Ada asked from nearby.

Alice was lying dead on the floor. Her face had been ripped apart, but there was just enough left to identify her.

Her mouth felt papery dry.

"They used clones of me..."

Ada nodded slowly.

"Of course. You were one of the basic models."

"Basic models..." Alice shook her head in disgust, then looked at her companion. "Why would your associates be in here?"

"We don't know that they..."

There was a creak of floorboards, a bumping sound from upstairs.

Alice drew her pistol and started climbing. Her mind was racing, though, making it difficult to focus.

Have I been here before? She shook her head. *No. It's impossible.*

Shc passed a rotting Undead and looked carefully, half expecting it to come alive. But it seemed to have died for good. Finally she got to the top of the stairs—where there was more disarray. An overturned table, clothing strewn everywhere. She walked down the hallway, feeling strangely drawn to explore it. She'd definitely seen something at the window.

Maybe just an Undead.

She hoped it would be something else—maybe Ada's team. Maybe a survivor.

Not likely...

She reached the door to the nursery—it was slightly open. No sign of a baby, or the family that once lived here. But there was something... someone.

The closet.

She moved past the broken crib and, licking her dry lips, she put her hand on the louver doors. Slowly pushed them aside—

The Undead leapt out at her. It knocked her back, tackling her, and they crashed heavily to the floor. Alice straight-armed the creature, knocking it back from her just enough that the mandibles emerging from its gnashing, reeking jaws snapped the air an inch from the end of her nose.

When the thing tried to force itself closer to her throat, Alice twisted, brought a knee up, and flipped the creature over so it crashed into a dresser, splintering it into a million pieces. She rolled the other way, got to her feet just as her slavering opponent was up, charging at her.

She fired, blowing off the top of its skull, and stepped aside to let the corpse fall limply beside her. Then she heard a scuffling sound from behind.

Spinning, she was startled to see a little girl in the closet, pushing aside the blankets that had hidden her, jumping up and rushing at her. Her first instinct was to shoot it, but she stopped herself—it wasn't an Undead charging her. It was a healthy human child.

As she recovered from the shock, Alice realized that the child who hugged her was deaf, and spoke to her in hand signs. Thanks to her training, Alice understood.

"*You came back!*" There were tears of joy in the little girl's eyes. "I hid—just like you told me to! I love you, Mom, I love you so much!"

Mom? What... Alice sank to the ground in shock, still holding the child in her arms.

The girl began to calm down. She looked up and signed again.

"What happened to your clothes? And your hair?"

12

Times Square was lit by strong ceiling lights. Jill Valentine and her squad halted in the midst of a forgotten traffic jam. The cars were there but the drivers had gone, as if they'd just gotten out and walked away.

Strange thoughts came to Jill, sometimes...

She led her squad onward, toward the enemy.

Why were they the enemy? Because the scarab said so. Umbrella said so. Reason enough, wasn't it?

An electric shock punished her, like a bee sting to the skull—a shot of electricity, warning her that she was having unauthorized thoughts.

Just keep going, the scarab said. *Do your job.*

The traffic lights hung like dead things; the cars showed no headlights, the signs were dead.

"How are our guests?" Jill asked. The African-American clone trooper put on a set of tactical glasses, checked the surveillance feed.

"Still alive."

"Let's change that," Jill said firmly.

"Yes ma'am," the trooper replied. He tapped the tactical glasses, peered at the heads-up display, and issued a few commands.

Luther and the others had taken shelter in the GUM department store—where they were trying to repel an army of Las Plagas Undead.

The strike team was crouched behind the display case podiums for the department store's front windows—the window glass was gone, shot away, and the mannequins were blown to pieces. Heads and limbs littered the floor around them.

The surreal nature of their situation struck him as he blasted at a motorcyclist plague soldier riding by. It hadn't felt so strange to be firing from the old prison they'd taken over, back in Los Angeles. But this place—with its ornate, neoclassical architecture commissioned by Catherine the Second—was a strange bunker in which to be hunkered down.

Luther popped shots from his auto pistol, out the store windows past remnants of mannequins wearing the hot new fashions of a few years back. He had the pistol set on single-shot to conserve ammo. The Undead hadn't organized into a charge, yet. They roared back and forth in front of the store, firing their weapons and presenting surprisingly inviting targets.

Windows shattered under the impacts of bullets, rocket launchers blew up pieces of the store's ornate façade—but so far no one on the team had been hit. It had been a close thing, running in here with bullets from that machine gun strafing up right behind them. But they'd made it to good cover.

Only, it wasn't going to last.

The plague soldiers, dim-witted though they were, would inevitably charge into the store. The strike team was heavily outnumbered.

What's gonna happen if we don't get out of here, Luther wondered, *before those explosives go off?*

Suddenly the fighting dropped off for a moment. The plague soldiers seemed to be regrouping.

And then they began to advance, moving forward like a wall of rotting flesh, eyes ablaze, firing as they came.

"They can't shoot for shit!" Barry said as the bullets cut the air overhead.

"Yeah, but there's plenty of them!" Leon said, firing a burst from his machine rifle. He hit a motorcycle's gas tank, and it exploded in an orange ball of flame, the Undead driver continuing to drive it, the ball of flame rocketing along on two wheels until it crashed through a false wall.

A rippling line of Las Plagas plague soldiers came at them, firing, creating a storm of bullets overhead. If Luther had stood up, he'd have been perforated—turned into raw hamburger. The noise of it racketed and echoed in the GUM store spaces; like someone was pounding directly on Luther's eardrums.

The enemy fire slackened for a moment. Leon jumped up and unleashed a long stream of machine rifle fire. The strafe cut a swath through the onrushing soldiers, many of them falling—but others came after them, stepping on the bodies of the fallen without even glancing down. Others, ripped across the middle by bullets, kept staggering onward.

"And they don't go down easy," Leon growled, as

he ducked down again.

Luther fired several more single shots, bringing down a couple of their attackers, And then, all at once, the enemy gunfire stopped.

Silence—except for the ringing in his ears.

"Now what?" Leon asked.

"Maybe they're giving up?" Barry suggested. Luther had to look to see if he was serious.

Leon gave Barry a look of mild disgust.

Luther looked back through the ruined window, wondered how the plague soldiers were communicating. He hadn't seen any of them giving orders, but somehow they'd all decided to hold off for a moment... and they'd decided it all at once.

Some kind of telepathic connection, maybe?

And what were they up to?

Then he saw it. On the back of a flatbed truck, a plague soldier was leveling a rocket launcher—aiming it right at the department store. And the deep cough of the rocket launcher sounded as he fired.

Oh, crap!

It was headed straight for Leon.

"RPG!" Luther shouted. "Down!"

They flattened, and the RPG round exploded, blowing out a nearby chunk of the GUM façade. Debris rained down on them. His ears ringing more than ever, Luther saw Leon lifting up to look accusingly at Barry.

Barry just shrugged, causing bits of debris to fall from his shoulders.

"Can't be right all the time."

A new sound caused Luther to turn. The plague soldiers had used the rocket attack as their moment, their opportunity. While the smoke was still clearing, they charged, pouring in through the ruined gap made by the RPG shell.

Luther and Leon jumped up, fighting side by side as the plague soldiers rushed them. Bullets whipped past—then a soldier was leaping at Leon, swinging its weapon like a club. Leon ducked under the swing and pivoted into a kick, slamming the Undead in the jaw with his boot, drilling shards of broken bone into its brain.

Luther kicked another in the balls, was surprised at how much effect it had—the Undead buckled up, and Luther stuck the barrel of his auto pistol in its mouth, firing—splashing the thing's brains into the glowing red eyes of the soldier coming after it, temporarily blinding the creature so that he was able to yank his pistol free and mix the first one's brains with the shattered gray matter of the second.

Leon shot two other charging plague soldiers, delivering quick, effective headshots, and then another came in—and Luther saw with a chill it was the one with the chainsaw. The big machine, held in both its hands, was grinding away, roaring, the chain whirring. Tony shot at the Undead but it blocked with the saw, the rounds ricocheting from the blade's metal.

And then, as Luther was trying to get a bead on the creature's glowing red eyes, it shoved its chainsaw past Tony's gun muzzle, slashing downward, cutting him from the left shoulder down, sawing through him stem to stern, ripping down through his flesh and bones, through his collarbone and ribcage and sternum, grinding his heart to paste, shredding his entrails—

Luther's gut twisted at the sight and he nearly threw up, but he squeezed the trigger.

Too late, dammit, you're too late! he told himself.

He fired... and missed. Leon was shooting at the chainsaw wielder, too, and hitting him, and so was Barry, but none of them were kill shots.

The thing turned to ram the chainsaw down Leon's throat—

And then Luther squeezed off three quick shots, precisely aimed. One each for the creature's eyes, puncturing right through, the third striking *between* the eyes.

The chainsaw soldier swayed, blood gushing where its eyes had been—then fell back, dead.

Leon looked at Luther with a new respect.

"Not bad."

Luther shrugged.

"For an advisor," he replied. He could still feel his gorge rising, but managed to hold it together.

Barry was firing through the smoking gap, taking out a biker who tried to ride in over the rubble. The riderless bike skidded out and lay, spinning its wheels and spewing exhaust by the creature's shattered body.

Then the smoke cleared, and the charge had stopped—the plague soldiers had eased off to regroup.

He looked at what was left of Tony—took in the horrified expression forever frozen on the man's snow-pale face. A nauseating smell rose from the ripped-apart corpse, fecal matter and blood and guts and a smell that might be bone marrow... all mixed with the heavy throat-scratching pall of gun smoke.

Luther sighed. Too bad about Tony... but he probably wouldn't be the last one of them to die.

He turned to Sergei—saw him in the midst of all the smoking chaos and rubble, poring over his laptop. The little computer was dusted with shattered plaster, its screen blurred, but he worked at it by sheer desperate instinct, fingers flying over the keyboard.

Leon stepped over bodies to look over Sergei's shoulder.

"We should be at the rendezvous already," he said grimly. "Find us a way out of here!"

"Downloading schematics now."

"Downloading?" Leon said. "You're still *downloading?*"

Sergei just shrugged in that way only an I.T. engineer would understand.

Dori found a tire iron lying beside a car that was up on a jack, one wheel off. She picked it up, hefted it, experienced a kind of inner click as her overlays and training merged. *Using narrow metal bars for weapons, parts one and two.*

She was most of the way across Times Square—making her way to the open door of a souvenir store that she suspected would offer a way out of the simulation—when the Undead came at her from behind a still-smoking, half-burned minivan.

The thing had been a woman. And for a moment Dori thought it was... her.

It was Alice. Only it wasn't Alice. It was *an* Alice. And it was extending its bloodstained fingers like claws to slash at her eyes, its mouth stretching wide for the rustling, bristling mandibles forcing their way out.

Dori let her reflexes guide her—she spun on her heel to work up the momentum she'd need, coming all the way around, driving the sharp end of the tire iron straight at the creature's face, hard as she could. The tire iron crunched into Alice's nose, sliding up a nostril, through her sinuses, and into the brain.

The creature hesitated, but didn't fall—the damage wasn't enough.

Gagging at what she was having to do, Dori twisted the tire iron around the way people scrape the innards from a pumpkin to make a jack-o-lantern. The Undead shuddered and fell back. As it did, she held tightly onto the tire iron so the corpse's fall would pull it free.

She turned away, and shook the rotting black glop from her weapon, gagging once more, then forced herself to go on, to run toward the storefront. She went through the open door, glanced at the souvenir props arranged on shelves inside. There were miniature Statues of Liberty, Empire State Buildings. Dori knew what they were—the real ones—because JudyTech had shown them to her on a computer screen. But the Empire State Building was mostly burned down, now, and overrun with Undead...

She'd never get to see them in their glory. The people who had come before had wrecked the world, had trampled all that they had built. And they thought they were better than clones? Dori laughed bitterly at that, and made her way to the store through the door.

She found a door marked "Emergency Exit Only," and when she went through it she discovered that she was in a kind of alley. There was no one there and, still carrying her bloody tire iron, she went through another door, emerging into a broad staging area, under a series of catwalks and an intricate mesh of utility wires.

It was shadowy here, dusty, and her footsteps echoed...

She thought she knew which way the clone crèche was, but she wasn't sure she'd be able to get into it. By now, JudyTech would be looking for her.

What would they do to her mother—to JudyTech— if they caught her searching for Dori... if the whole story came out? They'd either kill her, or implant her with a scarab. And the scarab might be worse. She'd see Dori, and simply turn her over for the recycling vat.

Her own mother would turn into one of those robotic, empty-eyed people. She wouldn't know her; she would feel nothing for her.

It would be better if they killed her.

Alice, Ada, and the little girl traversed the iconic suburban neighborhood that had been the killing floor for so many. Alice held the girl's hand with one of her own; with her other hand she carried her auto pistol, with the safety off.

Ada was frowning, looking from side to side for her strike team.

There were no Undead to be seen—Umbrella must have disposed of the ones they didn't want kept alive for tests. They'd put the facility at risk if allowed to wander randomly about. Did the corporation send in troopers to kill them? Did they use nerve gas?

The girl tugged to get her attention.

"Mom, who are we looking for?"

"Ada's friends," Alice signed back. "Who'll help us get safely out of here."

"You know sign," Ada remarked, glancing at them.

"Of course," Alice said. "Basic training, just like you. You forget, we worked for the same people."

Ada glanced at her countdown watch and shook her head.

"We should have waited at the rendezvous point."

"And what if they never came?"

The woman in red made a sound of exasperation, deep in her throat.

"What the hell is taking them so long?"

"You know it's strange," Alice said, "when I woke up in the interrogation cell, I had this... dream, I guess, fading from my mind. About this street, these houses. I had a husband, and we had a house we lived in. With a daughter."

It occurred to Alice that the technicians working for Umbrella must have decided to *make* the girl deaf, to make it all seem more real, another fanatically crafted detail in the background of a family. A pointless detail, really. It was almost as if some of them enjoyed creating the maximum believability—just so they could enjoy the suffering of people as their "lives" were taken away from them...

Sick bastards.

"But how could I know?" Alice muttered, mostly to herself.

"How could you have had a dream about it?" Ada said, still looking around. "When it happened to a clone—and not you?"

"Yeah," Alice admitted. "Somehow... it was like I was experiencing it myself."

"After you... left the company, they found out that the people who were cloned often retained a kind of telepathic connection—especially if the experience was emotionally powerful enough. It's not unlike the experiences encountered by identical twins."

It was just an echo from someone else's mind. Alice looked at the girl.

And yet the connection between them was more than an echo. She knew, now, that she would defend this child with her life.

13

Luther picked up Tony's rifle and dropped down on one knee, firing through the still-smoking gap in the wall, nailing two plague soldiers that were rushing at them. Eventually these guys were going to figure out flanking. And then, Luther figured, he and his companions were screwed.

As if the creatures had heard him thinking, a group of them came from his left flank—three of them, one firing a shotgun that took the head off the last standing mannequin.

As one, Luther, Leon, and Barry all swung left, firing as they did, the three of them ripping into the oncoming plague soldiers, making them dance with the impacts of the bullets, splashing the walls and ceiling with blood and brains. But there were always more where those came from. They were going to run out of ammo—and then what? Maybe scrounge weapons from the Undead.

If they had a chance before they were overrun...

Two more soldiers went down. Pretty soon they'd

be able to stack them up to use them as cover, a bunker of human flesh.

Spent cartridges from Luther's gun rained down on Sergei's laptop. He glanced up at Luther.

"Do you mind?" He sniffed, then went back to trying to find an escape route. "Trying to work here..."

A readout indicated that the door was malfunctioning.

Thank goodness, Dori thought. At least she would be able to go through. Before she did, she tossed the tire iron away. Peering down the corridor, she looked both ways, saw no one. So she turned and jogged along in a direction she hoped would take her to the crèche, the place she might find JudyTech.

If she could find her before being caught.

Corridor after corridor, corner after corner, stairway after stairway. What limited staff there were must have been confined in the lockdown. According to JudyTech, they'd lost a great many personnel to Undead outbreaks—there weren't many people in the world left to recruit. And clones required both time and expense.

Tired and footsore, unused to so much activity, Dori was close to tears—sure she would never find her way back—when she recognized the warning sign over a door, at the other end of the latest stretch of hallway.

BIO-DEVELOPMENT PERSONNEL ONLY
UNAUTHORIZED PERSONS SUBJECT TO RECYCLING

There was a security camera over the door. If she

got much closer, the camera would pick her up.

She heard the troopers coming before they spotted her. Their boots, moving in lockstep, sounded to her left, where the hall vibrated. They'd reach her in a matter of moments.

Frantically Dori moved down the hallway, trying doors. Locked. Next one—locked. Another one—locked.

She had to find someplace to hide... She was already within the security camera's range, and the sound of boots was getting louder.

Then a knob turned, a door opened, and she slipped quickly through—found herself in a lavatory. There were no booths, just toilets and sinks. No place to conceal herself, but perhaps none of the troopers would need to stop. Pressing her ear to the door, she heard them go tramping by.

She slumped, and suddenly realized that she had been holding her breath.

What should she do next? Where could she go? From experience, she now knew that the door to the crèche was locked, but she needed to get past it.

And there was the security camera. She'd been close enough for it to see her. She wasn't dressed properly—these jeans and this sweatshirt—for a worker in the facility. Her look would scream, "AWOL." If anyone was monitoring that camera, they'd be here in just a minute, or two.

Dori went to a sink, and drank some water, splashed some on her face. She had to make up her mind.

She had to *think*...

Then the door opened.

Without daring to look at the newcomer, she

walked toward the entrance, trying to act as if she'd just finished using the bathroom. Trying to look calm. But a hand restrained her, and she tensed. She turned and saw—

"JudyTech!"

The woman just grinned at her. She had buck teeth and showed a lot of gum when she smiled. She had lines at the corners of her small green eyes, a snub nose, and graying brown hair braided close to her head. There was something deeply kind about her face. She wore a green lab smock and dull-green lab pants, and she carried a blue satchel.

"I saw you on the security camera, Dori," she explained. "I took over a shift so I could watch for you."

Dori threw herself into JudyTech's arms.

"I'm so sorry I wandered off," she said, tears welling up in her eyes. "I just wanted to... I don't know... I was..."

"It doesn't matter," JudyTech said. "Listen—we're going to get out of here now. Right now. I monitored a conversation on the security system—I think there are bombs set to go off. This place is going to drown in seawater. We've got to escape!"

"But how?"

"Look..." JudyTech opened the satchel. Inside it were folded clothes for Dori—and on top of the clothes were two of the metal scarabs Umbrella used for mind control.

At the sight of them, Dori felt her heart sink to her knees.

"No... *no!*"

"Take it easy, hon," Dori told her. "They aren't real. The electronic guts, the drug infuser, all that has been taken out of them. There's just the shell and the lights. They're our tickets out of here."

They arrived at Alice's house—the house she had shared with Todd, and their daughter.

The clone Alice.

The clone Todd.

And the clone daughter...

Alice walked through the open front door, gun at ready, not sure if the place had been cleared. The girl and Ada came in behind her. A quick look around told her there were no creatures.

"We have to find Daddy!" the girl signed. She ran off down the hall before Alice could stop her.

"Do you know what you're doing?" Ada demanded.

"No," Alice admitted.

"Didn't think so."

Alice looked at the blood splashed on the walls. She could almost remember. But it hadn't been her. It had been something that *resonated* with her. Almost a part of her. Yet not quite.

The girl came running back to her, her face drawn with disappointment.

"He's not here!" she signed, shaking her head.

"Good!" Ada said curtly. "So let's move!"

Alice took the girl in her arms.

"You tried," she signed. "But now we have to go."

The girl looked her mother in the eyes.

"You won't leave me, will you?" she signed. "Like before? You won't leave me alone again?"

"I won't leave you," Alice replied, smiling gravely.

"You promise?" the girl signed.

"I promise."

She tried to smile—but her lips trembled. Alice hugged her.

"Are we coming back?" the girl asked her.

"No," Alice signed.

"Then I need to take some things." Without a sound she ran back down the hall.

"Just hurry," Alice signed. "And stay where I can see you." But the girl was already gone.

Ada checked her watch.

Alice looked at the framed pictures on the wall—of Todd and Alice at home, the three of them in the backyard, on holiday at a beach. Again the perverse attention to detail shown by the test planners. A picture perfect family life—that she'd never lived. That *no one* had ever lived.

"None of this is real," Ada said.

Running feet sounded again, and the girl was coming down the hall, stuffing things into a backpack.

"It is to her," Alice said.

"I know," Ada responded. "That's the point." She was studying them—watching Alice with her "daughter." Alice had the feeling that Ada saw the developing attachment as a problem, an unnecessary complication.

"She's not your daughter," Ada added softly, almost whispering. "She's not even a real person."

Alice shot Ada a glare. It infuriated her—the utter bullshit, the idea that a clone, with just as much capacity for suffering, for tragedy, just as much joy, just as much potential—could be seen as "not even a real person."

But Ada pressed on.

"All these feelings she has for you," she insisted. "They were imprinted. A short time ago she was a blank slate. She didn't even know who you were."

It's useless, Alice thought. *She's too much the professional killer to let herself feel anything. I'd never convince her.*

"I could show you a room with a dozen just like her in cold storage," Ada added. Alice just stared at her, until her ally shrugged. "I'm sorry," she said, "but it's true."

"Ready!" the girl signed, trotting up to them, smiling now. "I was fast," she signed. "Wasn't I?"

Alice tousled her hair.

"Yes you were."

"Oh, just—come on," Ada said. "Let's get the hell out of this place." She led the way through the front door, Alice and the girl followed—then stopped, staring.

Waiting on the manicured grass of the front lawn were Jill Valentine and her squad of troopers. Rain was sitting casually in the swing-set— the "Rain" clone, anyway, with an MP5 machine gun in her hand. Another trooper, sans mask, was familiar to Alice. His name was—or had been—Carlos, and he'd fought alongside her a while back. Until he had died. He was pointing his own assault rifle at her chest.

He looked exactly like Todd.

Yet strangely, Becky didn't seem to notice...

"Welcome home," Jill said dryly. "Nice place you have." She picked up a fallen pink bicycle and stood it up straight. "Now, surrender, or die."

"There's a child here," Alice said. She pulled the girl closer.

"Your problem," Rain remarked casually, getting up and raising the MP5, racking it back to fire. "Not ours."

"All heart," Alice said, looking at her. "You haven't changed."

"I don't know you, lady," Rain said, frowning.

"So what's it to be?" the Carlos trooper asked.

Alice glanced at Ada.

Ada looked back her, eyebrows raised.

Jill's eye-projected IUD was explicit, its scrolling text identifying targets and prescribing action.

ADA WONG—*KILL*

CLONE—*KILL*

PROJECT ALICE—*CAPTURE/KILL*

But past the heads-up, Jill was peripherally aware that Alice was stepping in front of Ada. Her instincts told her that nothing Alice did lacked purpose.

In the next instant the nearest Umbrella trooper was shot off his feet with a burst from Ada's weapon. Alice herself fired at "Rain"—suppressing the trooper's fire as she was forced to dive for cover. Then Project Alice bolted for the house, pulling the girl along by the wrist. Ada fired again, and then darted in behind them.

A spray of bullets perforated the door the split second they closed it behind them.

Alice pushed her daughter down behind a sofa. The child's head popped up as Alice put fresh clips in her guns.

"What are you doing?" she signed.

"Mommy stuff," Alice replied. More bullets ripped through the front door, leaving it in shreds, a mere splintery frame.

Alice pushed the girl down again, turned, and fired past the archway and through the front door.

Bullets whipped over Jill's head, and slammed into a parked Honda Civic—hitting the gas tank. The car exploded, the fireball kicking it into the air, flipping it upside down. She grimaced as the car smashed down onto the pavement behind her, flaklike pieces of exploding metal trailing smoke as they sang past.

"Suppressing fire!" Jill shouted.

"Yes, ma'am!" came the response.

"Yes, ma'am!" another trooper shouted. He signaled to the others and all the troopers let loose, firing full out from behind trees, flat on the ground, and in kneeling positions to the right and left, tearing the house apart with bullets...

In the living room Ada and Alice dived for cover as the house was put through the meat grinder by a storm of bullets. The walls were shattering, being chewed apart and beginning to sag down, their undermining threatening to collapse the entire structure around them.

The bullets were like swarming angry insects just

over Alice's head, blackening the air. She was lying on her stomach, half turned to aim out the shattered front door, where she could just make out the black trooper, reloading.

He looked up at her.

That familiar face—a clone of an old friend—made her hesitate.

And then the moment was gone as he rolled out of the way.

She fired—hitting the trooper right behind him. At the same time she was aware of Ada, crawling past her toward the kitchen, probably to check for troopers who would be trying to flank them from the back.

Alice fired out the front door again—as the house groaned, settling, still threatening to collapse, its timbers nearly eaten through by bullets.

In the kitchen, Ada dropped to a low crouch, deploying her hook gun. There was a noise from the back door, and she turned—the door was open, so the only barrier was the closed screen door. Through it she saw a masked trooper, his rifle leveled at her.

Ada fired, aiming the hook gun with pure instinct. The harpoonlike weapon went through the screen and impaled the trooper just below the sternum. He screamed—but he didn't die. Coughed-up blood leaked from the corner of his mask as he tremblingly raised his gun to fire at her. She pressed the rewind button and braced herself, holding firmly to the handle.

The hook jerked him toward her, reeling him in, smashing him through the door and into a cabinet where he came to rest with a nasty crunching sound.

A relative quiet fell, the gunfire diminished, the storm momentarily abating as the troopers reloaded their weapons. Pieces of rubble and plaster pattered down from the shattered walls; broken light fittings swung.

Nearby, Alice fired out the door again—then slipped up closer to Ada.

"What are we going to do?"

"You can't stay here." Ada took off her digital glasses, and handed them to Alice. "These will show you the way out. I'll hold 'em back as long as I can." She peered outside, then back at Alice. "I'll meet you at the elevator."

Alice looked at her.

"Thank you."

"For what?" Ada demanded. "I'm not dying for you, lady. I have a plan B. Now take this." She disconnected the used cartridge from the hook gun, then held it out to Alice. "The less I have with me, the better."

"I've got something for you," Alice said, handing her an unprimed grenade.

"Thanks. See you at the elevator."

Sure, Alice thought. *If there's life after death.*

14

Outside of the house, the troopers finished reloading, slamming magazines home into their weapons.

"Set!" a trooper shouted.

"Advance in teams!" Jill called. She reiterated the command in hand signals.

The clone that looked like Rain called out, "Alpha team forward!" They began to advance—and as they went they opened fire, ripping the house apart with long automatic-weapon bursts.

"We've got movement!" a trooper shouted, peering at a heads-up on his digital goggles. "Behind the house! Two targets!"

Jill signaled a halt, and ran to the trooper. "Identify!"

There was a moment's hesitation as he touched the goggles, zoomed the camera in on the figures.

"It's Alice," he said.

Jill frowned. Two targets *behind* the house?

So Alice and the clone kid were running, while Ada stayed behind to keep the squad busy.

Okay. One kill at a time.

She pointed at the house.

"Take this bitch out!"

Ada looked out the back way, saw Alice and the girl slipping away—and saw a trooper coming around the side of the house, aiming at their backs. She chuckled

He figures he's got the drop on her.

She fired her auto pistol, unloading half a clip into the guy, just to make sure. He spun around, yelling in pain, and fell. He tried to crawl for a moment or two... shuddered... and lay still.

She turned, looked through the archway toward the front door—and saw a line of troopers running toward the house, blazing away. Bullets ripped through the walls—and a big section of the living room collapsed, burying the sofa and coffee table, spewing a cloud of plaster dust.

Ada fired out the front door with one hand, while with the other she prepped the grenade and threw it out the front door. It bounced—

Ada grinned, seeing the troopers dive out of the way. The grenade blew. Someone screamed. She saw a severed arm go flipping past the door, pinwheeling blood.

Smoke obscured the scene for a moment. Then as the smoke cleared, she saw the "Rain" clone shouldering a portable missile launcher, smiling maliciously as she aimed it, adjusting the sights.

"Damn!" Ada blurted out.

She slapped a clip into the auto pistol, and aimed it at the wooden floor, fired it in a tight pattern, concentrating her fire, cutting a kind of manhole in the wood. There wasn't much left when she was done.

She jumped on the spot she'd drilled with bullets. The wood collapsed under her, and she dropped down to the ground underneath—a thin covering of dirt over the concrete that was part of the test floor.

She got to her hands and knees, flattened, and began to creep along in the crawlspace under the floor. Crawling for her life.

Up above, she saw the launcher fire, envisioning in her mind's eye the missile load as it split apart into six mini missiles—which impacted on the floor, not far behind her. Ada felt fire singe her feet and ankles. Shockwaves banged her around, and the house disintegrated.

Smoke and fire and debris swirled... and she felt a heavy weight press down on her back.

Alice looked over her shoulder when she heard the detonation—and saw the fireball rise. Could Ada have survived that?

"They'll be coming!" she signed to the girl. "We have to hurry!" They continued running along the sidewalk, cutting between houses, then down an alley.

She had a stitch in her side. Or something worse. The pain was increasing, was viciously throbbing, burning... Alice reached down, felt her left side—and found hot blood pumping out. She was wounded. She'd caught a bullet somewhere in the fusillade back at the house.

She pressed her hand against the wound, trying to staunch the flow of blood and encourage clotting.

It hurt like a bastard. And every step made it hurt worse. But she kept going.

She always did.

As they ran, the young girl panting, Alice glanced over her shoulder—saw someone back there. They were being followed.

Up ahead, Alice saw herself appear in a mirror wall, the girl beside her.

They ran up to the mirror, gasping. Alice paused, turned away so the girl wouldn't see, and checked the injury in her left side. It had clotted—was no longer bleeding. For now. But it ached and she'd lost some blood. She hid the wound under her clothes, and turned back to the mirror wall, where the girl waited.

Alice strode to the wall, and opened the door. They stepped through, and found themselves in a Moscow train station. She looked around in a kind of sickened fascination. Was there no end to these proving grounds? Was there no end to the perversity of this place?

Dori and JudyTech were in a utility passage, hurrying along over dusty concrete, under the aluminum pipes and fluorescent tubes tracing the narrow ceiling. They'd passed some unarmed bio-lab personnel—though no one had challenged them.

Dori had changed into the clothes JudyTech had brought her, so she was wearing a tight-fitting combat outfit, complete with a trooper mask. So was JudyTech. It was hard to breathe in the mask. She hated the smell of it, and the way JudyTech looked in the trooper mask. Both wore the inactive scarabs, and it scared her to see the one attached to JudyTech, even though Dori knew it had no power over her.

"There's no time for us to get out before the flood starts," JudyTech said as they reached the end of the passage. Her voice was muffled by the mask. "The only way is to be able to survive underwater..."

The door was standing slightly open, and they both peered out.

Dori was awestruck. The cold air struck her as she poked her face out; as she stared at the mist rising from the water in the submarine grotto, toward the high, carved-out ceilings of stone.

"Are we... are we *outside*?" She'd never been *outside*, in the upper world, in whole of her short life. She was really only a few years old, technically. She'd been imprinted with a degree of maturation and borrowed experience, and some socialization. But she knew she was really a kind of infant; and she knew that the world was a vast mystery to her. That she was locked in a box, within a bigger box, under the sea, and now underground.

JudyTech had explained all that to her.

She wanted out of the boxes—she wanted, more than anything, to see the great outside. To see the sky and the sun, not just pictures of them; to feel the world's unrestrained wind, to see animals in the wild, to see birds soaring, and hear great beasts roaring.

"No," JudyTech said gently. "This isn't the outside, not yet. We're a little closer. But no... You see those vessels? Do you know what they are?"

"I don't think you ever showed them to me."

"Those are *submarines*, love. The Russians built them once, long ago. They still operate. They're big, and there's a lot of room in them. And I don't think they're being used now. With luck—we can get inside one, and hide. Others will come, and pilot it out, after the flooding. At least I hope so. And we'll find our way past them then."

"And—to the outside? The real outside?"

"Yes. To the real outside."

Dori stared at the enormous, red-and-black-painted objects.

"On that one—that thing sticking up—there are men lying there. I think they're dead. I see blood, dripping down."

"Yes. That will work to our benefit, I believe. Come, child..."

They stepped out into the chilly air, and their feet echoed in the great, silent grotto.

They were on the platform of a Metro subway station—or what was supposed to resemble one—somewhere near Red Square, in Moscow. On the wall were billboards and a station name, all painted in Cyrillic lettering.

Площадь Революции

They'd stepped out of a mirror wall which reflected the station so that the tracks seemed to stretch on endlessly. To the left was a set of stairs, leading upward.

"Where are we?" the shocked girl signed. But before Alice could respond, she heard a sound behind her. She turned, raising her gun, preparing to fire at whoever was there.

It was *Rain*, coming through the door in the mirror. She must have followed them through.

Alice aimed for the heart.

"Wait!" the little girl signed. "She helped us! Don't you remember?"

Alice stared. That outfit—the top with all the buttons. No gun in her hand. Her hair entirely different... this was a *different* Rain. She'd have seen it sooner, but she was getting woozy from loss of blood.

Alice lowered her gun.

"You two made it!" The Rain clone hurried over to them, and surprised Alice with a hug for them both. "I'm so happy there's someone else left alive!" Alice untangled herself from the awkward gesture, wincing at the pain in her wound.

The young woman looked around, amazed.

"What is this place?" She looked Alice up and down. "And what's with the get-up?"

In the distance, Alice heard the sound of gunfire. There was a battle, somewhere. A considerable battle.

"You know how to use this?" Alice held out one of her automatic pistols to Rain.

Shaking her head, Rain looked at the gun with undisguised disgust.

"I campaigned for gun control!"

No you only think you did. That's a false memory they planted... Alice considered saying it aloud, but there was no time to explain. And how could she convince her that her whole past life was an illusion, that all her memories were overlays?

Instead she stepped behind Rain, pressing the gun between her hands. Before the young woman could object, she stretched out her arms, aiming the gun for her, pointing it at the wall on the opposite platform.

"It's just like a camera," Alice said. She pressed her cheek to Rain's, and showed her how to aim along the top of the gun. "Point and shoot."

Rain squeezed the trigger, and across the tracks a section of tiled wall flew apart under the impact of a burst. She shuddered, staring at the smoking muzzle.

"Congratulations," Alice said dryly. "You're now officially a badass."

Rain's lips curved into an odd little smile.

Somewhere above, the sound of battle intensified, echoing through the station.

"What the hell is going on here?" Rain asked, still staring at the gun in her hands.

"I'll explain everything when I get back." She nodded toward her daughter. "Right now I need you to keep her safe."

The girl looked up at her with big, astonished eyes—Alice felt that look like an arrow through her heart.

"You're going?" Becky signed. "You said you wouldn't leave!"

"I'm going to be right back," Alice responded.

"You *promised*!"

Alice knelt down beside her. The girl looked away, hurt. Alice put her hand where she could see it, and signed.

"Look at me," she said. "You can trust me—you *do* trust me, don't you?"

The girl looked at her—and nodded.

"What I say is true," Alice signed. "I will be back for you."

The girl's lips trembled. Alice could see she was

working to hold back tears.

"Okay?" Alice signed.

The girl nodded, and signed, "Okay." So Alice stood up, started to turn away.

"I love you," the girl added quickly.

Alice stared. She wasn't sure how she should react. This wasn't really her daughter. The child desperately believed, though, that Alice was her mother. She looked at her—and saw a girl desperate for reassurance.

"I love you, too," she signed.

The Rain clone turned to the girl.

"She'll be back. Don't worry. Come on—let's find some place to hide."

The girl seemed to get the gist by reading Rain's lips. She nodded and took her hand.

"I met your sister," the girl signed.

Rain looked at her in puzzlement—she didn't understand hand signs.

"What?"

"She's not very nice," Becky signed.

Alice turned away, the wound in her side aching—but what hurt worse was the pang of uncertainty, her fear for the little girl. She wasn't used to this—she was used to being confident in herself, trusting herself to make the right move.

This was uncharted territory.

Was she lying to this child? Her instincts were strong, and she would defend the girl to the death—

out they weren't a mother's feelings. Not exactly. She'd have to tell the truth eventually. Was she leading an innocent deeper into betrayal?

When it was all about surviving, Alice told herself, about not getting shot, or killed when a bomb went off, there was no need to worry about hurting people's feelings. That was where she had to be now.

But still, those trusting eyes haunted her...

They'd lost track of Project Alice.

Waiting by the ruins of the house, half a dozen troopers standing at ease nearby, Commander Jill Valentine listened to reports from her troopers. The security cam system for this scenario had been damaged by explosions, but it seemed likely she'd moved over to the next test floor—Moscow. Perhaps Alice was hoping to join Ada Wong's team.

Jill growled. How was she supposed to do her job with so few personnel? So many clones were thrown away on these incessant tests.

She felt a strange dissonance inside her—as if something in her rejoiced at Alice's escape, temporary though it would prove to be. She had to suppress those feelings, however—or the scarab would punish her. She might end up in a bio-vat. Parts from non-cloned humans were recycled in the bio-vats. Their proteins, amino acids, and other fundamentals were used to create new clones—more cannon fodder for Umbrella.

Jill forced herself to concentrate on the task at hand—confirming that Ada Wong was dead. She was about to order the excavation of the smoldering remains, when the blackened floorboards not ten steps away split open.

Ada Wong forced herself out. She swayed, coughing, in the smoking wreckage, looking bruised, bloodied, and blackened with ash—yet fundamentally unarmed.

The Rain trooper stepped onto the foundations of the house and pointed her weapon.

"Going somewhere?"

At Jill's hand signal, the other troopers closed around her.

Ada stared at them, looking overcome and weak. Then she slowly raised her hands in surrender.

Well, Jill thought. *This could be useful.*

1 5

Leon, Barry, Sergei, and Luther crouched behind a pile of bodies and debris, firing only when they had to. Their improvised "bunker" was made of piled-up dead plague soldiers, along with fallen cornices and display props from the GUM store. The limbs of mannequins were mixed up with the limbs of dead men.

Sergei was still hunched over his laptop, desperately poring over the schematics of the Moscow test floor.

"We're running out of time," Leon shouted at him. "You have to find a way around them!"

"Almost there!"

Luther looked at his countdown watch. Only thirty-three minutes left to go.

Make that thirty-two.

No make it thirty-one minutes and fifty seconds...

A plague soldier with glowing red eyes came out of the smoke and vaulted over his dead compatriots, right at Luther—who raised his gun, squeezed the trigger—

And nothing happened. He'd lost track of his ammo. The weapon was unloaded.

The soldier had a shotgun in his hand. He swung it toward Luther—then the top of his head flew off in a corona of blood, as Leon shot him.

Luther nodded his thanks and reloaded his weapon. He sighed. His mouth was dry, his heart was banging in his chest, and he was hungry and tired. And he still saw Tony, in his mind's eye, getting sawed in half by that roaring chainsaw, blood spraying everywhere.

So here I am, Luther thought. How the hell had he got himself into this? Trying to find Alice, was how.

Women. That's what got you into the worst—

Suddenly Sergei slammed his computer shut.

"Got it!" he shouted triumphantly. "This way!"

Barry, Leon, and Luther fired suppressive rounds and threw the last of their grenades to keep the plague soldiers back, and then turned and bolted after Sergei. He led them along the inside of the wrecked façade of the GUM store, past more tumble-down, smoking displays, toward a far corner of the building.

Their sudden departure left the plague soldiers momentarily confused, still focused on the "bodies bunker" the team had left behind. So the team made good progress, and safely reached the corner of the building, all of them breathing hard. Ahead was an intact glass display window.

Sergei picked up a steel chair, swung it with one hand and tossed it, sending it flying high. It crashed through the store window, breaking most of the glass out.

"This way!" Sergei shouted.

He jumped up on the display and past the bashed-out window. Luther followed, with Leon and Barry close behind.

"Move, move, *move*!" Leon urged them.

Then they were out on a street corner, in the Moscow testing set, their boots crunching over broken glass. It was in an "evening" mode out here, the lights dimmed down.

"We can work our way..." Sergei said between gasps, "around the perimeter... and..."

And suddenly something pink and wet and serrated and big as a power line cable whipped out, wrapping itself around Sergei. Luther could see his ribs cracking as the screaming Russian was lifted off his feet, and up...

Luther looked up, following the wet pink cable. Up, up, farther up—and he stared.

The cable was a tongue—an impossibly long tongue, extending from the dripping maw of the most hideous thing he had ever seen. Hanging upside down in the shadows, clinging, somehow, to girders far overhead, was a gigantic flesh-colored creature, at least twelve yards long from head to tail, with the general heft of a fairly squat elephant.

Sergei shouted in pain and struggled as the tongue reeled him in, bringing him to its mouth—and he screeched hideously as it bit him in half, calmly chewing him up. The lower half of him fell to the ground, landing with a wet sound.

Shit!

Luther had to look away, try to control his gagging.

He forced himself to look back as the others began to fire at the creature. That's when he realized that to either side of big pink mutant, pasted to the ceiling in translucent, glutinous cocoons, were human beings—clones who were supposed to have taken part in the tests. Writhing in their restraints.

Still alive.

The bullets had little effect on the monster—except to make it want to come down and take them out in person. It released its hold and dropped, flipping itself in the air, landing in front of them on its four sets of claws. The street shook with the *whump* of its landing.

"What the fuck is it?" Luther asked.

"A Licker," Leon told him, his voice shaking as he aimed his gun. "The biggest one I ever saw or heard of. Mutated from a variant of the T-virus. Believe it or not, that thing was once a human being..."

"Umbrella must've had it developed in a lab," Barry said, slapping a clip in his rifle. "Released it here to stop us."

Luther could see the monster more clearly now. It looked as if the outer layer of skin had been scraped off, down almost to the muscle. The top half of its skull—including its eyes—was entirely missing. Where they should have been there was a big, leathery, overgrown brain, looking like some hideous fungus. Though apparently blind, the thing somehow sensed them. It stalked toward them on dragonlike legs—four of them, its front limbs almost as much like legs as the rear. Scything claws scratched the street with each step, its dripping serrated tongue whipping out, feeling its way along.

Luther backed off—then a bullet cut the air just over his head, coming from behind. He turned and saw plague soldiers running up toward them, firing sporadically.

They were boxed in.

RESIDENT EVIL:RETRIBUTION

He fired at the Licker but it stalked implacably toward them, squealing and snarling, apparently unhurt. It was so big their bullets were just irritants.

Then Luther heard something that had no place here—a roaring car engine. He saw the double pools of headlights illuminate the creature, making it turn. A Rolls-Royce Silver Phantom, gleaming and thoroughly pimped out, was doing eighty miles an hour as it rocketed toward the Licker.

The giant creature roared in fury, then the driver engaged the brakes and the tires squealed as the car skidded, deliberately power-sliding, striking the hulking flesh-colored monster side-on. The impact knocked the Licker sideways, and then over onto its back so that it tumbled through the plate-glass window of another fake store.

Stunned, the monster thrashed about in the window display, crushing mannequins underfoot, confusedly lashing at them with its tongue, trying to right itself.

Leon and Barry began firing at the plague soldiers, forcing them to take cover behind cars parked on the street. The Rolls-Royce Silver Phantom jolted to a stop, and a door opened, revealing the driver.

Alice.

"Hi," she said, casually.

Luther was dizzy with emotion, just looking at her. Too much had happened in the last few minutes.

But he swallowed hard, and smiled.

"Nice ride," he said.

"Well, this *is* Moscow," she countered. She gestured and the three men ran to the sedan. They climbed in, Luther up front beside her.

"Let's get outta here before that thing figures out that dummies don't make a good dinner," he said. She nodded. The wheels spun, and the Rolls-Royce peeled out. Bullets from the plague soldiers smacked into the side. She ran over what was left of Sergei's body as she went, but Luther didn't criticize her for it. They were in a hurry.

Barry looked over his shoulder, up at the ceiling.

"Those people—were still alive!"

"The creature was cocooning them," Alice said. "Saving them for food."

She barreled down the street, and Luther introduced the other two men.

"Barry, Leon... Alice."

"Pleased to meet you," she said.

Luther looked behind them, saw that the Licker had freed itself. It was racing after them—and it was pissed off. It killed a couple of plague soldiers on the way, for good measure, with casual snaps of its jaws.

Still, the Rolls was outdistancing it.

"You might want to buckle up," Alice said. They were coming to a blocked cross street. It was stop, crash into the blockade, or turn.

She'd better decide, Luther thought, looking at the speedometer. *We're going seventy miles an hour.*

Without slowing, she pulled a hand-break turn, the G-force making the men strain to keep their places in the car.

"Nice driving," Barry said.

Luther smiled. Aware of the absurdity of the situation, and yet somehow not caring. Here, anyway, was Alice.

"Nice to see you again," he said.

Alice returned his smile.

"Nice to be seen."

Leon glanced back.

"It's gaining." Luther looked back and saw that the Licker was running like a rabid racehorse, coming on strong, moving closer to them.

"Not a problem," Alice said. She turned to Luther. "So... did you miss me?"

"Really?" He looked at the Licker. "We're going to do this right now?"

Alice shrugged, then smiled. She looked pale, at least to Luther.

"No time like the present," she said.

Luther considered asking her how she'd found them—but probably she'd lucked onto "Moscow," and then followed the sound of gunfire.

Up ahead the street was clogged by abandoned and burned-out vehicles, many of them overturned. Alice slowed just enough to weave skillfully between them, like a stunt driver on an obstacle course. The giant Licker didn't bother weaving. It charged straight through the vehicles, bounding up, and crushing them as it came down, or shouldering them aside like a rhino tossing bales of hay.

Alice looked in the rear-view mirror, and Luther saw that she was becoming worried. The Licker was getting close. Real close. It was whipping its tongue out ahead of it, slapping at the rear window.

Nasty, Luther thought.

He looked up ahead—and saw something bearing down on them. Another pair of high beams, their source obscured.

"Alice..." he said. She didn't seem to hear him.

"*Alice!*" The car's headlights were glaring in his eyes—it was coming right at them, head-on.

"*Car!*" Luther shouted.

Instead of slowing, Alice accelerated—drove straight on instead of turning, apparently intent on hitting the other vehicle.

Too late to do anything but brace for impact.

Then Alice jogged the wheel and hit the brakes, doing a "bootlegger reverse." The car spun around through a sickening 180 degrees, but avoiding the pursuing Licker—which *couldn't* stop. It did so suddenly as it hit something with a sickening crunch.

It wasn't another car that had been coming at them—it was the Rolls, reflected in the mirror. The creature smashed through the glass, and was flailing wildly. Luther hoped it was cut to pieces.

He held on as Alice squealed the car around, sent it burning down a side street. Then he turned to Barry with a "did you see that?" look—and was surprised when Barry high-fived him.

"I can see why we came for her," Barry said.

But Leon was scowling.

"Where's Ada?" he demanded, leaning toward Alice.

She shook her head sadly.

"I don't think she made it," she said. "I'm sorry."

Leon took a long ragged breath.

"You saw her die?" he asked.

"No," Alice admitted.

Leon nodded to himself, and he actually seemed to relax.

"She always has a plan."

At that moment the rear window shattered in a sudden fusillade of bullets. There were two flatbed trucks pursuing them, one mounted with a rocket launcher, the other with a machine-gun turret—the vehicles they'd seen at the Red Square, driven by plague soldiers.

Persistent bastards, Luther thought. *But what else are they going to do? Go bowling?*

The machine gunner opened up again, and bullets hammered the back of the Rolls. It wouldn't take much more of this kind of bullet storm, Luther mused.

"Boys," Alice said coolly, "would you mind?" There was an odd strain to her voice, though—as if she was in pain.

"Shall we?" Leon said to Barry, like a gentleman asking another if he'd like to go duck hunting.

"My pleasure," Barry responded, clamping his perpetually unlit cigar in a corner of his mouth. He leaned out the back of the shattered back window and fired his machine rifle, Leon followed suit.

"This is for Sergei, you pricks," he muttered.

The machine gunner lost the top of his head in one of Barry's bursts—but he was quickly replaced by another. Leon aimed very carefully at the muzzle of the RPG launcher—and fired when he saw the flash of its ignition. His rounds impacted neatly with the rocket-propelled grenade, before it had quite exited the barrel. The whole assembly exploded, tearing the Undead gunman apart.

Luther didn't have much ammo—he looked for a shot but he was afraid he might hit Leon or Luther. So he leaned out of his shattered side window, and fired at the pursuing trucks, trying to hit the drivers.

* * *

Driving furiously, screaming through turns, trying to evade her pursuers, Alice noticed a Las Plagas Undead riding a motorcycle, pulling up close to her, a machine pistol in his right hand. She ducked as he fired and a spray of bullets knocked out her side window.

She lifted up enough to see, and jerked the wheel in order to sideswipe the motorcycle. That sent it crashing into a newsstand, where the bike flipped over and slammed down on the Undead like a hammer.

Then she veered around a burning wreck in the street, looked in the mirror, and saw another RPG launcher pop up from the back of the flatbed that held the machine gun. There was a flash, a puff of smoke, and she saw the rocket streaking toward the rear of the Rolls.

Timing it carefully, she jogged the steering wheel so the Rolls swerved and the rocket whipped on by, passing the car and exploding in the street up ahead. There was no choice but to drive right through the ensuing fireball and Luther—leaning out a window to fire at their pursuers—shouted a curse as the flames licked around the sedan.

"*Son of a bitch!*"

He pulled back into the vehicle, driven in by the blast. He slapped some small flames out on his coat, and turned to Alice.

"Let me know when you plan on doing that again," he growled.

Alice glanced in the rear-view mirror—and saw another RPG round rocketing toward them on a tail of fire.

"Heads up!" she called out, and she jogged the

wheel again so the projectile exploded beside the Rolls, making the car rock.

She jerked the wheel into a sharp turn, taking them into the midst of Red Square—and saw a motorcycle coming straight at her on a collision course. The Undead rider was firing a machine gun over the handlebars as it came. Bullets sparked off the hood.

"Down!" Alice shouted, ducking. Luther and the other men ducked down just as the front windshield imploded, and bullets flashed over their heads.

She peered over the top of the steering wheel, saw the motorcycle about to impact with the Silver Phantom. She spun the Rolls into a 180-degree slide, opened her heavily built side door—and smashed it into the motorcycle. Acting like a fly swatter, it flattened the Undead, knocking him and his bike into a twisted, spinning heap of bloody, burning slag.

Alice spun the car again, back on course... and Barry spoke up.

"Guess who's back."

In her rear-view mirror, she could see that the giant Licker had found its way back to her. It was in hot pursuit.

16

The gigantic Licker was gaining. It was mangled, badly cut up from crashing into the mirror wall. And it looked seriously pissed off. She wasn't going to be able to shake it—not the way she'd been doing it. And if they happened upon the Las Plagas soldiers again, chances are their luck would run out.

They couldn't survive another hailstorm of bullets.

She was going to have to do something extreme—for a change. And she saw exactly what she needed, up ahead.

The Red Square Metro station.

"Almost there!" Alice shouted.

"Where?" Luther asked.

She looked in the mirror again. The Licker was closer yet—shoving the pursuing Undead out of the way, crashing their vehicles into the ornate walls of the Resurrection Gate. The gigantic pink mutant was one good bound away from leaping on the Rolls, big enough to smash what was left of the Silver Phantom.

No time to do this delicately.

"Hold on—this is going to get bad!"

"It's going to '*get*' bad?" Luther laughed bitterly. But she didn't bother to respond.

Alice slammed on the gas, crashed through a construction site at the edge of the square, and jumped off a ramp of piled chunks of asphalt. The Rolls soared twenty feet off the ground, arcing through the air, coming down with a squealing, bone-rattling crash at seventy miles per hour.

And then it plunged down the steps that led to the Metro.

Luther, Barry, and Leon yelled as the car bounced and clattered down the steps, their shouts wavering like yodels with the impacts on the stairs. They all held onto whatever was handy, their heads whipping around with every impact. Alice gripped the steering wheel, got a jerky glimpse in the rear-view mirror of the mangled Licker, still following her down into the underground station.

If it caught up, it would leap onto the Rolls, rip it open like a sardine tin, and begin feasting.

At the bottom of the stairs was an archway that appeared to be under repair—heavy stones curved along the arch. Scaffolding held up part of the ceiling. The car reached the bottom, and ignoring the shooting pain in her side, she deliberately slammed it into the scaffolding—just as the Licker leapt.

Alice slammed her foot down on the accelerator and crashed through the scaffolding, knocking it down behind the Rolls. The stone arch it had held up was knocked down with it. Tons of stone and girders dropped onto the Licker, burying it and plugging up the tunnel behind her. A cloud of dust rose up around the falling debris.

She ground the car to a halt and looked back. The Licker was at least half buried.

That should slow it down.

"Everyone okay?" she asked, looking at Luther. He looked as if he might be sick to his stomach.

"We'll live," Leon said.

"Time to get out and walk," Luther said.

Alice led the way, carrying the hook gun that Ada had given her, as well as the machine pistol. Not far down the tunnel they came to an abandoned station

"Hello!" Alice called. "You can come out now!"

The Rain clone and a little girl emerged from the darkness at the other end of the tunnel, where they'd been hiding. The girl ran straight to Alice and threw her arms around her waist. Alice hugged her.

"She was very brave," Rain said.

Luther looked with undisguised surprise at the little girl holding onto Alice.

"Who's this?" he asked.

"I'm Becky," the girl signed.

"Becky..." Alice murmured. Suddenly she realized that it was the first time she had heard the name—though it sounded familiar.

That strange telepathic dream...

"I'm very pleased to meet you," Becky signed. She indicated Alice. "This is my mom."

Alice translated.

"She says she's Becky, she's pleased to meet you, and..." She sighed. "I'm 'her mom.'"

Luther looked at her with eyebrows raised.

"Her mom?"

"Long story," Alice said, and she really didn't feel like telling it.

Leon stepped up to them, pointing at his countdown watch.

"Twenty-two minutes left." Everyone looked back at the collapsed archway—they could hear the sound of claws on metal and stone; the muffled squeal of frustrated mutant. Alice thought she saw the tip of a cablelike serrated pink tongue, licking out through a crevice in the fallen masonry. The Licker was still alive—and trying to break through.

"There's no going back the way we came," Luther pointed out.

"And we lost the map with Sergei," Barry said, nodding.

"I've got it!" Alice said. She took out the spectacles Ada had given her, pulling them from a pocket of her battle suit. She unfolded them and put them on, tapped the frame, then moved her finger up and down the stem, scrolling up and down till she got to the schematics of the test floor. She studied them, seeing the glowing outlines of the buildings, the streets, the tunnels.

Her trained mind sorted through the data—and quickly found a route.

"We can take this tunnel—" She pointed at a side tunnel that led into inky darkness. "At the end there's a service shaft that connects with the submarine pens."

"Then let's go!" Leon said, striding quickly that way.

Alice urged Becky along ahead of her, taking up the rear because she was worried about the Licker. The others entered the tunnel—and just before she followed, Alice glanced back. The rubble past the wrecked Rolls-Royce, was beginning to shift, to shrug about, and she thought she glimpsed a Licker's talon.

She hurried on, wanting to get under cover now. Up ahead of them, not quite running, were the Rain clone, Barry, Luther, and Leon. Alice and Becky caught up with Leon, who had a small flashlight in one hand. A little light glowed up from the flashlight, eerily illuminating his grimly determined face.

"How did you end up working for Wesker?" Alice asked.

Leon's response was a harsh snap.

"I don't work for him!" He glowered over at her for a long moment. Finally he went on. "But things on the surface have changed. Everyone thought it was important to have you with us. Wesker said you knew of some weapon... something that could turn the tide." He shook his head, perhaps thinking of Sergei and Ada. "But I don't know if I would have risked so much, just for one person."

"Okay, then," Alice said. There was no time—no political room, in a sense—to push for more information. In time, it would all come out.

But as long as Wesker was involved—she was pretty sure it'd come out badly.

"Dead end!" Barry said, pointing.

The tunnel—just "window dressing," after all—came to a halt in a wall of rough stone. But in one corner, a metal staircase led upward. Alice took off Ada's glasses and looked up the staircase. There was a little light coming down from above.

"Access shaft to the submarine pens," she said. "Come on!"

She led the way, wincing at the spiking pain in her side that came with every step now. When she thought she was out of sight of the others, around a turn in the staircase, she checked the wound. It was bleeding again. She already felt lightheaded, weaker than usual.

Come on, Alice, she told herself. *Find the energy and do what has to get done. One more time...*

She heard a scratching sound on stone, from back in the tunnel. It didn't seem human. Was that the sound of a Licker's claws, as it crept along, searching for them? She glanced back, and saw Becky hurrying to catch up with her. Alice smiled at the girl and waved.

Could she really keep Becky alive, while she was slowly bleeding out? With the bomb ticking toward an explosion, with the troopers looking for them, and with the Licker once more on their trail, the odds weren't good.

Jill and her team hurried across the underground Metro platform, past the imitation Russian billboards on the tiled walls. Ada Wong, in handcuffs, her head hooded, stumbled blindly ahead of them.

Even so, Ada was dangerous. Very dangerous. Cuffing her hands behind her, the hood, constant surveillance—it was all necessary. Just give her a sliver of an edge—just for a moment—and she would use that advantage to cut someone's throat.

Probably mine, Jill mused, *If she can get to me.*

She could see that the way was blocked up ahead by a fall of masonry. The rubble was moving a little as if something was forcing its way through. That would be one of the Lickers. She'd objected to releasing the experimental monsters from their pens, just to go after Ada Wong's strike team. The creatures would kill allies just as likely as enemies, and they were a threat to Jill and her squadron. But she'd been overruled and the things had been set free.

It looked to Jill as if one of the Lickers had already broken through the stone barricade. The other was still digging its way out.

We won't be going that way, she mused. It was possible that Alice was dead—but somehow Jill didn't think so. Project Alice was too resourceful. Trying to think like her quarry, Jill worked out the route the strike team had probably taken. She signaled to a trooper, instructing him to check his computer.

He nodded and stared into space, scrolling through imagery.

"They've reached the submarine pens," he indicated. "Headed for the elevators."

"Bring up the power grid," Jill grunted.

"Yes, ma'am."

He tapped his goggles, and issued the orders.

The spiral stairs ended in a concrete hallway, lit by flickering emergency lights, which gave the passage a strobe effect. Alice was feeling a little disoriented from loss of blood, and the flashing didn't help.

Focus, Alice, focus...

They pushed through a steel door, Leon taking the lead, looking around for troopers. Not spotting any, judging from his reaction. Then they all emerged into the gigantic, echoey stone room—into the chill, where their breaths plumed, and there was the briny smell of saltwater.

"Are those submarines?" Becky asked, her eyes huge.

"Yes," Alice responded. "Russian submarines."

Leon looked at his watch and let out a long slow breath.

"Eleven minutes," he said. "We're going to be okay." But Alice wasn't so sure. There still were a lot of wild cards, a lot of unknown factors, that lay between them and the surface world.

Leon led the way, jogging along toward an elevator that would lift them up to the boarding level. Alice trotted behind him, holding Becky's hand and trying to ignore the pain in her side; the way the room seemed to bounce around as she ran, as if it might start spinning at any moment. She needed food and rest. She needed blood pressure. She needed to...

Get to the elevator shaft, Alice. Put one foot in front of the other. Keep going. Do not lose consciousness. Not allowed.

The room swirled—but she stayed on her feet. And there was the shaft.

"Get on board!" Luther called to them, jumping onto the big freight platform.

"Hold on!" Barry said as Alice and Becky climbed up. He tapped the elevator's controls. "Next stop, menswear and sporting goods." He hit the switch, and the elevator began to rise. It looked like they were going to make it after all...

It got seven feet up the shaft—and then jolted to a stop.

The lights in the chamber went out, to be replaced

by dim, flickering emergency lights. The shaft suddenly seemed like a shortcut to Hell.

"Barry?" Leon asked, licking his lips. "What is it?"

"I don't know…"

Alice looked down at Becky—saw the fear on the little girl's face. She hugged her close.

"It'll be all right…" she signed.

Luther went to the edge of the platform, lowered himself from it, and dropped to the floor.

"Where are you going?" Leon demanded.

But Luther didn't need to answer as he went to the control panel. Leon and Alice climbed down and followed—Becky whimpering as Alice left her on the elevator. The Rain clone put her arms around the little girl, whispering to her. Barry looked around nervously, gun at the ready.

Leon was staring into the submarine pens as he walked over to Luther. So far, no sign of pursuers…

"Looks like somebody cut the power remotely," Luther said, trying to reactivate the control panel.

"Can you get it back online?" Leon asked.

Luther shook his head.

"Not my specialty."

Leon glanced at his countdown timer.

"Nine minutes. Looks like we're going with plan B." Luther looked enquiringly at him. "There's a reason we planted those explosives."

Suddenly a shadow fell over them. Claws clicked on stones. Alice felt a chill and looked up to see a gigantic Licker clinging to the wall just below a big open-air vent. The creature was limned flickeringly in the strobing emergency light as it hung above the elevator platform. A narrow, fragile-looking iron ladder, affixed to the wall, led up to the yawning vent.

Its tongue extending, lolling, seeking, its muscles rippling, its exposed brain pulsing, the Licker moved down toward them, half slithering and half creeping. The enormous pink mutant got within reach of Barry, and before he could bring his gun into place, it slashed at him with vicious speed and accuracy, raking him with its giant claws. He screamed as the powerful blow knocked him back, hard, into the concrete wall. He sagged down it, groaning, his face streaming blood, his scalp torn loose and hanging in an ugly red flap.

Alice was running toward Becky, but it was too late—the Licker shot its tongue toward the little girl, wrapped it around her, dragging her from Rain's grip. She screeched in sheer terror.

"No!" Rain yelled. She raised the gun Alice had given her, and charged the Licker, firing. One slash of its giant claws and she was flung away like a child struck by a drunken thug, spun through the air, hurling her off the elevator platform. She fell, screaming in pain, then struck the concrete below and lay there like a crushed rag doll.

The Licker dragged Becky, still alive, up the wall toward its maw, drawing her closer as it reeled in its ropy, serrated tongue. Alice aimed carefully, trying to get a shot at the Licker's brain that wouldn't hit Becky. But suppose she did hit the Licker, enough to make it drop the child? She was high up on the wall of the huge room now, and almost certainly would be killed in the fall.

Alice hesitated—and then it was too late. The Licker tucked Becky up close to it, like a lion dragging its prey to a den, and ducked into the big air vent high above.

Feeling sickeningly hollow inside, Alice lowered the gun. She glanced over at the Rain clone—saw Luther kneeling beside her, checking her pulse.

"She's dead."

Alice looked up at the vent, and she made up her mind.

17

Moments later Alice was on the freight elevator, checking her weapons, making sure they were primed and ready. Aware that the seconds were ticking by, wondering if Becky was still alive.

She looked over at Leon and Barry.

Leon had returned to the platform, as well, where he knelt beside his friend.

"Talk to me, Barry."

Barry grimaced. His face was laid open, one of his lips slashed through.

"Feel like shit."

Leon began unwrapping a sterile medi-pad from the kit on his belt. He pressed the pad to Barry's clawed face.

"Here, this should help. Hold it in place."

Barry reached up weakly and pressed the pad against his skin, so that the medication would be drawn through the epidermis. He looked up at Leon, locked eyes with him.

"Tell me, honestly. How bad is it?"

"You know," Leon began thoughtfully, "I think that thing improved your looks."

Barry laughed, and then grimaced with pain.

"Son of a bitch! Don't make me laugh."

Leon looked at his countdown watch.

"Seven minutes then we're out of here. We'll get you help topside."

Barry nodded. Leon stood up and looked at Alice, who was walking toward the base of the ladder. He stared.

"What are you doing?" he asked, in disbelief.

"I'm going to get her," Alice replied, simply.

Leon laughed bitterly and shook his head.

"I didn't lose this many friends just to have you walk away!"

"I plan on coming back," she said calmly.

Leon strode over and blocked her way.

"Don't do this. You're more important than she is."

"Well, that's where you're wrong," Alice said firmly.

"This is a mistake!" Leon insisted.

Alice gave him a diamond-hard, ice-cold look. A look that spoke eloquently of danger. It said, *Try to stop me and I'll cut you down.*

"Step aside," she gritted.

He took a long, slow breath—then he stepped out of the way.

Alice walked over to the ladder—and so did Luther, offering her a small flashlight.

"Take this," Luther said.

Alice took the flashlight and smiled at him.

"Don't be leaving without me."

Luther chuckled.

"Are you joking? I'm coming with you."

Alice smiled—and then the smile froze on her face, melted away as gunfire cracked, and bullets ricocheted around them.

Luther spun, groaning, and went down.

Alice looked up and saw two Umbrella troopers, running toward the elevator shaft, firing their weapons. She drew her pistol, and fired back. Luther fired from a prone position, and Leon lit up the troopers, too. The two clones staggered back, dancing with bullet impacts—and then fell, twitching.

But more were coming, Jill Valentine and her squadron had reached the submarine pens.

"Are you okay?" Alice asked Luther, hunkering beside him.

"Clean shot..." But they both could see that his arm was mangled, broken. Alice shook her head, dubious.

"Clean shot?" she said. Smashed by a rifle bullet, Luther's arm was an ugly mess. He could bleed to death pretty easily.

Clenching his teeth against pain, Luther sat up, using a piece of torn cloth to fashion a makeshift tourniquet. He glanced up at the ladder, and shook his head—then handed Alice a belt of grenades.

"Go get her back."

Alice nodded, patted his cheek, strapped on the grenades, and jumped to the ladder. She started to climb.

Leon and Luther watched her climb rapidly up; watched till she vanished into the air vent.

"Don't be late," Luther called hoarsely.

Leon got his weapons ready and looked for a

secure firing position. The troopers came into sight, and began striding toward them.

Alice climbed over the lip of the vent shaft. It stretched horizontally, a grey metal tunnel, into the wall and beyond. It was dark and close and claustrophobic and it smelled foully of Licker.

It was hard to tell what was up ahead, in that murk—the creature could be thirty feet in, lying quietly, waiting for her, and she wouldn't be able to see it. She was reluctant to turn on the flashlight—it could make the Licker charge her, and she preferred to catch it unprepared.

Move, Alice. No time. Go.

She stepped forward, feeling her way, listening—and then reminding herself that time was short. She pushed on faster, five padding steps, ten, twenty, thirty... and then she stopped, feeling the movement of on her face. She'd reached a junction where the tunnel was crossed by another.

There was no choice, now—and she needed the light.

Alice switched on the flashlight, keeping it angled low, so the light would be as unobtrusive as possible. The shaft stretched endlessly on, both ways, right and left. She saw no sign of the Licker, not even a claw mark.

But there—something was lying a short distance to the right, on the metal floor. She went cautiously toward it, and realized it was Becky's backpack. She picked it up, hefted it, then slung it over one shoulder.

Had Becky dropped it to show her the way? Or had she dropped it as she'd died?

Either way, Becky was this way.

Alice continued on, and the darkness seemed to thicken around her, to whirl about, sucking at her like a drain. It pulled her down... She fell to her knees, shuddering, felt a warm wet trickling from the wound on her side. Bleeding again. Too much blood. She was on the verge of blacking out.

Gritting her teeth, Alice forced herself to stand. She knew from experience that if she got into action, her blood pressure would rise, giving her a temporary lift, an inner crutch that could carry her. But she also knew that it might force blood from the wound in her side. Regardless, she had to chance it.

She imagined Becky, clutched close to the monster, perhaps pasted to the wall with the webbing it issued from its mouth, cocooned until it was ready to tear her into pieces. Fury flared up in Alice, and she found herself striding forward, picking up speed, on into the tunnel.

Most of the little signs and directions stenciled on the walls and doors were in a language Dori didn't understand. JudyTech said it was something called "Cyrillic," a Russian lettering. But here and there were cardboard signs, taped on, giving English translations. One said MEN'S HEAD. What did that mean? Were there men's heads in there? She'd seen stranger things.

She had no wish to go into that room.

Creeping along the narrow steel and plastic passage, her boots clinking on the metal, Dori wished she'd taken JudyTech's offer, and let her come along on the search for food. But once they'd boarded the submarine, she'd seen how tired JudyTech was. So she'd insisted that her friend rest in their new hiding place—a room filled with old canvas hoses. It had something to do with emergency firefighting, and JudyTech said it wouldn't normally be entered, so they would do well to stay there.

The cramped, low passages were lit by dull red lights, some sort of emergency lighting. She'd taken off her mask so she could see better, and she'd taken off the scarab, too, though she knew JudyTech wanted her to wear it in case they ran into anyone. She just hated the scarabs—even the ones that didn't work.

She kept moving through the red-lit dimness. It was very oppressive, all that red light and metal. It made her think of blood—and robots.

Dori didn't like robots. There were maintenance bots in Umbrella Prime, and if people got in their way, they were known to scoop them up and recycle them.

She saw no robots, or people either, on the submarine. It must not have been staffed. There didn't even seem to be a caretaker.

Suppose she got lost? The submarine was so big, and most of the corridors looked alike, to her. She was already turned around, perhaps irrevocably.

Maybe I should turn back...

Then up ahead, a hand-printed sign on that oval metal door said GALLEY.

Dori went to the door, and put her hand on the lever. She hesitated, then tried it, and it turned. The thick metal door swung inward. She stepped over the lower frame of the door, and into the galley. The lights were on, showing a room with white-metal walls and long white-metal benches and tables, all running the same direction as the corridor and the general thrust of the vessel.

On the other side of the room there was an open window with a stainless-steel counter, where food was passed through, she supposed. She crossed over to it, climbed onto the counter, and through the window. Inside, there were microwave ovens, electric stovetops and—there, at the other end, a walk-in freezer, its stainless-steel door standing open.

Feeling a warm glow at having succeeded at the task JudyTech set her, Dori crossed the tile floor and stepped into the cold of the freezer—when suddenly a hand closed over her mouth, an arm clamped her about the middle, and a gruff male voice spoke.

"Well I wonder what we got here? Could it be one of the ship's rats?"

Alice came to another airshaft, this one directly above her—going straight up. She could hear air whispering along in it—and some other sound, perhaps a whimpering, perhaps just something breathing in a plaintive way. There was a cool-blue light coming from above, and it reflected off of a wet coating of slime on the metal walls. The light fell on a cocoon, glued to the wall of the shaft some distance up.

It was a cocoon big enough for a little girl. And it was *moving*. Eyes peered down at her.

Alice's heart twisted at the sight. At least she was alive...

She started to step forward, looking for a way to climb up to Becky—then the girl broke one hand free from the cocoon. She used it to sign to Alice.

"Trap," Becky signed frantically. "It's a trap..."

Alice peered past her, up the shaft, where the shadows had thickened like dust-coated spider webs, and she could just make out a bulky shape, a shadow darker than the rest, shifting slightly, poised up there—waiting to drop on her.

Waiting to pounce.

Lickers appeared to be the embodiment of murderous rage, and nothing more. But they had been human beings once, and they retained human cunning. There was an evil hibernating in the human brain, and it could be fanned by genetic engineering, she knew. It could be spurred into wakefulness, an insect inside that could take over the mind and make its monstrous appetites, its rapacity, the center of all meaning. Lickers weren't just mutations—they were the personification of the most primeval impulses in humanity, the animal within the animal.

Don't underestimate these creatures, she told herself. *Not if you want Becky to live.*

Leon and Barry were crouched in the hallway, firing at the troopers. Return fire churned the concrete walls as if by a dozen jackhammers. Luther was firing from the elevator platform. They were trying to conserve ammo—it was getting sparse.

The troopers were fifty yards off, crouched behind crates and columns near the pens, sniping at them, sometimes firing long machine gun bursts. Luther picked out a target, a black-masked head poking out from behind a concrete post—dropped the crosshairs of his sights, and squeezed the trigger. The gun bucked in his hand and a pink mist spread from the jerking figure as the man tipped over, dead before he hit the ground.

But bullets from another enemy weapon sizzled overhead and he had to flatten down to give them less of a target. It seemed to him that he recognized the woman who was firing at him. It was that mind-trapped commander, what was her name—Jill Valentine. The bitch was shooting at him personally.

He wondered for the hundredth time if Ada was dead. They were pretty close, him and Ada. Maybe it was superstitious, but he thought he'd feel it if she were killed. And he wasn't feeling it.

You get crazy thoughts under fire, he mused. *Believing in the supernatural. No atheists in foxholes.*

But if Ada was alive—where the hell was she?

Don't think about it. The mission is a mess. They'd probably never get Alice out of here, as per the plan. *A fucking waste, and I may not even salvage my own life.*

Leon looked at his countdown watch and felt his stomach contract in dread.

1:47 — 1: 46 — 1:45...

He looked up toward the ladder Alice had climbed. No sign of her. And no more time to wait.

Another long burst of gunfire came from the enemy. Bullets cracked and ricocheted around them. They couldn't take much more of this—the troopers were bound to charge soon. And his watch was still counting down.

He had to make a move.

"Get back to the elevator!" he shouted, over the racket of gunfire. "Less than two minutes! We have to move! *Now*!"

Barry shook his head.

"You go. I'm just gonna wait here awhile..."

"Barry..."

"When the countdown hits zero, you have to be on that elevator, and someone has to stay here. Besides..." He let loose another volley of shots, driving back a tentative charge by the troopers. "...I'm kinda enjoying myself."

Leon shook his head. He'd known Barry a long time. They'd already lost Sergei. Maybe Ada, too. He was failing to keep this mission together—at least he should get Barry back. And he knew damn well what Barry planned to do. Playing the goddamned hero. There had to be another way.

Barry loosed another burst, slapped in a magazine—then turned frowning to Leon.

"You still here? Go!"

Leon sighed—and turned away.

Sometimes there just wasn't any other way.

Standing just a step back from the overhead shaft, Alice checked the hook gun to make sure it was ready to fire. She knew if she stepped into the square of light under the shaft, the Licker would strike. Unless she struck first.

Alice held the gun in her right hand, angled upward. Split seconds mattered now. This had to work—she'd only have one chance. And she'd better be right about where she thought the Licker was roosting...

The mangled creature had set up this trap for her personally. She was sure of that. She had tricked it into running headlong into that mirror wall; into getting itself badly sliced up. She'd toppled a stone archway on it. The Licker knew who its enemy was. And if it caught her, it would probably take a good long time to kill her. It might keep her alive for days, slowly chewing her up.

You're not going to get that chance, monster. You took the wrong hostage.

The moment had come. She was dizzy with blood loss, but she was also adrenalized, and ready to fight.

Alice stepped into the square of light, aiming and firing all in the same motion. The Licker struck, too— shooting its tongue, the pink cable streaking right at her. But the grappling hook zipped up, up, and past the Licker, just as she had planned—and drove itself into the concrete of the wall. Alice pressed the "wind" stud and the cable pulled tight. She braced herself, ready for what was coming.

Suddenly she was jerked into the air, pulled up the cable at seventy miles an hour, using every last erg of energy to hold on with her right hand. In her other hand she had her auto pistol.

The long serrated tongue licked past her—missing. But Alice didn't miss. The cable pulled her up close to the creature, and she could see it clearly, outlined against the darkness. She pressed the gun muzzle to its head as she was pulled past it, too fast for it to grab her—and she fired, holding the trigger down, tilting the gun to keep the muzzle pointed at the thing's leather brain as she whipped past it, up to the hook.

The bullets tore that brain to shreds. Instantly the Licker shuddered and collapsed... falling down the shaft.

As she reached the top, Alice adjusted the hook gun, then lowered herself to the girl, landing on a ledge beside her.

"Becky!" She used a knife, cut her free. Immediately the little girl was signing.

"Thank you, Mommy—I knew you'd come!"

Alice hugged her—then froze, listening. The unearthly cries of more Lickers filled the ventilator shaft. She looked down—and saw a swarming crowd of Lickers crawling up toward them. Umbrella must have released all its mutants, in a desperate attempt to stop her and the strike team.

If those things reached her and Becky, there'd be nothing left but a couple of blood puddles. She couldn't fight them all. So Alice braced herself and jerked on the cable. The grapnel was stuck in the concrete and didn't want to come loose. She gave it one more hard tug and the grapnel pulled free, unreeling back to the gun.

"Come on!" she signed, and, taking Becky by the wrist, she led her down the horizontal shaft, deeper into Umbrella Prime.

She had no idea at all where they were going to end up. They simply ran—into the unknown.

18

The strike team member who remained was firing burst after burst, using up his ammunition—but effectively keeping Jill's squadron suppressed. Crouching behind the concrete post, she shouted orders.

"Bring up the prisoner!"

With luck the team would react stupidly, blindly emotional enough to sacrifice themselves in the hope of saving Ada Wong.

The Rain clone pushed the bruised and battered woman up, into the line of fire. She was wearing a hood, and Jill reached over and pulled it away so they could see clearly who it was. Electronic handcuffs secured her wrists behind her, and "Rain" pressed a gun to her head.

"Cease your firing!" the trooper shouted. "Or I execute her!"

Ada struggled to pull free—but the trooper cracked her upside the head, hard, and she sagged to her knees.

The firing from the strike team cut short.

"Now!" the trooper yelled. "Throw down your guns and step out!"

And Jill waited.

Clambering onto the elevator platform, Leon muttered to Luther.

"Strap yourself down!"

Luther wondered what exactly Leon was expecting. But when he thought about the placement of the explosives, and the fact that the tide would be at its high point, up there, he thought he knew.

So he pulled off his belt, working with one hand—the other limb mangled, mostly numb—and wrapped it around a rail on the platform, then wound the other end around his good arm.

Leon tried to see what the troopers were doing—but there was a post in the way. He couldn't tell what they were up to. Then he peered at his comrade.

"Barry! What are you doing?" he gritted.

The wounded man looked up at Leon and Luther—nodded to Luther, then turned to Leon.

"See you around, old friend!"

"Barry—*no!*" Leon yelled.

"Step out now, or she dies!" the trooper shouted.

Barry stepped into plain sight, hands aloft, guns held high—and the trooper opened fire on him.

Several slugs hammered into his chest and he lost his grip on his guns. He was knocked off his feet and fell back, feeling cold and hearing broken bones shattered by bullets, grating on one another. Before he quite hit the ground he looked up to see one of his guns falling toward him, end over end. Time seemed to slow down for Barry, in that moment. As if it were letting him prolong, and fully experience, his last moments alive.

He watched the gun fall toward him. And he hissed, "Fuck it!" between his teeth as he snatched it out of the air, his fingers instinctively finding the grip and the trigger. The strength was flowing out of him, but he had just enough left to aim and fire.

One shot.

The black trooper went down with a bullet in his head.

Ha, see you in Hell, you bastard.

The other troopers opened up on him, their rounds tearing him apart, kicking him around the floor as if there was an invisible thug there, stomping him. The darkness welled up from the wounds—it was as if he was bleeding darkness, and the world was flooding with it. Then he was drowning in it, was sinking in it.

But he smiled as he died.

"Who are you? What are you going to do?

The grimy man didn't immediately answer. He just grinned at Dori with uneven yellow teeth. He was older, with a red face and curly red hair streaked with gray. He wore a mechanic's coveralls, oily and greasy, and had a big black gun in his hand—which was pointed at Dori.

They were sitting at one of the tables, across from one another, as the stranger took time to evaluate her—at least, that's what it seemed like he was doing. Who knew what he had in mind? He was looking at her pretty oddly...

Finally he spoke.

"My name's Tom Pepper. I used to work for Umbrella. Like maybe you did—only probably you didn't know it. I'm guessing you're a clone. That right kid?"

She nodded, and he continued.

"It's what I figured. That combat suit doesn't fit you very good—you're too young to be a trooper. So I figure you're hiding out, like me. Doesn't prove I can trust you, though." He paused a moment, then continued. "Me, I'm a mechanic. When the Undead started overrunning the place like cockroaches, why, that ended my job. My partner at the truck garage tried to eat me. I had to run the poor bastard over. Sorry to do that to him."

"JudyTech says it's not them anymore," Dori said, trying to sound reassuring. "She says the people they used to be are dead. This is just their bodies with a disease in it. She says it's like the virus is using the body for a car to drive around in, and it gets its fuel from eating people."

"Whoa!" he laughed. "That's a lot of information out of a little slip of a girl."

"You're the one talking so much," she replied, feeling a bit indignant. "And I'm not that small—I'm only three, chronologically, but I'm fifteen in 'effective maturation.'"

"Yeah? Well I'm fifty-two," he said, "every inch of me. Anyway, you friend's right—he wasn't my partner no more, really. Just his body turned into a nasty thing. So I had to find me a job with Umbrella, because they were about the only ones who had anything happening. You'd see a chopper go over, and it'd have their insignia on it. You didn't see any other aircraft around anymore. And I got a smart younger brother—half-brother, really—who I don't even know that well. We grew up separate places. But he worked at Umbrella, and I had a cell phone number for him. They were still working back then. So he got me in here—and turns out it's not much better than being out there."

"Are you a mechanic for the submarine?"

"Nah, I'm..." He tilted his head and looked at her with pursed lips. "Can I trust you? That's the question. You don't have the scarab on you... you don't seem like you're old enough to be any kind of trooper or... an agent for them. But who knows? You could have cameras in your eyes. You could be a robot or a mutant. The world's crazy—and it's Umbrella made it that way."

"Well, how do I know if I can trust you?" Dori responded. But she found that she wasn't afraid of Tom Pepper. She wasn't sure why, since he'd grabbed her, and he had a big gun in his hand.

"Why shouldn't you?" he asked, seeming surprised.

"To begin with, you're pointing a gun at me."

He looked down at it.

"Kinda forgot about it," he confessed. "Okay, I'll put the gun down—but don't make any funny moves." He laid the gun down in front of him, and then looked philosophically at the ceiling, seeming to consider how to continue his story. She had the impression he hadn't talked to anyone in a long time, and that he was enjoying it.

She kept her eyes on him—but she darted her hands out and grabbed the gun, pointing it at him.

"Is that what you mean by a funny move?" she asked.

His eyes widened.

"You are fast, girl!"

"I have an Alice overlay for certain fighting reflexes." She waved around the pistol.

"Be careful with that thing!"

Suddenly a voice came from behind her, and Dori jumped, almost dropping the weapon.

"You didn't answer her question," the voice said. She didn't have to turn around. She knew JudyTech's voice.

Tom turned and looked.

"You're that Judy, maybe," he said. "Judy Tucker or Tecker or whatever she said?"

"I'm Judy Gordon. She calls me JudyTech. Keep your eye on him, Dori. We don't know if we can trust him." Then she looked around the room. "But first things first—is there any food here?"

Tom sighed.

"Yeah. Yeah there is…"

"Then we'd better eat soon. There's gunfire outside—and things could get worse. Who knows what'll happen. We might be safe in here or we might not. But we'll need our strength."

Alice dropped from the vent, then caught Becky as she dropped down. They turned to look around. They were in a cavernous circular chamber a hundred feet high. Around the walls were transparent, cylindrical growing vats—and in them were clones, hooked up to tubes and wires, each floating in a state of dormancy, awaiting someone or something that might at last awaken them.

A dozen of the clones seemed to be Rain. She was a popular model, it seemed. Alice supposed they'd acquired the actual Rain's DNA when she was working for Umbrella.

In the corner of her eye, Alice detected movement, somewhere off in the shadows. She watched—and waited.

The next group of clones was all Alice.

"Mommy, who are they?" Becky asked, her voice betraying shock. She was signing as well as talking as she stared at all the clones. Of the woman she thought of as her mother. And beside them, a line of other clones...

Becky. Lots and lots of Beckys.

More movement in the shadowy part of the big room. A Licker, creeping into view. All around them. She began pulling the pins on grenades, adjusting the timer on each one...

"Mommy, who *are* they?" Becky repeated, staring at the other clone little girls, sleeping so peacefully in their vats. She turned to look at Alice.

"Mommy, who are *you*?" she asked.

Alice had no idea how to explain the clones to Becky, not in brief—and there was no time for any kind of discussion. So she didn't answer, just kept preparing one grenade after another.

"You are my mommy... aren't you?" Becky asked, signing desperately.

As the Licker crept closer, Alice dropped the belt

of incendiary grenades Luther had given her. The grenades rolled free of it, humming warningly.

"I am now," Alice signed. All of a sudden she swept up the little girl with her left arm, her right hand firing the hook gun at the ceiling. As she did, the gigantic Licker reared over her, throwing its shadow across them. Its jaws were wide, its razor teeth glistening, its tongue unreeling...

And then the grapnel caught the ceiling and Alice hit the rewind so that she and Becky were pulled straight upward, just as the scattered grenades exploded across the floor. A lake of napalm fire spread across the room, consuming the monster and sending a wave of heat after them.

The creature screamed almost piteously as it was cooked alive. But Alice felt no pity for it.

The trooper crept along the wall, hoping to get to the elevator without being seen—and planning to nail his two targets the second he got there. He'd get the drop on them and blow their heads off. His name was Carlos, and he'd volunteered for this.

He had to make good.

Today was the day he was at last going to make Jill Valentine notice him. He lived to please her—it was what kept him going, kept him pretending. His scarab didn't work very well. Something in it had broken down, and it wasn't transmitting to him much. So a lot of unfamiliar impulses rose up in him—things the others couldn't feel.

Sometimes he fantasized about removing her scarab, and taking her with him, out of here. But where would they go? The world was a worse hell outside than it was in here. So he waited. And when he could he tried to impress her, so she'd keep him close to her.

Now he crept up close to the elevator—and stepped out from the wall. There they were. Designations "Leon" and "Luther."

Well, Leon, he thought, *your new designation is 'terminated.'* He sighted through his rifle's scope, and settled the crosshairs on Leon's head.

The target was looking at his watch and saying something to the man who was with him, shaking that head.

Up on the surface, high tide surged up around the bases of the ventilator towers. At precisely the right moment, the bombs affixed to the towers exploded, shattering the rotating fans, causing the structures to collapse inward.

The debris went tumbling down the shafts, followed by countless tons of rushing seawater...

19

Just as Carlos was about to squeeze the trigger and send Leon to his maker, the triple boom of a series of powerful explosions made the floor quake... and caused Carlos miss his shot.

The bullets zipped past Leon—who jumped back, deeper into the elevator platform. Carlos fired again but he no longer had a good shooting angle. And then he was aware of a thunderous roar, a roar that was getting louder and louder.

"*Run!*"

It was Commander Valentine, and when Carlos turned to see what she meant, he saw an oncoming tidal wave, sweeping toward the submarine pens. A wall of sea-green, flecked with ice, as if the ice floes were its teeth, roaring right at him...

He stared, and realized there was no place to run. He couldn't get under cover—he'd be drowned wherever he ran. There was no time to get to the submarines.

The temperature dropped, a cold exhalation of the

wave as it rushed toward him, pushing super-cooled air before it. He didn't have to wait long. A moment later, the green jaws closed over him.

As the upper levels of the facility were quickly flooded by seawater and crushed ice, the invading elements exerting colossal pressure on the inner structures of Umbrella Prime, so that the giant underwater framework could no longer maintain its integrity.

It began to implode.

To the crescendo of the roaring waters was added the cracking, booming, and squealing of metal girders breaking apart, a pandemonium of sound generated by a breakdown on a titanic scale.

On the elevator platform Luther stared up at the ladder that Alice had climbed to the vent.

"She didn't make it," he said. He was shocked that she hadn't made it. He'd have thought that if anyone could've, it would be Alice... Because she was larger than life.

Leon gripped the railing and shouted above the noise of the oncoming wall of water.

"Hold on!"

The seawater hit the bottom of the elevator shaft first and surged upwards, jarring the freight platform from its stuck position and sending it rocketing up.

"This was your *plan*?" Luther demanded. *This was their plan B?* They'd planned use the water to get up to the surface?

Crazy motherfuckers...

The water surged around them, painfully cold, but the movement of the platform kept their heads above it. Luther wondered if he'd die of hypothermia before they got out of this. This water was the coldest damn thing he'd ever felt in his entire life. The only good part was it numbed his wounded arm. A sharp chunk of ice hit him hard, and he didn't even feel it.

That's okay, he thought, *I'll feel it later.*

The wave roared like a dozen speeding locomotives and a hundred bulldozers, filling up the coliseum-sized room, slamming the submarines with chunks of ice... making the vessels rise up out of their pens.

And then the room was out of sight, and Luther and Leon were still rising up, through the shaft. They left the water behind, and it drained away around them, to Luther's enormous relief. Pieces of ice littered the platform at their feet.

Leon stepped over it to the control panel, flipping open a plastic cover, revealing a button labeled Emergency Brake.

He kept his hand poised over the button as they rushed upward, shivering, cold air blasting past them.

New York City. Times Square.

Undead wandered through the streets—those the maintenance bots hadn't got hold of yet. They staggered about, mouths open, endlessly hungry, *maddeningly* hungry, no relief to be found. Something deep down inside each one of them, a little spark of humanity, yearned for an end to it. For an end to the wandering. For an end to the mindless searching, the perpetual pain, the feverish hunting that never ended... as hours became days without sleep, without rest, without end.

And then, the ice-cold hand of the world blessed them, at last. It offered relief. It offered surcease from their unliving hell.

Because that's when the tidal wave, the internal tsunami, swept through the testing floor, smashing buildings, flattening false fronts, picking up cars and flipping them around as unruly children played with toys. Sparkling billboards crackled and short circuited, spitting sparks; windows shattered and blasted broken glass through the air, speckling the rising waves, mixing with the ice; debris churned like the blades of a garbage disposal, cutting up anything and anyone in it.

Charged wires spat and leapt over the water, then the lights went off across "Times Square," as if the seawater was throwing switches methodically as it went.

The Undead were caught in the wave, and made instinctive efforts to thrash out of it, to escape. But at heart—deep inside—something at the cellular level whimpered in release as the cold of cosmic entropy crushed them to itself, smothered them, and ended their suffering at last, at long last...

If you can drown joyfully, that's what they did.

Shibuya Scramble, Tokyo.

The JumboTron screens were shivering, shaking, their looping images flickering, the giant faces of pretty people—models who had died in the great rising of the Undead—were electronically corroding, warping,

JOHN SHIRLEY

pitting, as if they were becoming digital zombies. The distant false ceiling was dropping bits of paint chips and dust; a piece of a cornice fell down with a crash.

Puzzled troopers on clean-up duty looked around. Some of them seemed to take little dance steps backwards, as the ground shook...

And then the wall of seawater rushed in upon them. They felt a wave of cold air first, and then turned to find the great white curtain of foam sweeping down on them, tumbling cars and vans and the bodies of tester clones and prop furniture from storefronts along ahead of it. Mannequins swept from window displays seemed to thrash about as if trying to swim.

A thousand-pound dead walrus, sucked in along with the seawater, struck one of the troopers as the water rushed over him, crushing him.

Another trooper found herself lifted up by a rising surge of water, tossed this way and that until a gigantic face filled her vision—a giant, two-dimensional, lovely Japanese model, her mouth open as if to swallow the trooper. It was a digital face, fizzing out and re-forming itself on the gigantic screen. And it did swallow her, in a way, as she was thrown headfirst into the digital mouth, smashing through the JumboTron, her neck broken.

A moment later a minivan was heaved through the same screen, the electronic sign exploding in sparks. Within moments the Shibuya Scramble was drowned, the reproduction of Tokyo's commercial heart sunken under seawater, like some Nipponese Atlantis, where the bodies of troopers spun and tangled with the bodies of the Undead.

* * *

Moscow, Russia. Red Square.

The tsunami came inexorably rampaging through, hurling cars to the right and left, ripping buildings from foundations and turning them end over end, ripping up power cables and spitting the sparks, blue and yellow, into the air...

The Las Plagas Undead—the plague soldiers—tried to outrun the massive wave, the great wrecking ball of ice and frigid seawater, but they were swept away as the mountain of water swept through the Moscow streets, crashing against the turrets and twisted minarets of the Kremlin. The wave picked up the Undead and smacked them hard against the walls of the faux Kremlin, smashing them to jelly, so that blood and innards colored the sea.

A pilot whale had been sucked down, alive, with the seawater and found its way here—it ripped into the thrashing Undead, tearing them apart with its great white teeth. As it surfaced, an errant Licker swam up, like some primeval behemoth in a prehistoric sea, and swarmed onto the mammal, biting into it, its tongue winding around the pilot whale's jaw. The two predators fought, rolling over and over in foamy rage, dying the sea crimson and black.

The waves sawed at foundations until the model of the Kremlin collapsed, and another tsunami surge crashed through the enormous proving ground, turning the minaret towers into giant spears that were flung about. The shattered walls and windows were turned into disposal blades, whirling around broken ends of concrete and sheets of metal and glass in a spinning whirlpool, an aquatic meat grinder, slashing whale and Licker to shreds. Decapitating some of the zombies, and drowning the rest.

Leaving Red Square's Undead quite dead at last.

The internal tsunami roared over the quiet, tree-lined streets of suburbia, picking up houses and making temporary vessels of them, crashing them against one another till they splintered and sank.

The gigantic wave of seawater tore up telephone poles and sent sparking electrical wires whipping through the air, cutting through the foliage of the silk-leafed fake trees. It flooded the streets and cleansed them of the vile bodies that decayed in their intersections.

And the wave crashed into a large house where the clone of Alice had been killed trying to save her daughter. Here the clone designated "Todd" was still creeping about, having been missed by the clean-up teams. He was caught in a basement room, busily chewing at the leg of one of the troopers that Alice had killed, gnawing on the leg like a senile lunatic chewing on a raw chicken drumstick.

Suddenly the water swirled and rose round, and with the detached, ragged leg clamped in its mouth, the zombie tried to grab the rising water, to choke it, to drive it away.

But the Todd Undead was swept off its feet, sucked up the stairs by a powerful current, then out through a broken window. Still clamping the half-eaten human leg in its mouth, it made vaguely remembered attempts at dog paddling, till it was drawn into a whirlpool where broken window frames, edged with fangs of glass, sawed through its spine and belly, cutting it in half, and sent its halves waltzing together, dancing in rotting black blood, down into the cold depths.

In the submarine, Dori, JudyTech, and Tom were sharing a quite remarkably large can of pork and beans, when they heard a distant booming, followed by a strange vibration that grew by the moment.

"What the hell," Tom grumbled.

Within a minute the submarine itself was shuddering, the deck seesawing under them, and Dori was thrown against the bulkhead. She sucked air through her teeth, at the pain in her bruised shoulder.

"You okay, kid?" Tom said, grabbing her arm. The sub lurched once more, and he held her so she wouldn't fall again.

JudyTech, who had the gun now, looked at Tom closely.

"Let's get out of here," she said, waving the gun toward the door, "back to our hiding place."

Tom nodded. He already had a rucksack filled with canned goods, and he grabbed it, then they headed down the narrow passageway—Tom leading the way, JudyTech keeping him covered with the pistol, Dori coming behind—past the Cyrillic signs and wheel-opened doors, till they got to the door marked with a crude sign: FIRE ABATEMENT STOWAGE.

"In there!" JudyTech instructed him. "Go!"

Tom went in without a murmur, and they followed, Dori hesitating in the door, listening as she was about to close it.

She'd heard something...

"There's someone up there—voices!" she said. She could hear footsteps, too, and people shouting commands.

"Come in and close the door," JudyTech ordered. As she said this, she turned to Dori, and half turned from Tom—who instantly snatched the pistol from her hand.

"Ha! That's *mine*, thank you!" He pointed the gun at JudyTech and told Dori, "Now both of you get inside here and girly, you close that hatch!"

Dori didn't know what else to do. She couldn't abandon JudyTech, and it sounded like there were troopers in the other parts of the submarine. So she and Judy stepped through; Dori closed the door, and locked it.

Inside, the light was yellow and the long hold—sixty feet long—was mostly filled with old fire hoses stretched out on aluminum racks, many of the hoses were mildewy and pitted, probably useless in a fire. Soviet-era workmanship.

Tom put the rucksack down.

"This where you picked to hide?" He looked around approvingly. "Smart! Real smart! They probably wouldn't be coming in here, less'n they really got to, and those hoses are okay to lay down on, get your forty winks—maybe even to hide under. Good thinking." He nodded to himself. Then he looked at the gun in his hand. "I'm a mechanic, not a soldier. I don't like guns much. I'm getting too old for all the stress of not being able to trust nobody at all. Can't take it.

"That's why I deserted from Umbrella, and hid down here. They were gonna put me on one of those damn scarabs soon, like they done my brother. Not me, no ma'am. Anyway..."

He flipped the gun around in his hand and offered it to JudyTech, butt first.

"You hold onto this. If I'm gonna trust you—well, you'll have to know you can trust me."

Alice and Becky entered a ceiling vent above the clone room, clambered from there into a maintenance crawl space, and moved hurriedly along a catwalk used by engineers who worked on the facility's intricate electronic, hydraulic, and aeration systems.

The walls shivered and groaned; the sound of rushing water roared louder and louder. They'd felt the reverberation from the explosions overhead— Alice had heard the internal tsunami thundering through Umbrella Prime, and she'd guessed what had happened. The countdown had reached its completion.

As much as she could, Alice answered Becky's questions, sketching in a little about the facility and the clones. How the real world was outside. How everything she'd experienced was artificial, used to give her a sense of a past.

"All a test," Becky signed, shaking her head with sad wonder. "Just a test. That's..." She hesitated, unsure how to put it.

"It's *cruel*," Alice signed. "They're cruel people. But not everyone is." *But most of the good people have died*, she mused. She'd explained a little about the Undead, and the Lickers. But it was all too much—too shocking for the girl to take in.

All a test...

Sometimes Alice thought all of existence was a

test. Just another proving ground, set up by some unknown entity. Because she constantly felt tested. So far, she'd passed the tests that determined survival. But there were others she felt she'd failed.

And someday she'd fail the survival test. Still— everyone failed it someday, whether they died in a bed... or were shot by a trooper clone.

Alice tried to angle toward the elevator shaft, using the blueprints she'd memorized, and then a girder suddenly rammed right through the wall, spewing chunks of concrete, squealing as it came. Partly blocking the catwalk, it was a heavy steel strut pressed out of place as the imploding facility shrugged and shifted about. It seemed as if the entire structure was buckling inward.

Becky began crying to herself, and Alice put her arm around her.

"We've gotten this far," she signed. "We'll make it! Come on..." She kissed the top of the girl's head, took her hand, and helped her climb over the girder, wishing she felt as confident as she sounded. They hurried onward, with the building making grinding sounds all around them, sounding as if it were about to collapse completely.

They came to a service elevator. Alice pried the doors open and looked down the shaft—it was filling up with rising seawater, churning with broken ice.

"Not that way," she said. "Come on, I think it's more this way..." She remembered the girl couldn't hear her, and repeated herself with signing.

Then they forged onward.

* * *

The freight elevator carrying Luther and Leon had been rammed up by the geyser of seawater, propelled into the broader silo, rocketing them upward toward the cold outer world. It seemed for a while as if they'd never slow down.

But at last the pressure was equalizing, the force of propulsion was spent, and the elevator began slowing. As it did so, the only thing keeping it suspended in the shaft was water pressure, which was sure to drop.

Luther knew that when the water pressure under the platform subsided, they'd be dropped down into the water... icy water, in which a man couldn't survive—not for long. It was just a matter of time.

And then it happened—the platform began to drop. And drop faster...

Leon punched for the emergency brakes. And the platform slowed, gratingly coming to a shuddering stop, locked in place with water swirling around their ankles. Unlatching his belt from the railing, and shivering uncontrollably, Luther glanced up. They were still a hundred feet from the surface.

Not going to be easy to negotiate that with one hand—if he could do it at all.

"Now we climb," Leon said.

Luther had his doubts—but he started toward the ladder.

And then there was a banging noise above them. It was a metal utility grate that was moving, creaking—then swinging down out of the silo wall. Leon and Luther sighted in on it—ready for troopers or Lickers.

That's when Alice and Becky stepped out on the grating, together.

Well I'll be damned... Luther smiled.

Alice looked down at them with mock reproach. She put her hands on her hips.

"I thought I said not to leave without me!"

Leon grinned.

"Well, maybe this mission isn't a complete bust after all," he said. "Okay, Alice. Lead the way. Up the ladder!"

Alice looked at Luther.

"How's he going to...?"

"I think I got it figured," Luther said. He stepped up to the ladder, swung his good arm behind the ladder, and put his feet on the lowest rung, pushing himself upward. Each time took another step upward, the arm slid a bit higher, hugging the framework. It was awkward, but he could do it.

Alice led the way, Becky behind her. Excitement replaced fear on the girl's features as she climbed. She was going to see the outside world in person, for the first time in her life. She was going to have real memories of the real world—not clone overlays, lies printed on her mind.

Alice hoped she wouldn't find the outer world to be worse than Umbrella Prime...

20

A storm was blowing in. The cold had been steadily increasing, the last fifty rungs or so, and Alice was afraid her hands might freeze to the metal of the ladder. But she got to the top, climbed over the lip onto the snow in front of the bunkers, and turned to help Becky up.

"The... outside world..." She tried to say it aloud, but her teeth were chattering too hard. She signed the rest, "...so cold."

"Not so cold," Becky signed, "most places. We'll go where it's warm."

Alice helped Luther up, and then Leon came over the edge, teeth chattering.

"Damn!" he said. "Let's get in the Spryte! Come on!"

Alice glanced at the cratered area where the sea was still sucking into a powerful whirlpool around the wreckage of the vents. Then they hurried to the waiting vehicle. Becky had never seen anything like it, and looked around in fascination, though her teeth were chattering and her fingers were blue.

First Alice bundled her into the vehicle, then they all got in, Leon closing the door, settling in the driver's seat and starting the engine. He immediately cranked up the heater. Both he and Luther were shivering almost uncontrollably, wet from the seawater in the elevator shaft, with ice on their noses and eyelashes.

They moved to a compartment in back, and when they returned they had changed into dry paramilitary togs. Luther's injured arm was bound so that it wouldn't move.

"That feels better," he said, coming back to the front, the warm air from the heater soothingly rising around them. He was wearing a thick parka, and Leon brought two for Alice and Becky.

Luther looked sallow, sickly. He sagged into his seat with a soft groan, and Alice and Becky sat close by. Leon settled into the driver's seat, looked at the instrument panel, then checked the fuel and the weather scanner.

"Storm is three miles out. Headed this way."

Alice peered out the window. She could see it coming in, a billowing wall of snow approaching in the distance, down the beach, across the plateau up above, and whipping up the waves on the sea.

Leon put the vehicle in drive, and headed it down the beach, where the peninsula jutted out into the pack ice. Luther groaned every time they hit a bump— and Alice didn't feel so good herself. Her adrenaline was wearing off and she was dizzy again.

Leon glanced at her in the mirror, guessed what was on her mind.

"There's emergency supplies in that locker right in front of you." She opened it and found a medical kit, as well as cans of quick-consume food. In the Arctic, where the body labored to survive in plunging temperatures, food *was* emergency supplies—consuming calories, carbs and glucose at the right moment could spell the difference between life and death.

Against his protestations, she removed Luther's parka and shirt. As the steadily warming Spryte trundled along, Alice sprayed antiseptic on his bullet wound, confirmed that the bullet had gone all the way through, and dressed it. Becky watched the procedure with big eyed fascination.

"Looks like a cracked bone," Alice observed. "Must hurt like a broken heart."

He chuckled.

"Worse."

She put a med patch on his shoulder, seeping painkiller in through his skin.

"There. That should help without putting you to sleep."

"What about you?" he asked. "I saw you limping."

She nodded. No use pretending anymore. She lifted her shirt and peeled away the cloth stuck to her side. Becky gasped with alarm. Alice sprayed it with cleanser and antiseptic, and a styptic blood clotter. Then she put surgical glue over it, and a dressing.

She gave herself a pain pad, too—not as strong as the one she'd given Luther. She liked to keep her head clear. Just in case.

Then it was time for the food.

"Instant heat cans in there," Luther said. "Great invention."

Alice looked at Becky, then pointed to the food and repeated his words to her in sign.

"What's that?" the girl asked in her uneven voice, unconsciously signing the words at the same time.

"You try it," Alice signed. She handed her the can and signed, "Just open it the top, and that'll start a chemical reaction in the sides. That'll heat it up really fast. Then when it bulges up... right, just like that. Now pull off that cellophane stuff, and there it is, hot stew! That one's yours. Here's a spoon."

"She cooking for me, too?" Leon asked. He turned around enough to point inquiringly at the food and then himself, to get his question across to the little girl.

"Yes!" Becky said, making an effort to speak out loud. It was a bit hard to understand her, but Alice made out, "You can have this first one!" She seemed to be enjoying it, like a little girl at a tea party.

She handed the heated can up to Leon, he shook his head at the spoon and drank it with one hand, like coffee from a cup.

Before she gave Luther his food, Alice added powder from a packet marked "blood loss," then dropped the same mixture of vitamins and minerals into hers. She began to feel better within a couple of minutes. Sleepy, but better.

Becky and Luther dozed as the storm threatened to catch them, and the growing wind battered at the vehicle. The girl sometimes opened her eyes, stared out at the bleak landscape, and shook her head, as if vaguely disappointed.

Leon turned the snowcat to follow the peninsula out onto the frozen sea. On they trundled, in the shadow of the peninsula, and eventually he drove out away from the land entirely, keeping to the places where the pack ice seemed thickest. He caught her looking at him questioningly in the mirror.

"The choppers will meet us on the pack ice," he explained. "We rendezvous in an hour. So just sit back and relax."

Alice was feeling better, stronger, but a certain disorientation had set in, a flat feeling after the adrenaline rush of the last few hours. Becky was slumped against her shoulder, snoring softly. The kid was simply exhausted. She twitched in her sleep, and moaned. Her hands signed, unreadably, as she slept. Alice thought she saw the sign for *sisters*. And one for *glass*.

She must be dreaming about the clones, she mused, *the ones in the vats*. That was a damned hard thing to process. Alice had seen the same thing herself, at another Umbrella facility. She'd liberated hundreds of copies of herself—hundreds of Alices—and later on she'd seen them die. She'd fought beside copies of herself and watched them get shot down. She hadn't been able to help them, not really. And each dying clone looked exactly like her.

She still had nightmares about it, sometimes. And she was sure Becky was going to have nightmares about what she'd seen in the last couple of hours, maybe for years to come. If she lived that long.

Thinking about clones, and the Shibuya Scramble in Tokyo, remembering how she'd been sure she'd killed Wesker, Alice wondered.

What the hell is real, anyway?

She bent her head to look out the window, trying to see the sky. She could see the broken clouds flashing past, driven by the stormy wind, in a hurry to get somewhere. The dull sunlight came angling through from time to time, stabbing down, cutting off as the clouds raced over, then stabbing down again.

Sure looked *real*.

"Are you okay?" Luther asked her. He was staring at her, a worried look on his face.

Alice nodded.

"What are you looking at?" he asked.

"The sky." She hesitated. "The real world."

He smiled wanly.

"You had doubts?"

"Just checking."

They churned out away from the peninsula—and further onto the ice as the weather congealed around them.

"We're sure this ice is... is thick enough, here, Leon?" Luther asked.

Leon glanced back at him with that a look of irritation, then he seemed to reconsider—maybe thinking about all they'd been through together—and nodded.

"It's thick enough, bro. Trust me."

Alice thought she could hear the ice groaning under the weight of the Spryte. She thought about global warming, and she wondered if Leon wasn't a little too confident.

The storm really hit them then, hundred-mile-an-hour winds buffeting the windows, making the metal frame of the vehicle creak, blowing snow around them, whining and sighing. Outside, it was a total whiteout. The blizzard darkened the world as it at last completely swallowed the vehicle.

Alice expected Leon to slow the vehicle—but he

kept right on at the same steady speed.

"Better hit the lights," Luther said.

Leon nodded, and flipped a switch.

Alice glanced at Luther, and thought he was swaying a little in his seat. He'd lost more blood than she had, she guessed, and he might have the start of an infection. The treatment she'd given him would help—but he needed hospitalization.

Something which really didn't exist anymore...

She was feeling better, but still wasn't up to snuff herself. Her hands looked pale and they trembled when she lifted them off her knees. Alerted by the movement, Luther glanced at her.

"Are you okay?"

"Better than you." She patted his good arm. He really did look sickly. *Bullets will do that to you.* Then she put her arms around Becky, and the child snuggled against her. She laid her head against the child's hair, taking comfort in its simple homey smell of her.

Are you my Mama?

I am now.

She hoped she could live up to it.

Alice closed her eyes, and slipped into an uneasy sleep.

The dream started more or less benignly—it was based in genuine memories.

Alice was reliving a night at an award ceremony, where she was expected to accept one of the employee appreciation plaques the Umbrella Corporation had given out, back in the days when the company was still just another major multinational.

Back before the scarabs were invented.

Mind control was so much easier than old-school human resources. Mind-controlled employees never asked for raises, never started unions. The scarabs were the perfect tool for corporate human resources.

She had received two such plaques for her work in security. To get this latest honor, she'd protected the lab from something she'd been told was a "terrorist break-in." Alerted by the security computers, she'd shot all three of the criminal commandos who'd broken into the lab. That was a year before the Hive was opened. The incident had led to her becoming Head of Security.

Right before things fell apart, she'd realized that the "terrorist commandos" she'd shot had been activists trying to confirm rumors that the company was secretly experimenting on human beings—homeless people taken by force, prisoners requisitioned from privatized prisons. The experiments often killed the subject... or did something to them that was worse than death.

Alice had accepted the company's plaque partly because of her "husband," Spence Parks. Spence had been in charge of protecting the entrance to the Hive from snoopers and investigators... and they'd pretended to be the rich couple living in the mansion. And yes, there'd been some romantic connection between them, there—or maybe just a sexual one. He's been an evil son of a bitch, but the guy had been good in bed.

She'd accepted the plaque, and up to that point the dream was fairly accurate. But then, as she turned,

Alice glanced at the audience and saw a man in a tuxedo. He started convulsing, spitting up red foam, and falling... only to jump to his feet and sink his jaws into the face of a woman in an elegant dress, shaking his head like a pit bull with a grip, hard from side to side, to rip her face off her skull. The woman screamed and died, and then almost instantly jumped up and started chasing other members of the screaming audience.

A little girl who was clutching her mother screamed as a fat Undead tore the woman's throat out. The little girl ran in abject terror toward the stage, but then she turned into Becky, and Alice was trying to help her climb onto the stage as an Undead clutched at the little girl's ankles, chewed off one of her shoes.

Alice grabbed the screaming child and the two of them ran offstage, into the wings, past ropes that were supposed to control the curtains. They became hangman's nooses that turned into living, predatory things, one tightening around Spence's neck, lifting him off his feet, choking him. His kicking feet were out of reach.

I can't help him, Alice thought.

Holding Becky's hand, she ran under his twitching feet, toward an exit door. Then Alice heard evil laughter, very close by—she looked down at the plaque and saw a face on it, the brass relief image of Oswald Spencer.

The brass face tittered evilly and jeered.

"You made it all possible, Alice! People like you! All the people who did what we told them, who looked the other way when they knew that the sickness was taking hold! You protected the T-virus, Alice—and you

protected Umbrella's madness.

"Thank you! We honor you with this award!"

She threw the plaque away, and it spun in slow motion, laughing, to shatter on the exit door...

...which swung open, on its own, to reveal a burning world, a world of smoke and fire, a world of crashing planes, of exploding skyscrapers, of bloody-faced living dead men staggering about.

And Becky screamed.

"No, don't take me out there," she cried. "Don't take me outside of Umbrella Prime!"

"...Going to be a shock for that little girl, being outside Umbrella Prime," Luther said as Alice woke from the nightmare. He was talking to Leon as the Spryte drove out onto the creaking ice of the frozen sea.

"Nothing down in Umbrella Prime but seawater and frozen bodies now," Leon answered. He was hunched over the steering wheel of the "snowcat," watching the ice closely. He was driving more slowly now, Alice saw as she tried to shake the nightmare off.

"How're they going to set down in this storm?" Luther asked, looking out the window at the whiteout of the blizzard.

"Weather report has it abating, out this way."

"Doesn't look like it to me."

"I think we're almost through the worst of it."

Alice looked down at Becky, the sleeping child twitching and squirming in her arms, still having nightmares. The child's lips were quivering, her hands jerking, her eyelids jumping with R.E.M. movement. Alice considered waking her out of it.

But sometimes you need nightmares, to process the horror of life.

"One click from the RZ," Leon said, glancing at an instruments on his dashboard. The blizzard did seem to be clearing away a bit.

Suddenly the Spryte lurched violently to the right, skidding on the slick surface. Leon braked and the vehicle slid to a halt.

"What is it?" Alice asked.

"I'm not sure," Leon said.

Becky woke up, stretching, looking sleepily around. "What's going on?" she signed.

"We're not sure yet," Alice replied. But she could see giant cracks appearing in the ice outside the big vehicle. As she looked around, from one window to another, she could see that the cracks were spreading in all directions. And the Spryte lurched again...

If the vehicle fell through the ice, the chances of getting out of it—getting alive to shelter—were probably zero. They'd be killed by hypothermia, or simply drowned when the snowcat plunged through the ice and into the sea.

The cracks continued to spread, in lightninglike forks...

But there was something strange. It didn't look as if it was the Spryte breaking the ice. It looked like something was cracking it from beneath, off to the right. There was something dark out there, pushing upward, shouldering great floes out of the way. And suddenly rearing into view, a monolith of metal came squealing up through the ice, shedding chunks of frozen sea as it came.

"What the hell is that?" Luther burst out.

Then the shockwave reached the Spryte—and the world turned topsy-turvy. Alice and Becky and Leon and Luther were tossed around inside the vehicle like rag dolls as the vehicle was flipped over.

Becky made a shrill sound of terror as the world seemed to spin. Luther cursed and even Leon wordlessly yelled as he clutched at the steering wheel. The Spryte turned completely upside down. Its roof struck the ice with an ear-splitting clang.

Leon ended upside down on the ceiling of the Spryte's cab, alongside Luther and Alice and Becky, all of them twisting about to get their feet back underneath them.

"Becky!" Alice shouted, signing as well. "Are you hurt?"

"No, I'm okay," the girl replied.

"You're sure?" she signed, insistently, while her other hand checked Becky for broken bones.

"I'm okay... really," she said out loud in her uneven voice.

"Stay here," Alice signed.

Luther was the first to drag himself out of the vehicle, and Alice followed close behind. Carrying a machine pistol, she crawled to a window, its glass shattered now, where she wormed through and stood up on the slightly rocking surface. She scooped up two sharp ice axes she found lying in the debris, for use as backup weapons. Shoving them into her back straps, Alice looked around.

There was a grinding sound, and she turned to see that the blades of the Spryte's tracks were still going around, whirring away at the sky.

It was cold as death out here. Her teeth started to

chatter; the gun felt icy in her fingers. The blizzard was waning, but there were still sheets of snow slanting down. She stared at the monolithic shape looming a dozen paces away—great streams of seawater poured off the steel monolith as it stabilized.

The monolith was the conning tower of a Typhoon Class submarine—it was one of the submarines from the Umbrella base.

Leon joined her, watching as a hatch opened at the bottom of the conning tower, and several figures emerged. One was the "Rain" clone trooper; another was Jill Valentine. Both held guns in hand.

The third was Ada Wong. She was still handcuffed, badly bruised and battered, but staring defiantly, spirit unbroken.

Leon turned to Alice.

"I told you she'd have a plan..."

This is her plan? She glanced at him. Was he serious?

Then Alice looked at the three figures by the submarine, and called out to Jill Valentine.

"Only the two of you?" She nodded toward the Rain trooper.

"It'll be enough!" Jill responded. She and "Rain" both had the scarabs on their chests.

There was a moment when the weather forced hesitation on them—another burst of snowfall, carried on the howling wind. Alice had the machine pistol ready—and she was weighing how she might shoot Jill and the Rain clone without hitting Ada.

Rain reached into a pocket, and produced a cylindrical device—some kind of high-tech syringe. Alice could see a red fluid in the formula chamber.

And then Rain stabbed the business end of the syringe into her own neck... and injected herself. Was there something writhing within that red fluid?

"The Las Plagas parasite," Leon muttered.

And then "Rain" began to transform.

21

Rain's whole body contorted. She seemed to swell up, her clothing splitting at the seams, and her eyes began to glow with an unearthly red light. Jill's attention focused on her, and Ada Wong took the opportunity to run.

Before she had gone more than a step, Jill spun and viciously backhanded her, knocking her back. Ada fell heavily to the ice, stunned.

Alice's weapon was up, aiming at Jill—but the security chief was already in motion, charging across the rocking ice at Alice, Leon, and Luther. The transfigured Rain sprinted alongside her.

Jill leapt into the air, flipping to make a difficult target, and Alice missed her shot—missed her by microns.

Luther raised his weapon, aiming at the Rain creature. Leon followed suit.

Still in mid-mutation, she was charging toward

them. They fired, their rounds tearing into her, and she halted as they ran through their clips. She seemed to sway, and blood ran from her nose...

But she didn't fall. Luther could see something moving under her skin—like dozens of small, sluglike creatures making their way from the center of her body to her extremities. Then they reached her fingers—and burst from her fingertips.

The things dropping from her fingertips... were bullets. The very slugs they had shot into her—she'd used her Las Plagas mutation to expel them from her body. They rattled on the ice, and Rain raised her head. She howled in triumph.

Leon recovered first, raising his gun to fire, trying to get a headshot—but the mutated Rain—eyes glowing, limbs swollen—was rushing them again. She was just too fast, and her spinning kick sent him flying back against the side of the overturned Spryte, making it resound with a hollow thump.

Jill Valentine closed on Alice, and with stunning speed knocked her weapons aside. Alice had the ice axes, which she plucked from her back straps. Jill had a telescoping metal attack rod in her hand, which she used to counter the flashing axes.

The wind blasted around them; snow swirled into their eyes, the ice was slippery and both of them struggled for good footing, but still they fought—even as Rain and Leon and Luther fought nearby.

Alice was slowed a bit by her injury and the medication she'd taken—and Jill seemed to anticipate every move she made. No matter what Alice did—and she used every trick she knew—Jill seemed to predict it, block her, or avoid the cut completely. It flashed through Alice's mind that Jill's scarab might be helping her, using its expert systems to anticipate Alice's moves, prescribing defenses and counter attacks.

Back and forth they ranged, arms flashing, weapons making only minor strikes—but with the attack rod, even a glancing blow to the shoulder was excruciatingly painful. One struck just above the wound in her side, so that she gritted her teeth with agony, forcing herself to counter attack. Her axes slashed, cutting Jill's left arm, but only slightly, but enough that the blood was flecking the snowy ice at their feet crimson.

She was being driven back by Jill's attack, pushed toward the Spryte. In her peripheral vision she saw Leon and Luther's fight with the Rain clone—the creature laughed nastily, and Alice suspected it was only toying with the two men. She felt the icy air stabbing her lungs as she labored to block Jill's attacks, and it was getting harder by the second.

Alice's arms were beginning to feel heavy as she tried to slash past Jill's blur-fast defenses. She managed to nick Jill's right ear—but that gave Jill an opening and she cracked Alice glancingly across her right cheekbone, laying open her skin and sending a thrill of pain that reverberated to the core of her being.

Normally Alice could detach herself from the pain, but that one was hard to ignore. She groaned and slipped to one side, almost losing her footing. Blood was slicking her neck, running onto her fingers. It was becoming difficult to hold onto the axes. They seemed to double in weight every few seconds, as Alice's arms trembled with fatigue. Sweat trickled, mixing with blood, then freezing in the shrieking wind.

Seeing Alice panting for breath, increasingly on the defensive, Jill grinned in murderous glee and moved in for the kill, her scarab glowing as she attacked with resurgent fury.

The fight had been carried out almost as much by the scarab as by her own brain and body. She was in hyper-sync with the object, its impulses and flow of data making her like a ballet dancer in sync with music, and the scrolling computer text projected onto her eyes gave her data on her own condition.

ADRENALINE SURGE - 150%

Behind her opponent, the upturned tractor-tracks of the snowcat continued buzzing along, their blades still slashing at the sky. They, too, could be used as a weapon, if the occasion arose.

And Jill saw her opportunity. As Alice crossed her axes to block a particularly vicious down-slash, it left her middle unguarded. Jill threw her weight onto her right foot, cocked her left, and slammed it with all her strength into Alice's chest.

She was sent crashing back through the windshield of the Spryte. Stunned, she lay inside in the broken glass. Jill heard the girl—the odd little clone with which Project Alice had saddled herself—shrieking from somewhere inside the big snowcat.

"Mommy!"

And in the background, ice floes crunched and

squeaked against one another; the two men gasped and cursed; a gull squalled somewhere overhead. But that was all background noise. Jill was keenly focused on the business of killing. She reached through the broken glass, grabbed Alice's legs, and pulled her back out into the icy wind

Leon and Luther were running out of steam, too.

Luther's arms felt like sandbags as he raised them up to block their attacker. He was trying to see where they'd dropped their weapons... if he could grab one, shove it against her head, blow her brains out, she wouldn't be able expel *those* bullets.

But she never gave him the moment he needed. And he only had one arm to work with.

Rain was laughing at them, slapping them around, and Leon, enraged, unleashed a punishing series of kicks, punches, and blocks, all with dizzying aggression. But the Las Plagas mutation hardly reacted to his onslaught. It laughed in his face, its swollen features swelling even more, its red eyes glowing a brighter crimson. She blocked him and drove him back with pile-driver fists, so that he staggered against Luther.

Got to find a weapon, Luther thought. He glanced desperately around. The snowfall had covered most everything—at least one weapon, too, had slipped through a crack in the ice, to be lost in the sea.

The Rain creature saw him fumbling in the snow, stepped in, and backhanded him hard, sending him flying back. He managed to keep his feet but his head was still spinning, he tasted blood in his mouth, and he choked as he tried to warn Leon, who was circling.

The creature was whipped around and slammed Leon hard in the chest with its right boot, sending him hurtling backwards through the air till he came to a stop on red and black metal: slammed hard into the conning tower of the submarine. Then the creature spun again and struck Luther—knocking him off his feet.

He lay there, trying to get the strength to stand...

The Rain mutant seemed to think he was done for. It turned away...

Alice got to her feet. She no longer had her ice axes, but she managed to use her fists to defend herself against some of the body blows that Jill was raining on her.

Seeing Alice react to strikes against the wound in her side, the trooper grinned sadistically and began to aim more and more blows there, making blood spurt freshly once more from the ruptured dressing. Alice blocked a blow of Jill's fist—but couldn't stop the metal rod from striking home.

The pain hit her like a stroke of lightning, making her arch her back, rising up through her to flood her brain with red glare... the color of a Las Plagas monster's eyes. And then she fell to her knees, pitching forward, almost losing consciousness.

An instant later she aware that she was being lifted up by the throat. Jill turned her face toward the tracks that had driven the Spryte across snow and ice. The razor sharp steel blades, designed to penetrate hard packed snow and ice, were still spinning. They would slash her face into chopped blood-and-bone salad in seconds, if she allowed it.

Alice was jolted into consciousness at the sight. She grabbed Jill's wrists, and struggled to pull the trooper's hands off her neck. The pressure was making flickers appear before her eyes, cutting off her breath.

Then something occurred to her.

I'm fighting the wrong thing...

She let go of Jill's wrists, resisting only with her lower body, reaching downward instead...

Jill Valentine chortled, certain she'd won now. She started to force Alice into the blades. They were less than an inch away...

And then she gasped—as Alice clamped her bloody hands onto the scarab fixed to Jill's chest. She jerked it away, bringing with it tiny scraps of bloody flesh. Alice tore the scarab entirely free—and immediately Jill slumped to the ground, convulsing.

Alice straightened up and tossed the scarab away. It fell into the snow, and then flipped itself over. It started to scuttle about on tiny mechanical legs, seeking its host. Once it sensed Jill, it scurried back across the snow toward her.

Alice reached for Jill's holster and pulled out her gun. She aimed it at the mind-control device just as the small bug-shaped robot leapt, eager to fix itself once more to the trooper's nervous system. Several rapid-fire shots caused the scarab to explode in shiny, sparking fragments of titanium and glass.

The sound of a gunshot brought Luther partly to his senses.

His eyes fluttered, and his head hummed—but he didn't want to move. He wanted to lie there and let the numbness that was gripping his limbs have its way, and take him into the warm dark escape of death. Every joint ached, and his damaged arm was screaming with pain.

But his friends needed him. Leon and Alice. The kid.

Had to get up...

Get your ass up, Luther.

Gritting his teeth he placed his feet under him and stood, looking blinkingly around. Saw the Rain mutant stalking over toward Leon.

Leon was slumped at the base of the submarine conning tower, half covered with falling snow, coughing blood.

Luther looked desperately around. There was only one thing handy—fallen from the overturned Spryte— that he could use as a weapon. He picked up the metal object and staggered, as quickly as he could, over to the mutant, coming up behind it, his feet slipping on ice.

At the same time Leon got shakily to his feet, seemed to gather his strength as the mutant loomed over him. He swung a haymaker at the creature's face, but it caught his fist in a swollen, vein-covered hand, its eyes glowing brightly as it tightened its grip.

Luther, slipping up behind the creature, could hear the bones breaking. Leon gasped in pain and went to his knees. Rain towered over him, raising her fist to finish him off.

But Luther was within reach. He swung the fire extinguisher with all his strength, cracking the mutated trooper clone hard in the side of the head, breaking her skull, spattering blood.

She fell off balance, stunned...

"Not bad, huh?" Luther said, smiling weakly at Leon.

"For... an advisor," Leon managed.

Luther looked at the mutant, and saw that the damage he'd done to Rain's head was *healing*. The Las Plagas parasite was rebuilding her skull from within. Before he could react the creature stood up once more, glowering at him with burning red eyes.

Only one thing to do, he thought. *Smash that skull to jelly. Crush it into something that can't be repaired.* So Luther brought the extinguisher up, readying himself to hit the creature again.

But the mutant moved lightning fast, knocking the extinguisher away with one hand. With the other it put all its mass into an open palm strike, directly to his chest. The impact was so powerful that he knew—instantly—that all the bones of his chest were collapsing. He could feel the shockwave moving through his chest, shattering ribs and pulverizing his lungs—and reaching his beating heart.

He could feel his heart's last beats.

The very last beat.

And then—his heart stopped. That warm darkness he'd wanted just a few minutes ago was back, swirling around him, and this time he had no choice but to go with it.

The was only time for one last thought.

Alice...

22

Leaning on the Spryte, getting her strength back, Alice looked up just in time to see Luther's body buckling under a devastating blow. She had seen many men die—and she knew just what this meant.

When she saw him collapse, utterly empty of life, she knew this time he was finally gone.

"Luther!" she shouted, knowing it would do no good.

Then Alice raised Jill's gun and ran toward the monster that had once been a pretty clone named Rain. She fired as she came.

Jill Valentine, the former Commander of Security for Umbrella Prime, was trying to remember who she was.

She lay there, shivering in the cold, huddled against the wind, lying fetuslike in the snow. Her chest ached, throbbed, and bled where something had been removed. She felt drugged, but she also felt the influence passing out of her.

With the scarab gone, her memories seemed both distant and tantalizingly near. She could almost touch them.

Who am I?

It began to seep back to her. Her childhood. Her interest in police work. Raccoon City. Her signing up with...

With what?

S.T.A.R.S. Special Tactics And Rescue Service. A branch of the Racoon City police.

Arklay Mountains. She'd been a rising star in S.T.A.R.S. until then. Then the Arklay Mountains incident—and Leon Kennedy. His death... was it real? They'd blamed her.

Umbrella—trying to control her—with money, at first. Using their influence to destroy her. Then taking her prisoner, and controlling her mind.

What had they made her do?

She had a nightmarish memory of trying to murder someone—to murder them horribly. Trying to force their face into the grinding blades of the Spryte's tractor treads. And it was someone she respected—even liked.

It was Project Alice.

Just... Alice.

A voice—the uneven voice of a deaf child who'd learned to speak by feeling the vibration of her voice box. It was crying out, somewhere. She couldn't understand the voice clearly, but she heard one word—

"*Mama...!*"

Something piquant in the voice made her open her eyes—and she saw someone she knew. Was that her? Wasn't that... Alice?

JOHN SHIRLEY

Jill sat up, shaking with cold, and brushed ice crystals from her eyelashes, watching as Alice ran, firing the auto pistol at the monstrous creature that had once been designated "Rain." Formerly one of her troopers—ordered to taint herself with the Las Plagas parasite. The creature was swollen, vein-marbled, losing some blood but seeming to absorb the bullets that struck her. And then spitting them out, some of them issuing from its mouth, some from its fingers.

The creature had its right hand raised, with an open palm—and Jill knew what that meant. The death strike. Alice was shooting, trying to destroy the creature's brain—but not hitting it straight on enough.

And then... Alice was within reach. She tried to block the blow, but failed, and it slammed her in the chest, open handed with precision and power.

Alice gasped—and fell to her knees, choking. Blood seeped from between her lips.

Jill got to her feet. Her legs were like jelly under her. She found her back-up pistol in a holster. Held it in her shaky hand—and didn't think she could fire it accurately. Not yet. Anyway, it seemed to be too late. Alice's eyes were glazing... she seemed to be dying, or perhaps already dead.

The creature was turning away from her.

Jill looked around. She saw nothing but cold emptiness... the inevitability of death. She saw ice, and the flying clouds, and snaking spits of snow coming down, and the deathly cold dark sea. The man called Leon, dying, and Luther's corpse. Ada Wong, trying feebly to get up, but she probably wouldn't make it. She would likely die here, and so would they all.

She could feel it creeping into her flesh, her bones.

She could see it like a stark message written on the barren face of the world.

And then—Alice raised her head. And she struggled to her feet. She raised her fists, to defy the creature who'd been Rain. Seeing that, Jill felt a sudden surge of hope. If Alice could live through that, if life could stand up to death even now...

The Las Plagas horror turned back, its eyes glowing, the veins throbbing on his swollen head and neck, and it struck. It hammered Alice with a flurry of blows, ending with a spinning kick that sent her flying.

As she was flung through the air, Jill saw the weapon she had tried to use, slipping from her hand, whirling away, to be lost in a crack in the ice.

And then Alice fell heavily on an ice floe, groaning...

But *still* she tried to get up, tried to fight, as the creature came stalking over her. The ice creaked under its feet, but held.

Jill knew, then, what had to be done.

"Alice!" she shouted, her voice ringing out over the frozen sea.

The woman looked blearily in her direction. Jill marshaled her strength, and threw the gun. It hit the ice, skidded, and slid over—just as Rain was about to strike.

She snatched it up.

Eyes shining with a fierce red glow, the monster sneered gratingly.

"You can't kill me!"

"I don't need to," Alice said, hoarsely. Then she fired, using most of the clip—but not at the creature. She fired at the ice under its feet, blasting a line of holes in the frozen surface.

Already weakened by the submarine, the pack ice cracked—and broke apart. The mutant roared in fury, but its roar became a gurgle as it suddenly slipped into the water, as quickly as dropping through a trap door. "Rain" was gone from sight—then rose up again thrashing, grabbing at floating pieces of ice, trying to claw its way back onto the pack.

But the creature wasn't alone.

A pair of zombies, pale grey and wearing Russian military uniforms, appeared in the water. Then they were clinging to her, biting her, dragging her down. The Rain thing tried again to drag itself out of the icy death trap, but two more of the Undead appeared, grasping her limbs and pulling her back.

"I'm coming back for you!" the mutant howled, locking eyes with her intended prey. "You wait! I'm coming back!"

"Good luck with that," Alice replied. The creature clawed futilely for purchase, and then was dragged underneath once more.

Bubbles seethed where it had been, and then even those were gone.

Alice knelt by the edge of the ice, shivering, and looking down.

"Mom!"

Jill and Alice both turned to see the little girl, picking her way across the ice toward her mother, signing frantically.

"I'm okay," Alice signed. "Don't... worry."

Alice didn't look okay. She looked as if she was on death's door. Becky stared at the freshly bleeding wound on Alice's side.

"You're hurt!" she said, repeating it with hand signs.

"I'm just fine. I'll be okay…"

The storm, which had seemed to slacken away, now appeared to intensify with a booming sound and the whipping up of snow in a new surge of wind. A drumming sound made them look at the sky—where floating lights illuminated the storm, like a vision of a U.F.O., a giant spaceship descending from the clouds.

Jill made herself stagger over to Leon, to see if he was still alive. He was. She reached down, helped him to his feet.

"So you're free again," he said into her ear, as she helped him stand. "Don't leave Ada behind…"

"I won't," she responded. They moved painfully, like two injured people in a three-legged race, picking their way over the cracks toward Alice and Becky. They stopped to help Ada to her feet. and the three of them continued on.

"What is it?" Becky said, signing the words and saying them as best she could. She pointed upward.

"It's help," Leon told her, as he and Jill staggered up, dragging Ada between them. "You're going to be okay." Alice smiled weakly and tried to stand—but then her eyelids fluttered… and she fell. Becky knelt to try to help her.

Jill could see clearly now: helicopters. Several of them. Their rotors were sending flurries of snow across the ice, a miniature mechanical storm in themselves. As they moved in, Jill prayed that they were friends.

* * *

"The question is," JudyTech insisted, "do you know how to pilot this thing? They've abandoned it, it's all ours, but we can't survive in here indefinitely."

She and Tom stood in the submarine's "attack center," the equivalent of a ship's bridge. It lay under the conning tower, at the bottom of the craft. Tom had just explained that it was the nerve center of the vessel.

They didn't understand much of what they saw, looking around the intricately outfitted room, but she had some scientific training, And Tom had some engineering training. So maybe...

"Well, Tom?" she persisted. "Can we drive this thing?" She was wearing an old Russian sailor suit, and was staring at him expectantly.

"Ah, well," Tom said, "I *think* I can get it under the water a way. It's just a matter of the right filling of the ballast tanks. And I think I can point it pretty good, too." He cleared his throat, noticing she still had the gun with her, tucked in the waistband. Tom still wore his coveralls, though he'd made a point of washing them. "Where's the girl at, by the by?"

"She's taking a nap in the crew quarters." Judy said. "Tom—if this thing is nuclear... I mean, what if we make a mistake? Run it too hot or something?"

"You know, the nuclear power's not as complicated as it sounds," he replied. "Really it's just a complicated steam engine. The nuclear reactors heat up water, that turns the turbines. It's just that they don't need diesel, and it provides a lotta power. I've watched them start 'er up more than once, and Umbrella put a manual on the computer. Now, some of it's Greek to me, but I'm pretty sure I can use it to get the thing down forty feet, maybe fifty, get us under the ice.

We're out on the northern edge of the Pacific Ocean, here, and if we head south, why, we can maybe find somewhere safe... someplace we can fetch up, as my old dad would say."

Now she was giving him that fish-eye again, that funny look she gave him sometimes. Kind of amused, kind of suspicious.

"You talk a lot of 'we,'" Judy said slowly. "I'd like to think we can trust you. It helped that you gave me the gun back. But... we're two females, and we're alone in the world."

"I know," he said. "Seems like there's nothing in the world but things to be afraid of. But there's a chance for something more, seems to me. Look here, Judy, we *should* stick together. There ain't very many real, human people left... people without those damned scarabs on 'em, folks who aren't trying to bite your face off.

"We got to stick together, or no one gets past this thing. And the whole... the whole history, the whole..." He struggled to find a way to say it. "The whole history of the human race—it'll mean nothing but a big bad joke. If we're all afraid of each other all the time—life's got no meaning! Because what gives it meaning is..." He cleared his throat again and looked away from her. "...is other people."

When he looked back at her, it like she was a little more relaxed. She smiled a little—and that lit up her face. She wasn't a pretty woman, but she wasn't unpleasant to look at, especially when she smiled. A man could get to...

Crazy thoughts, Tom.

"This vessel—we've really got it all to ourselves?"

she asked, looking around at the blinking indicators, the streams of data running past on monitors. Some of it, implemented by Umbrella, was in English, and some of it was still in Cyrillic.

"We do. Believe me, soon as those people got out there and started fighting with each other, I closed and locked that hatch. They were so busy trying to kill each other, they didn't notice. Then I searched every inch of this thing, from sail to rudder."

"Sail?" she said. "There're no sails on this ship."

"Oh, not that kind of 'sails.' The 'sail' on a submarine, that's an old American Navy expression for the conning tower up above, where the periscopes are. They call it the sail."

She nodded. That seemed to satisfy her.

"Let's try to get this big hunk of metal out of here soon as we can. I want to get away from Umbrella Prime. First thing—we need to get it under water, and out of sight."

23

Alice woke to a drumming sound, and—was it some kind of electronic music? The drumming sound would be the percussion...

She opened her eyes. The room was blurry. She made out a light source, and tried to concentrate on it. It came into focus, and became a portlike window in a concave, metal hull—a helicopter window, she decided. So she was in one the choppers operated by Ada's people; also Leon's people.

And Wesker's people.

Ada and Leon, she might trust—a little. But Wesker. Who should be dead, seemed unkillable. *No.* She could never trust him.

And someday she would kill him.

Straps held her to a cot. But looking at them, they didn't seem to lock—they were held in place with Velcro. So she wasn't being restrained like a prisoner. That much was good, anyway.

She tried to move—and sucked air through her teeth in agony. Everything went blurry again. She was hurt, and badly. There were wires attached to her arms...

Alice looked to her right, following the wires back to their source. She could make out a medical monitoring device, beeping repetitively with her pulse. The room was big, for a chopper—probably a cargo hold, outfitted to be a medical bay.

She wasn't wearing much—just a loose fitting shirt. She had fresh bandages on her side, and arms.

Then there was the scuffing sound of a footprint on the deck, and Jill Valentine came in, bent over to look at her.

"Glad to have you back," Jill said.

Alice gave her a weak smile.

"Glad to have *you* back." Suddenly she remembered. "Where is she? Becky?"

"Taking a nap, last I looked, in the comfiest spot you can find on this chopper. She was sitting in here with you for hours."

Alice nodded.

"And Leon?"

"He's here, with Ada—they're both doing pretty well." She nodded off to one side, and Alice turned her head. Leon and Ada were sitting together. Cautiously, Leon moved one of his hands to place it on Ada's knee. But she brushed it aside.

Alice turned back to Jill.

"Luther..." she said. "Did we leave his body there?"

"When the helicopters came down, the ice shifted, and his body went under. Maybe it'll freeze in there. Make a nice tomb for him. He's out of our reach."

Luther. She'd felt a real rapport with him. And a powerful attraction. He'd been breezy, likable, easygoing, but brave as hell, and instinctively loyal. And there had been a chemistry between them...

But of course—of *course*—he had been taken away from her. Everything was taken away.

Stop feeling sorry for yourself. At least you're alive. You've got hope. You've got Becky...

But, Luther...

Alice closed her eyes, bit her lip, not wanting Jill to see any weakness in her. But inwardly she felt all the emotional pain fighting free, all the anguish she'd suppressed just to get through it all. She'd pushed it all down just to survive, and keep Becky alive.

All those other people for whom she'd felt herself responsible—the prisoners she'd liberated on the *Arcadia*, Claire and Chris Redfield. Where were they now? Prisoners of Umbrella, she thought. They might've been turned into monsters, like the horror she'd sent to the bottom of the sea. They might be in interrogation cells, screaming as they were tortured, as she had been. She'd barely managed to keep herself and Becky alive. But those people?

She could almost hear them screaming.

"Think I'll..." She cleared her throat, aware it was hoarse. "Think I'll nap, myself."

"Sure," Jill responded. "We've got a long way to go."

"To where?"

"We're headed to Washington, D.C. What's left of it."

Jill left the room, and Alice let the emotions well up in her.

It'd been a long time since she'd cried. Tears had welled in her eyes when she'd seen the open grave of all the Alice clones that Umbrella had toyed with, played with like psychotic puppet masters. But actually crying—how long had it been?

At the very thought, the sobs came. And then she remembered the last time she'd wept. She'd been with Spence Parks, her "husband." What a bitter lie that word was to her. *Husband*. Role-playing. Sometimes the roles got a little too real. Other times the reality of their relationship came rudely between them.

They'd been in the mansion, guarding the Hive together.

Years ago. Before the rise of the Undead...

Alice came home from Raccoon City, feeling both tired and wired. The training session in the city had been about interfacing with technological enhancements, about the possibility of new biological enhancements—some of which seemed kind of fanciful to her. She'd had a chance to try out some new hand-to-hand fighting techniques, and had found it both exhausting and stimulating.

It was a summer evening, and she was looking forward to having a vodka lime juice with Spence. They had to spend a good deal of time together at the mansion, playing house, in a way, acting the roles of husband and wife. Maybe tonight was the night to get back to the other part of playing house.

Making love to Spence had a certain appeal. He was a compact guy with dark-brown hair and a light-hearted, ironic manner. A good-looking guy, but his was the face of a lovable thirty-two-year-old sitcom star, not a hunky action hero.

They'd tried resisting the sexual attraction, for a while—they were just role-playing, after all, as part of the cover story. But the sexual chemistry was strong, and Spence came through in the sack—plenty of strength and staying power, and even a willingness to show some masculine dominance, now and then, if he wasn't too over the top about it.

She didn't easily allow anyone to dominate her.

As she drove up to the mansion in the Arklay Mountains, nodding to the guards outside, she reflected that any emotional distance wasn't necessarily Spence's fault. He might just be protecting himself. After all, why would he risk himself by getting too deeply attached?

She parked the car, chuckling at herself.

Vanity! Assuming he's got to work at it, to keep from falling in love with you. She hadn't allowed many people to get close to her—not sexually and certainly not emotionally. She was a professional warrior, a trained killer, a martial artist, a detective, and a security specialist, all rolled into one. She was highly paid, she was expert, and she'd asked for the job, once upon a time. No place in all that for a marriage, or for kids.

But she'd felt lonely, in the last couple of years. Then this assignment at the mansion had come up.

"You and Spence Parks are to pretend to be married." That was a bitter irony, since she would never be a stay-at-home housewife. Still, she had family instincts, like everyone. What was that line from the Rolling Stones?

"The gangster is frightening with his luger in his hand, but when he gets home he's a family man."

Alice went to the door of the mansion, aware that the camera was scanning her as she went. She

performed the entry identification protocol, opened
the door, and went in, humming to herself, tossing
her purse on a chair.

"Spence?" she called.

"In here," he called, from the "sitting room." She
found him sitting by the fireplace, his legs stretched
out, a drink in his hand. He was frowning at the
gas flames licking over the artificial logs. Even the
fireplace logs were fake here, she thought.

"Good trip?" he asked.

She went to the liquor cabinet and made herself a
drink, pouring Rose's Lime over Grey Goose.

"I'm tired. But not too tired." She looked closely at
him. "You look kind of down in the mouth."

"Turns out we're going to have visitors, and we'll
need to play our roles to the hilt. Not looking forward
to it. I don't know how they decided that acting was
my métier but it's not."

She turned and looked at him quizzically, sipping
her drink.

"What do you mean, visitors? Hasn't been
necessary to do anything more than be here for the
mailman now and then, show up at the place down
the road for a barbecue."

"Maybe they want to use this big expensive set," he
replied. "I don't know. Maybe it's got more to do with
Senator Salter."

"Salter? What about him?"

Spence sighed and put his drink down on the
redwood coffee table.

"He's coming here tomorrow night. They told me
a few days ago. I thought about calling you, but—
wasn't sure if it was secure to do that. I was kind of

hoping they'd cancel the whole thing. But it looks like he's coming, along with his entourage. Including his wife and kids."

"Here?" She sat down in the easy chair. "He doesn't know about the Hive does he?"

"No, no one in politics does," Spence said. "They want to keep it that way. But he's a big shot in defense appropriations. I guess they want to sell him on a new project. The 'T' project. From that whole Ashford gambit..."

The 'T' project. Meaning, she knew, the T-virus.

He gave her a significant look, then glanced up at the lights. They were being monitored by Umbrella, probably by the Red Queen. Theoretically they'd disabled the bugging and cameras in their bedroom, but it was hard to be sure. And there were topics they both knew they shouldn't talk about, even alone in the house. If they used a term like *biowarfare*, or the phrase *viral agent*, security computers sorted and parsed their conversation.

But Alice *did* know about the T-virus. She knew more than she wanted to know.

"How are we supposed to prepare?" she asked, wincing at the thought.

He shrugged.

"Just put on our best, look shiny and happy, play the role. The thing will be catered. Security taken care of. We just have to play hosts."

"But why us—why here?"

"Some locals are wondering about the house. The guards haven't been as discreet as they might've been. Our cover story's not all that convincing, to some of the neighbors. They've been asking questions. I guess

there were some disappearances in the area, so..."
He waved a hand dismissively. "They're blaming the
'mysterious mansion' or something. And somebody
with some campaign-money clout went ahead and
contacted Salter. He's their senator."

"So, Umbrella figures kill two birds with one stone.
We enhance the cover-up with Salter, and they pitch
him on their project."

"We're not doing the pitching?" she asked.

"Nah, it's 'need to know.' There'll be a guy here
from the company—Dr. Isaacs. You know him?"

"Sam Isaacs? I know of him." Supposedly Isaacs
had been deeply involved in the 'T' Project—and now
he was working on some variant called Nemesis. She
didn't have the goods on that one. She smiled ruefully
at him. "Well, if we've got to do it, what's the big deal?
You don't like parties?"

He snorted.

"Only party I'm interested in..." He came and took
her hands in his, pulled her to her feet. "...Involves
just two people. Guess who."

"Show me."

And she was glad when he kissed her.

Several nights later, they were at a different sort of
affair, a subdued dinner party. Alice and Spence
dressed elegantly but not too formally, seated at the
opposite ends of a dinner table. Senator Salter and
his wife, Laney, sat on Alice's right. Dr. Isaacs sat on
her left. A rather sullen teenage girl sat farther down
the polished maple table, closer to Spence, and across
from her was her younger brother.

Alice found Dr. Isaacs an object of some fascination. He was a blond man, in early middle age, still rugged, his cold blue eyes and distant, urbane manner both charming and off-putting. He wore a gray suit, clearly tailored for him, complete with a white silk handkerchief in the blazer pocket. He ate with complete attention to his chicken, his hands making little surgical movements with the silverware. Now and then he looked up and smiled when someone spoke.

There was something about him that Alice found repellent. And yet he had spoken to them, earlier, over cocktails, with some considerable charm—chatting incisively, wittily, about politics and art, his eyes rarely leaving her. He had seemed unwilling to speak of science, however, when Alice raised the subject, though he was a scientist. But she understood that. His primary interests were classified.

"So you're an investor, Spence?" Mrs. Salter asked smilingly, in a lilting voice. Laney Salter was an attractive, very slender brunette in early middle age. She had a Florida accent and a taste for Parisian designer dresses—dresses with a slit up the side.

"That's right," Spence said modestly. *And falsely.* "Securities, gold, real estate..."

"I don't dare ask you, then," Salter asked, winking, speaking in a blaring Florida voice. He was a white-haired man, wearing a cream-colored suit, twenty years older than his wife. His broad nose was mottled with blue veins and his slab of a face was the color of raw steak. "I don't dare ask about the good investments, that's probably breaking some damn insider-trading rule. But maybe later on you can give me a hint!"

"Of course, Senator."

The two children looked quietly miserable. The teenager was a pretty blonde with braces, and a dress that was too low cut for her age. The boy was about eleven, pale, already pimply, wearing a Marlins T-shirt. He kept stealing looks at some kind of portable game console on his lap, as he picked at his chicken chasseur.

Senator Salter, for his part, was frequently stealing looks at Alice.

At the back of the room stood two men and a woman in suits and sunglasses, looking uncannily like Secret Service agents. But they were Umbrella Special Security, Level 4. Alice had once worked at that level. It was tedious.

"I wonder," Dr. Isaacs suddenly said, "what Mrs. Parks thinks of living in so remote a place? She seems a dynamic woman, more suited to an urban environment. But perhaps I'm wrong. Perhaps she lives to hike and fish?"

He looked at Alice, smiling faintly, raising his eyebrows to indicate that the question was meant for her.

The smile ended at Isaacs' eyes. They were as cold as chips of ice.

Alice put down her Chardonnay.

"Oh, I love it. I keep very busy. I help Spence with his research—investment takes research, you know. We go on trips all the time, of course, sometimes business, sometimes pleasure."

"But—isn't it rather too large a place for just the two of you?" Laney Salter asked, eyebrows raised. "Gosh, it seems... just huge!"

Spence chuckled.

"We hope to fill it up—with children." He raised his glass to Alice. "The time hasn't come yet. But it will."

Alice remembered to smile shyly.

"Thinking ahead, I like that!" the senator boomed. "Speaking of that—" He nodded to Dr. Isaacs. "Maybe we can adjourn here, pretty soon, and talk about that little matter..."

"Certainly," Isaacs said, smiling coolly, as unruffled as ever. "Whenever you like."

An hour later, Isaacs was meeting with the senator in the library. The children were watching television in an upstairs bedroom and Alice, sitting on the sofa, was watching Spence—who'd been cornered by Laney Salter in the sitting room, where they'd gone for drinks.

Spence was standing in front of the fireplace, his back to it, his face frozen in a polite smile, a drink in his hand. Mrs. Salter seemed to inch closer and closer to him, her eyes on his as she chatted earnestly about sports. How she liked *vigorous* sports. *"You know— men who really get out there and take that ball. Just... take it!"*

As she said that she threw back her shoulders, making her breasts pop forward. And making Spence inch back a little more.

Alice smiled to herself, amused by the woman's brazenness. Spence was going to back into the fire soon. Laney was something of a cougar. She'd probably have preferred a teenage boy, but Spence would have to do. He was a pretty youthful thirty-two.

Twenty minutes later, she whispered something to him, then turned to Alice.

"I think I'll check on my kids... upstairs," she said. She gave Spence a significant look and sashayed from the room.

When she was gone, he rolled his eyes, and Alice laughed.

"Spence, I think there's smoke rising from the back of your pants," she warned. "Then again, she's pretty hot. Maybe it's the front of your pants—"

Alice broke off as the door opened and Isaacs came in, followed by Senator Salter. The politician strode directly to Alice, beaming at her.

"There she is, the glorious lady of the house!" he bellowed. "I wonder if I could have a bourbon and branch water."

As Alice made the drink, Isaacs crossed to Spence.

"A few words outside, Spence?" he said.

Spence nodded, put his drink on the mantel, and they went out into the hall, closing the door behind them. Alice finished the drink and brought it to the senator, who was standing by the fire, warming his chubby hands. The room wasn't brightly lit, and the firelight danced on his features, lighting them from below, making him look quietly demonic as he grinned at her.

"Look at that, the perfect hostess!" He saluted her with the drink, and took a long pull at it, watching her over the top of his glass.

"Do you and Mrs. Salter return to D.C. from here, Senator?" Alice asked, sitting on the sofa. It was the only conversation she could think of, at that moment.

"Ohhh, yes, yes, tomorrow. We'll be staying here

tonight, of course. Your husband was kind enough to invite us."

"Oh, well, of course," Alice murmured. She hadn't known they were staying. But she decided she should pretend she was in the loop. "I suggested it to Spence—we have so much room here, after all."

"You know it's kind of funny, some of your servants seem like they're more used to being bodyguards. Saw some gun bulges..."

"Oh, well, Spence likes people to... to multitask." She grinned. "Our upstairs maid is a crack shot."

"Is she? I bet you can hit any target you point at, yourself. I'll bet you have a lot of talents, Alice," he said. "All kinda hidden talents, a sexy lady like you."

Normally, Alice would've slapped him down for that kind of talk. But she just smiled blandly. He was a senator, and a critical contact for Umbrella. Plus her job paid her a very high six figures a year. She definitely didn't want to lose it.

Spence and Isaacs returned, Spence looking kind of flushed, Alice thought, Dr. Isaacs looking the same as always: like the cat who'd eaten the canary. He maintained a nauseating demeanor of self-satisfaction and superiority, whatever he did.

"Alice," Spence said, "a word outside...?"

Not liking the feel of it, Alice followed him into the hall. He closed the door and looked around.

"Well?" she asked. Before he could speak she said, "Oh, I know—they want you to make Mrs. Salter happy."

"As a matter of fact, yes."

"A happy Mrs. Salter is a happy Senator Salter? I'm not sure how I feel about that. I mean I know we're just..." She lowered her voice. "...Just playing parts, here, but you and I have gotten..."

"It's more than that. The senator knows there's something more going on here. He doubts that it's legal, whatever it is. And he isn't certain he wants to approve the appropriations for Umbrella's... special projects. Umbrella is a government contractor but they're trying to cut back on... that area of deployment."

He didn't say "biowarfare" but she knew that's what he meant.

"And?" She wanted him to say it. She wanted to see what his expression was like as he said it.

"And he hints that if you play nice with him, he'll play nice with us. He won't ask too many questions about the Hive. He's heard that term, somewhere. He knows it's connected to this place. And he'll approve the appropriations for the... project."

Her mouth was dry. And as for his face, as he said it, he *did* seem unhappy. But there was no hint that he wanted her to say no. She could tell he'd made up his mind that they were both going to play the game.

"This is... supremely sick, Spence."

"I know," he admitted. "But—we've done worse."

"Have we?"

He shrugged.

"I have. They sent me on an assignment where I had to shoot a whole roomful of..." He shook his head. "Never mind. It's just one night."

"Easy for you to say. Laney Salter is way more palatable than that bloated, bourbon-soaked satyr." She tried making a joke. "Maybe we could switch places. He might like you."

Spence didn't laugh. He didn't even smile.

"So... he likes to do it right there on the sofa, that kinda guy. I'm meeting her upstairs. Isaacs says we keep them both happy."

"Isaacs. He's behind this."

Dr. Isaacs likes to degrade people... she thought. Her stomach roiled, thinking about it.

She could walk away from this. They wouldn't kill her for it. She'd just lose any career opportunity in the future. They'd see to that. They punished disobedience.

And then again, maybe her life *would* be in danger. After all, Salter was a powerful man. He might worry that she'd talk about all this, in the media. He might demand they take care of her—completely.

It wouldn't take long. But the thought of it...

Even if Salter had been an attractive man, she'd still have felt degraded by the whole experience. Being bartered like a cheap whore.

"That's how you think of me, Spence? You and Isaacs? Like I'm... some fun girl in Bangkok, always ready to 'entertain' the businessman?"

"No!" He shook his head sadly. "Come on. Laney's an attractive lady, but—I'm not feeling any better about this. I don't like to be 'entertainment' either. Not that way. But we have to do it. There are billions of dollars—*many* billions of dollars—on the line here! Salter doesn't like anyone telling him no. He's really vindictive, and he's taken a fancy to you, big time. He couldn't take his eyes off you at dinner."

"Suppose I throw up my dinner on him, during all this?"

Spence sighed.

"You're tougher than that."

In the end, she gave in. The risks of refusing were too high.

Billions of dollars—many billions...

That was the deciding factor as far as Umbrella was concerned.

She kept her face neutral as she returned to the sitting room. The senator was looking at her attentively, licking his lips. Isaacs spoke as she entered.

"Well, I'll be off," he said. "My car is waiting." He gave the senator a little bow. "Good night." As he left the room, Alice glanced at the door, hoping Spence would rush in, say, *No, Alice, don't do it, I won't allow it.*

But of course he didn't.

She turned to Salter.

"Well. How can I... entertain you?" And she dropped the strap of her dress from her shoulder.

It took him longer to finish than she'd hoped. A good half hour. Afterward, once he'd patted her on her naked rear and left the room—closing the door behind him—she burst into tears. It was the first time she'd cried since childhood.

It would be the last time for years after.

Remembering that night, now, as she lay on the cot in the helicopter, Alice squirmed—and winced when the movement brought pain.

A black female medic came in, nodded to her and,

as if on cue, injected her I.V. line with a painkiller. The soothing drug almost blotted out the memory of that half hour on the sofa. The weight of him on her; the smell of him—sweat, cigars, bourbon, faint halitosis, a strong scent of deodorant and aftershave. The slobbery pressure of his lips. The moment she'd opened her eyes and seen his veiny, bulbous nose rearing over her.

His gasping, grasping, pumping. His murmured obscenities, stubby, probing fingers.

Bruises on her breasts.

She almost threw up, remembering.

But then she closed her eyes and let the drug ease her into restful sleep...

24

The screen in the attack room showed the prow of the submarine. It was a fairly clear video feed—Umbella had upgraded it—revealing the green-blue sea, becoming darker shades of blue as it went down. A polar bear swam by, which was exciting for Dori, and they saw a few fish, and a pair of walruses.

Tom was tapping a control screen, causing the ballast tanks to fill.

"You're *sure* the hatches are all closed?" Judy asked. She sounded like a wife already, Tom thought. He'd been married once—his wife had been shot by a cop. But by then, she was already dead. She was just "walking around dead." She'd been bitten by the walking corpse of her sister Edna.

Tom had to kill Edna himself.

Now he was watching the gauges, and he felt the enormous submarine lurch.

"What about... what about doing it all evenly?" Judy asked, looking around nervously as the vessel began to shudder.

"What you mean, evenly?" Tom asked, watching the gauges.

"I mean—making one side sink and not the other," she said, "unless you intend to. What if we flip upside down, or..."

"Naw, it's all set up to spread the ballast weight evenly around the ship. It might tilt a little to the forward, but not so much. Don't you worry." Truth was, he wasn't feeling as confident as he sounded.

"Oh!" Dori said, clutching at Judy as the ship lurched again. She, too, was wearing an old Russian sailor's uniform, a little too big for her, the pant legs rolled up. "Is it going to sink?" she asked worriedly.

"You say that like it's a bad thing," Tom chuckled. "It's supposed to sink! That's what submarines do. Look at the screen, there—we're going down!" He was a bit worried that they were going down faster than he'd intended, though. He needed to slow the process down.

The conning tower would be underwater now, and below the ice pack. They could hear the water rushing around the vessel, causing a soft rumbling. The video screen was getting darker.

Then it occurred to Tom that they weren't far off the coast—so the water might be relatively shallow here. Which meant—

CLUNK.

It sounded just like that, a metallic clunk, as they hit the bottom. The vessel rocked around them, and they clung to the nearest surfaces, Judy slipping an arm around Dori. The deck tilted—and stopped at a slight angle. A shuddering worked its way through the ship, but the deck was steady under them again, and they relaxed a little.

"Went down a little too fast," Tom said apologetically. He was listening for the sound of running water; for the alarms that would come if the hull was breached. Nothing. A wire-frame image on the ship's status monitor showed the submarine tilted a little, but there were no indicators of water pouring in.

"Look!" Dori said, pointing at the video screen.

Tom looked—and shuddered. There was something human out there; a dark silhouette against the light-colored sea bottom. Sea grass swirled around it, and fish darted past its head.

Human? But it wasn't really human—judging from the red glow from the eyes.

"It's a mutant," Judy said hoarsely. "Oh, God. A Las Plagas mutant, judging from the eyes. Looks like it might've once been a 'Rain' designated clone."

"That's a clone, like me?" Dori asked, wide eyed.

"Not like you, kid," Tom said. "That thing's mean. They get like that, only one person can control them. Chances are that person's dead. The thing'll kill till it can't kill anymore. But I don't think it can get in here, to us. It looks like it's about twenty yards ahead—it's got ice on its arms there, see it? We'll go back up, to right under the ice, and head out—and we'll leave that thing behind."

"It must've been one of those who were fighting, out on the ice," Judy suggested. "Any way we can put it out of its misery?"

"Nah. Not while it's down there. This vessel was used as a transport, for Umbrella's top secret stuff, see. It wasn't armed, though. They didn't want to mess with any nuclear missiles, torpedos—too unstable after all these years. They took 'em out. There's a machine-

RESIDENT EVIL:RETRIBUTION

gun emplacement up top, though, on the turret. It's all closed off but there's ammo for it. No way we could hit that thing with it. You can only operate the gun from outside."

"It looks like it's trying to get close to us!" Dori said, and she pointed.

Indeed, the ice-laden creature was trying to lumber toward them, walking along the ocean floor, its booted feet raising the sand like slow motion dust clouds.

"Dammit!" Tom muttered, sitting in front of the control screen. He tapped the control for the ballast tanks, ordering them to blow half their weight. The submarine huffed, bubbles surged up, rumbling past—and the vessel groaned, as if complaining. They hung on again as it stabilized, rising—and in a few moments the mutant was gone from the screen.

Tom blew out a long stream of air in relief.

"Whew. Now..." He checked their depth on the bathymetry gauge. "Twenty-seven fathoms," he said.

"What's that?" Dori asked.

"It's how deep we are. Judy teach you math? A fathom is six feet."

"Of course!" she sniffed. "One hundred sixty-two!"

"That's how many feet down we are. I'm going to keep us right about here, because I don't want to run into the bottom of any icebergs. And I'm going to head southeast, if I can get the engine to cooperate with me."

"Sure you know what you're doing?" Judy asked again. "That's a nuclear engine..."

"It's a steam engine powered up by nuclear generators. Anyway—you want to live here, forever?"

"We could fish, when we ran out of food."

"Umbrella will be back here, salvaging. Investigating."

Judy winced at that.

"You're right. Let's go. But... let's go slowly, till we get out away from the ice and the land."

"Now you're talking sense. We want to get to deep water, and away from all this ice..."

"Can you get the engine going?" Dori asked.

"Come over here," Tom told her. She walked over and looked over his shoulder, hunching a little, her hands on her knees.

"Now—see that green tab there on the screen? Touch that with your thumb."

She licked her lips—and touched the green tab. At first nothing seemed to happen. Then the submarine responded, grumbling deep within itself, whining, and then a vibration ran through it, from the back to the front. They could feel it passing through the attack center.

"Oh, look!" Judy said, pointing at the prow video.

They could see ice floes, up above, illuminated by light from the surface, passing by as they tooled along under them.

They were moving, and the compass indicated that they were heading south-by-southeast.

When Alice woke, she heard someone walking back to the rear of the big chopper. They remarked that they had just flown east over the coast of California.

Or what once was California, Alice thought. Now it was just another wasteland, haunted by the Undead. There would be some tough survivors down there, fighting tooth and nail, struggling every day for life. And she hoped the sight of the choppers flying over would give them hope.

But she wasn't sure they gave *her* any hope. It was Wesker's outfit, after all. Who knew what he planned? He was one of the men who'd destroyed civilization in the first place.

She was on her way to be delivered to her greatest enemy.

She lay there a moment, listening to the percussive roll of the rotors, aware of crosswinds buffeting the aircraft, making it jolt from time to time. She could hear voices up forward, but no one seemed to be keeping an eye on her.

They'd have to stop for fuel at some point, and that might give her and Becky a chance to escape. Maybe Jill would help her—even go with her. Maybe not. Could be Jill would think of Wesker as her new employer.

And why not? Wesker had access to resources. He might have partnered with one of the other surviving multinationals. Umbrella couldn't be the only one. And if they had medical resources, fuel, helicopters, they'd provide some kind of shelter in a world still overrun by horrors.

Were they as ruthless as Umbrella? Then again, in the world as it was now, maybe that's how you had to be.

No, Alice decided. *There's no world that could justify what Umbrella has done.*

Yet if Alice hoped to escape—she'd have to be ambulatory to do it. She stretched, testing her limbs, then grimaced—the "Rain mutant" had damaged her pretty severely. But rest and pain meds had helped. And she seemed to have some of her old healing ability, though to a lesser degree than when she'd had all her powers.

She carefully unfastened the restraints that held her in place and, grimacing with little stabs of pain, sat up. The I.V. was still in her arm—she pulled off the tape and jerked the needle out of the vein. There was a roll of surgical tape on the table, and some clean gauze. She made a bandage to stop the bleeding, and then plucked off the monitor wires. The monitor chirped repeatedly, emitting a prissy-sounding alarm.

And the medic came in. He was a tall, skinny black man with an afro, probably from not having access to a barber, and a fuzz of beard. He wore cammie-style paramilitary togs.

"Hey, you lay back down now!" he told Alice. "What are you doing, taking your I.V. out?"

"Am I a prisoner?"

"Not that I heard. Your friend Jill is walking around as she pleases. Your little girl is watching the pilots. Only reason you're strapped down is because you were injured, and we're going to land for a refuel in Nevada pretty soon. You've got to be strapped down when we land."

He seemed genuinely concerned for her, and Alice didn't feel like fighting him.

"I'll lay down, but no I.V., I already need a bedpan."

"I'll get you one of those," he promised. "Just lay down. How's your pain?"

"Not bad. When I move around, though..."

He shook his head, and looked at her as if he thought she was insane.

"You got cracked bones in there, lady. Just take it easy."

Alice was feeling dizzy anyway. She shrugged and lay back down. It wasn't the right moment. There was Becky to consider.

The medic brought her the bedpan, waited, looking out a port, then took it away to empty. Very professional. That touch of civilized care was comforting, after so long in a world under siege.

A few minutes later Becky came in, looking giddy, and sat on the edge of her cot, smiling and signing.

"Mama, I was watching the pilots!" she said. "I want to be a helicopter pilot!"

"Some day!" Alice signed, and she smiled. They continued to sign back and forth, Becky sometimes talking aloud in her squeaky way. Alice spoke aloud as she signed, to encourage Becky to learn to read lips.

"Jill can sign too," Becky revealed.

"I know she can. So can Ada."

"And she told me we're going to Washington, D.C.! The real one!"

"Right, not one of those pretend towns that Umbrella made. The real one."

"I sometimes think I can remember being outside— but Jill says I wasn't even alive before a few days ago."

"You were alive, but you were sleeping in a lab. Like those others we saw. They put some memories in your mind, so you wouldn't be confused when you woke up. But they aren't real memories. You're making real ones now."

Becky nodded gravely.

"I'll never forget any of this," she signed. "Never. I want to see Washington, D.C. Our nation's capital."

"It's not like it used to be," Alice warned. "The Undead have overrun a lot of it, for now. But someday we'll get rid of them, take it all back, and build it up again. A lot of it was burned down, you know, by the British, in the War of 1812. Centuries ago. They rebuilt it. It can be our nation's capital again."

"It's not now?"

"Maybe in some ways. But the nation's lost a lot of... organization." She hoped she'd signed 'organization' right. "We'll fix it. But it'll involve having to fight a lot, I think. I don't want to go there now unless I have to... but someday people like us will rebuild it."

Alice hoped she wasn't leading Becky into false hope. It occurred to her that before the second Fall of Man—before the rise of the Undead—there'd been new prototypes of artificial hearing devices, implants, transplants, various devices that were purported to treat deafness. Becky might've had her deafness effectively cured. And she could have become "a helicopter pilot" someday, in that world.

If she could get her hearing back, now, somehow, it would increase her chances of survival. If you can hear an Undead coming up from behind, you have a better chance of escaping.

But that world was gone now. People who weren't killed by the Undead often died anyway, for lack of medical attention when they got an infected cut. Hearing implants? Not likely.

Still—what about Wesker, and whoever he was working with? They might have a cure for Becky, somewhere in their labs. But then, their "cure" might be a horror, too.

The black medic came in, then.

"We're going down for refueling."

"Where?" Alice asked.

"There's an old Air Force fuel dump we've taken over, in the Sierras. Razor wire all around it—should be fairly safe."

Who are you talking about when you say "we," Alice wondered. But before she could ask, the medic busied himself hustling Becky to the opposite bulkhead, where he buckled her into a fold-down seat.

"You just take it easy right there, little lady," he said. She didn't understand his words but she smiled at him. He tousled her hair and took his own fold-down seat as the helicopter began to angle downward, coming in for a landing.

Becky looked happily around, and Alice swore to herself she'd see that the girl was taken care of. In time she'd have to teach her certain things—like how to use weapons, martial arts techniques. Probably start with judo. Work her way up, teaching her how to kill with her hands alone.

There was room for hope in the world, sure. But innocence? There was no room for innocence. As far as Alice could tell, innocence was dead. Umbrella had killed it.

The chopper's engine changed its tune, whining, and then, after the slight jarring of setting down, the rotors slowed, their song getting lower in pitch.

Now was her chance...

* * *

Alice had made up her mind that she didn't want to go to Washington. That would take them to Wesker—and that, alone, was enough reason to get away from the helicopter.

Albert Wesker, after all, had once tried to eat her alive. To literally *eat her*. He had transformed himself with the empowering variant of the T-virus, becoming a transfigurable superhuman. Sometimes he was just a pale man with slicked-back brown hair, shades, a long, black-leather coat, and black gloves. But when he chose, he could transform—his enormous mandibles extruding from between elastic jaws, his body swelling, muscles bulging.

Wesker didn't have complete control over his transformations, so he'd decided that consuming "Project Alice," as he called her, would allow him to absorb some key part of her DNA. Alice had told him that she wasn't "on the menu"—and she'd escaped.

Just barely.

His mind was the most monstrous thing about him—his intricate rationalization for wanting absolute power. But it came down to something simple: The only thing that controls power, he said, is more power.

Wesker had been chairman of Umbrella when the T-virus project had been approved. Alice couldn't prove it, but she suspected that Wesker might have manipulated Spence into releasing the virus. And now they were taking her to that monster.

Her and Becky?

No.

The medic got up, checked on her, patted her shoulder, and asked her if she needed anything.

"Maybe something nutritious to drink?" she

replied. "Have anything like that? One of those canned smoothies or something?"

"We do. It's about a year past its 'use-by' date but so is everything we got. I'll get it for you."

He went forward, and Alice unstrapped herself, ignoring the pain as she sat up. Becky unstrapped herself and came over.

"Listen," Alice signed, "maybe we should go our own way—just you and me, from here. I don't know much about these people. Would you trust me, to just go with me? You don't have to."

Fear flickered in Becky's eyes. Her mouth trembled.

"Don't leave me," she signed.

"I won't—I'm saying that you can go with me."

"Will they let us go?" Becky asked.

An astute question...

25

Watching a tern fly away, past the circling cloud of gulls and out to sea, Jack Tannager ached to leave the island.

But he wasn't sure he ever would. Uncle Chung claimed that wherever you were, it was enough. The world, he said, is small in the cosmos. Everything is a speck, ultimately, so why not live on a small island? The whole Earth was a small island in the infinite reaches of space, after all.

Yet here he was, standing on the stony beach at sunset, on the west side of Catalina Island, gazing out to sea, and every fiber of his being ached for exploration. There were, at least, other islands that might be clear of the Undead. At least *they* could be explored.

Uncle Chung wouldn't hear of it.

"The sickness that killed your mother and father— it will not have you, too. I loved my sister very much. When it took her, changed the vessel that had held her soul, dishonored her memory, I swore I would give it no chance to harm you, Jack. We have been safe here for a long time. We will not take the chance..."

And there was Bim to talk to, and Lony. Sure, they were a young gay couple, so he couldn't relate to them on every level, but they were nice guys. They liked to fish, and Lony had shown him how to handle a boat and how to surf.

Jack picked up a smooth disklike pebble, and tried to skip it between the rollers, but it struck a wave and sank.

Just like me, he thought, sighing. *Can't move on.*

"Jack!" Uncle Chung called from the little bluff over the beach.

Jack turned resignedly to the sound.

"Yes, Uncle?"

"Come on, it's getting dark, time for dinner... We must stand our watches, right after."

He nodded glumly and climbed the sandy path that wound up the face of the bluff, joining his uncle. The old man stood in a fringe of sawgrass, hands on his hips. His orange Buddhist robe was frayed, his sandals were falling apart, duct-taped together. His scraggly gray beard was blowing in the wind. He smiled at Jack—that half-toothless smile, piquantly vulnerable. It was impossible stay angry with Chung for long. Especially since his eyes were so like Jack's mother's: brown, almost black, gracefully epicanthic, penetrating.

Uncle Chung was the only family he had left.

Jack was half Chinese, though he spoke almost none of the Mandarin with which his mother and Uncle Chung used to chatter. His father had been a British airline pilot, and a good man, though Jack hadn't seen enough of him. An infected passenger had killed him—and the plane had crashed.

After they had eaten, he and Uncle Chung stood watch companionably, Uncle Chung carrying the old M1 rifle strapped over his shoulder. It would have looked strange to see a Buddhist monk with a rifle, before the rise of the Undead. Now, of course...

They were lucky to have rifles enough, and a good supply of ammunition. Lony's father had been a gun collector. He'd gone to Los Angeles just before the apocalypse, and was presumed dead. He'd been a fancier of World War II carbines, and he had laid in a sizeable supply of .30 caliber ammo in an old World War II bunker—designed to be prepared for a Japanese invasion that had never come. There were four M1 Garands, two German Lugers, a crate of ammo, and a "trench broom" shotgun. There was also a machine gun, but it didn't work. The Thompson, too—no ammo for that.

But there was plenty of ammunition for the M1. They'd all been checked out, and had gotten damned good at target practice. And they'd cleaned the island of Undead, quite a while before. Jack had shot his share of zombies. The first time he got a good clean headshot, he said, "I killed one!" and was rewarded by a deep frown from Uncle Chung.

"Do not say you *killed* one," Uncle Chung said. "I would not let you kill anyone. That thing is *not alive*. It is just a body, an inflamed nervous system, and a hunger. It is nothing more. You have ended the misery of an Undead, but it was killed when it transformed."

There had been a lot more people here, of course, the day that the outbreak had started. There'd been almost four thousand people. More than half of them panicked and crowded on two large ferries, to escape the Undead.

The ferries had gone west, headed to another nearby island. Jack had watched them from the top of Mount Orizaba, the highest point on Santa Catalina Island, where he'd fled with Uncle Chung, after his mother had turned... into one of those things.

After his Uncle, weeping, had shot her in the head.

He hadn't shot *her*, Jack reminded himself, whenever he thought of it. Just her body, animated. Her spirit was with the Buddha.

They'd watched the ferries head west, and then one of them appeared to veer wildly, to crash into the other. Soon both ferries sank. No one made it back to shore. Except a few they'd had to shoot.

A great many more of the folks had crowded into a gymnasium, to barricade themselves in, but one of them already had been bitten. The doors were locked when he began to spread the disease. The others, outside, had burned the gymnasium down, with all those people in it. Probably some of them hadn't been Undead.

That wasn't something Jack liked to contemplate.

They'd gone over the island with a fine-toothed comb, the few who'd survived. Thirty of them. And they'd killed Undead after Undead. Two of the hunters had been bitten—and become the hunted.

One day a boat drifted toward the island—and they could see Undead stalking back and forth on the deck. Three of the men, volunteers, went out in a motor yacht, shot the Undead on the deck from about thirty feet away, then towed the boat back out to sea and set it afire. They didn't look to see what might be below decks.

That infected boat had spooked the survivors, and most had chosen to go on a cabin cruiser, to the west, hoping to find a safer place, more remote. Jack and Uncle Chung and Lony and Bim were all that remained on the island, apart from a few wild animals, and the half-feral dogs that Bim had almost tamed.

Bim was a stocky half-Polynesian man with a considerable belly and a big toothy smile. He came strolling up to them as they got back to the bunker on the north side of the island. Uncle Chung was breathing hard from the climb.

"See anything interesting over there, Jack?" he asked, waving. Bim was about thirty, and usually wore a Hawaiian flower shirt, white duck trousers, and sandals. Neither he nor Lony seemed effeminate to Jack.

The bunker was on a beetling foothill of the island's small mountain, overlooking the small, sprawling estate house that Bim's father had kept.

"No, nothing as usual," Jack said.

"Anything float up—debris, something we could use?"

"Couple of fishing floats."

"Wowie-zow," Bim said, grinning. He liked to say "wowie-zow." He liked to smoke pot, too—he and Lony had a little "weed patch," as they called it, up on the hillside. Uncle Chung never touched it. And Jack pretended not to.

"The boy is getting bored," Chung said. "Hard for him here. Maybe we should go on a fishing expedition, next nice day. There's fuel in a lot of those boats still."

But as he said it he was frowning, staring out to sea. He seemed to be looking for something.

"What you see, Chung?" Bim asked, shading his hand to look.

The sun had mostly set—there was just a little twilight, and the rising moon's glow.

"I... nothing. Don't see anything. And I see everything—the waves. Everything is waves. But no ships. I just felt it was coming. And last night, I had a dream. Last night it was..."

"Last night?" Jack prompted. His uncle had precognitive dreams at times. And they always came true. He didn't mention his dreams unless he felt they were important.

Chung shrugged.

"Been looking all day. Seeing nothing. Perhaps not as soon as I thought."

"What was the dream?" Jack asked.

"Last night... I dreamt a submarine would come to the island."

Alice simply walked out of the helicopter, into the cool early evening, with Becky holding her hand. There was a ring of light around the chopper. A guard stared at her, frowning—he had a blond beard, and bushy hair caught up in a headband. Probably he wasn't sure what to do with her.

Alice looked at his gun, lusting after it. It was an M60, and would fire 7.62 x 51 mm cartridges at a rate of more than five hundred rounds per minute. The guy also had a sling with a lot of magazines stuck in it, all of them loaded.

She was weaponless right now, and she knew that gun well. If she could get hold of it, she could hold off a small army with that thing.

But she just smiled at him charmingly. She'd cleaned herself up before coming out, and looked as good as possible with all the bandages. She acted as if she was just getting the air.

The guard seemed to relax a little.

Out beyond the circle of light was a weedy field, and two fences, one inside the other. The inner fence, about twenty yards off, was topped by razor wire. The outer seemed to be electric—but she doubted that was working.

The light came mostly from lanterns—set up on fuel barrels nearby, at the edge of the tarmac—and from the helicopter's windows.

They seemed to be on a slanted meadow, somewhere on a mountainside. There was an outbuilding and several tanks, presumably filled with helicopter fuel. There were pipes connecting them, and a flexible fuel line running to the back of the helicopter. Other choppers were circling, overhead, waiting their turn.

"I see trees," Becky signed. "And the moon. I smell... I don't know what it is. A bad smell and a good smell."

"The bad smell is fuel," Alice said, though she kind of liked that smell. "The good smell is probably a forest, somewhere around this fueling depot."

"Not so cold here. That's nice. Is that the real moon?"

"Yes."

So far as Alice had been able to find out, they were on the east side of the Sierras, not terribly far from what had been the border with Nevada. Maybe this area would be relatively free of...

Then she saw them. The Undead.

They were shuffling toward the fences, growling. And there were hundreds of them.

She'd never get past them, unless she fought her way through. Impossible without a major weapon—and with Becky to worry about.

"Aren't we out in the boonies?" Alice asked the guard. "Why all the Undead?"

"Those all belonged to a military base, when they were people," he said, shading his eyes to squint past the lights. "It's about a mile from here. They see the lights when we come. Every time, they push the fences a little more. One of these days they're going to... *whoa*. I think we've got a breach on the outer fence. *Sarge*!"

"Mama?" Becky quavered. "Are they going to come in here?"

"There are fences still in the way," Alice signed. "If they get in, we have lots of protection." But she still pulled the girl close.

"Ferguson!" the sergeant shouted through a door behind them. "We've got twelve minutes till we're done here! Keep the damn peace out there! If you need back up, sing out!"

"Yes, sir!" Ferguson, the guard with the headband and the enviable M60, stalked off toward the fence.

"I wouldn't do that," Alice called. "Ferguson? Don't get too close!"

He ignored her.

"Where's he going, Mama?" Becky signed.

"Damned if I know," Alice muttered. But signing, she said, "To check that the fences are safe."

"Back off, you buzzard meat!" Ferguson yelled, approaching the barrier. Alice was betting that he hadn't had much experience with the zombies, or he'd know that it wasn't going to work.

She sighed. Plainly she wasn't going to get away from these people—not here. She'd have to wait—maybe till Washington. Her first priority was survival, for her and Becky. So she turned and smiled down at the girl, cupping her chin in one hand.

"Go on in," she signed with the other hand. "Get Jill for me. Will you do that? But don't come back out with her."

Becky nodded, and, happy to be on a mission, ran up the ramp into the big helicopter.

Ferguson was a few strides from the fence now. Alice started jogging toward him, wincing at the pain in her chest and side.

"Ferguson!" she shouted. "*Don't!*"

He glanced back at her.

"Lady, get back to the chopper! This is security business!" He turned to the Undead, who were pushing over the outer fence. They were starting to climb over it, as now that it was crimped down at a forty-five degree angle. Ferguson raised his M60. "I warned you, buzzard biscuits!"

He pushed the muzzle of the gun through a gap in the chain-link fence and opened fire, strafing at about head height. A half-dozen Undead fell back, their heads shot open.

"Wee-*hoo!*" Ferguson hooted.

Suddenly forty more piled over the dead ones and rushed at the inner fence. They were in tattered military uniforms, their faces bloodied, many without lips, some with mandibles that extruded to yank at the fence's links with unnatural strength. Ferguson had maddened them with his proximity and now they were working like a swarming carpet of army ants, seeking to break through.

"Ferguson!" Alice shouted. "Get back to the chopper!"

He turned her a furious scowl.

"Lady, I thought I told you—"

That's when the inner fence collapsed, clamping down over Ferguson like the jaws of a steel spring-trap. He staggered back as it fell on him, trapping him from the waist down. His gun was trapped too, the muzzle lying next to him, pointing back toward Alice.

He screamed, long and loud and shrilly, as the zombie—who'd once been a fat old two-star general—leapt on him, snarling, its mandibles ripping at his throat. Alice kicked hard at the general, breaking its neck. The walking corpse sagged on Ferguson, but the others were pressing through. She had just time to grab the muzzle of the gun and Ferguson's belt of ready ammo magazines, and pull them free of the fence.

But there was no time to get the gun into position. Two zombies who'd once been women, still partially in uniform, came side by side, looking almost like twins. Both caught bullets in the head, their skulls exploding under the impact.

Alice leapt back to avoid the splashing gore.

Then Jill, an assault rifle smoking in her hand, stepped up beside her.

"Thanks," Alice said as she brought the M60 up to face the charging Undead. "Nice shooting."

Jill didn't answer, she was busy firing at the onrushing horde, skillfully strafing a line of zombie heads. The front line, pressing through the gap in the damaged fence, went down like harvested crops under a scythe—but more clambered over them.

Alice propped the M60 on her hip, firing at the onrushing horde almost point blank, blasting rotting blood and yellow bone into the air, sending snarling creatures spinning into the sweet release of final death. But there were just too many of them, and she and Jill were going to run out of ammo pretty soon.

They kept backing up toward the chopper.

Alice felt something tug at her foot, looked down to see Ferguson, who'd gone Undead. Somehow he had squirmed out from under the fence and the bodies, half tearing his face off, and now he was clutching at her ankle, snapping at her toes.

"Oh, Ferguson," Alice said, shooting him in the head. "You moron—you just don't listen."

Gunfire came from behind them, zipping past to take out a line of stumbling zombies. Alice worried about "friendly fire"—some of those rounds were going past pretty close. She turned, emptied her clip into the Undead, then shouted at the soldiers who were firing from the chopper.

"Hold your fire till we get back there!"

The gunfire slackened as she and Jill turned and sprinted. She hardly felt the pain from her cracked ribs—half-healed wounds, now—and the adrenaline rush pushed away the remaining pain.

"You seem to be feeling better," Jill commented.

"Still feel like crap," she replied. "But that's kind of the high end of what I usually feel."

They got behind the three soldiers lined up in front of the chopper. Alice could see Becky peering out the hatch behind them, her expression a mix of relief and terror.

One of the Undead was dragging a dead, half-eaten deer behind it. Some of them had extruded mandibles that waved in the air in front of their faces, others were stalking along with single-minded determination, trying to get to the bloody objects of their desire.

Alice ran up the ramp, gently pressed Becky back inside, then slapped another magazine into her weapon. She fired—the high angle enabling her to avoid the soldiers below her—and nailed a couple of Undead halfway across the tarmac. One of them, though, kept coming. She'd shot it through its neck, and its head sagged to one side—hanging, it seemed, by an artery.

She noticed Becky signing from the corner of her eye.

"What?" she said, slapping in another magazine. Becky read her lips.

"I want to learn how to do that!" She pointed at the gun.

Alice nodded at her.

"Some day soon," she signed.

No innocence left...

It was a killing field, a charnel slaughterhouse floor, out on the tarmac, covered with bodies—some of them squirming, most of them unmoving—but still the Undead came. That was how they overwhelmed defenders. Sheer numbers. You could only pull the trigger so many times. And the Undead had no fear of bullets. Either they sought true death, or they were too blind with bloodlust to consider it.

One of the soldiers ran out of ammo, and panicked, and turned to run up the ramp.

"They're coming! Get us out of here!" he shouted, his voice high-pitched.

"The fuel line's still hooked up!" Jill shouted. They didn't dare take off. It could cause them to crash—or to explode into flame.

Alice swore and jumped down off the ramp, ran to the back of the chopper, then fumbled at the interface where the fuel hose was plugged into the fuselage. It took her a moment to figure out how to release it— and then the Undead were upon her. Three of them, all burly soldiers once, now looking like drunks who'd taken terrible beatings, one boot off and one on, clothes in disarray, faces masked in blood. The one in the middle was extruding mandibles.

Suddenly the fuel line came free, and gas was still gushing out the big plastic and fiberglass tube, pouring out on the ground. If she fired her gun now, it might turn the chopper into a fireball.

One of the Undead grabbed her arm. Then Jill was running toward her, and she put a round into the side of the Undead's head, putting him down.

"Hold your fire, the fuel's still flowing!" Alice shouted. She grabbed the hose and turned it toward the two closest Undead, who were snapping at her face. They snarled and clawed at their eyes. Then she tossed the end of the hose—heavier than it looked—at the wave of Undead running toward her so that it gushed under their feet. They splashed through the gasoline as she turned, shut the fuel gasket on the chopper, and ran.

She felt and smelled hot rotten breath on the back of her neck.

Alice reached the ramp, and jumped up beside Jill. The sergeant was shouting at the soldiers to get into the chopper. One of them made it, running up the ramp, but the other—a heavyset man who was covered with sweat—tripped and fell on his face. He was instantly swarmed by Undead, four of them biting into his legs, a fifth into the back of his neck, another crunching through his skull with its mandibles, ripping out his spine with its bare hands.

His screams echoed across the mountainside.

Alice shot him in the head to put him out of his misery and save him from turning into a zombie, then emptied her clip into the nearest group. She turned and jumped through the hatch as the ramp began to pull itself up.

As the chopper began lifting into the air, a Filipino woman in a military nurse's uniform leapt onto the ramp as it closed. The creature's head was caught in the doorway between the ramp and the frame, growling, mandibles extruding and waving about. The helicopter angled upward, turning so that a gunner could fire at the Undead swarming the tarmac.

The bullets struck the still spreading pool of fuel and it burst into flame, taking the refueling tank with it. A lake of flame consumed the crowd of roaring Undead.

Jill slammed at the head of the creature stuck in the frame of the door, crunched it to jelly, then knocked it free so it could fall into the lake of fire... and the hatch finally shut completely.

Becky was crying. Alice took her in her arms and looked out the port at the fiery hillside receding below. She was going to Washington, D.C. after all.

26

Tom was looking through the periscope at the sea up above—they were just below the surface, rumbling along south-by-southeast. It was early morning out there. He could see seaweed, gulls, and a floating wreck of a ship—fortunately the ship was a mile to port, so it shouldn't be a problem. He hadn't figured out how to use the sonar yet, and was worried about running into debris..

He heard Dori's unmistakable footsteps, light and quick, on the deck.

"Tom? There's a trap door in the floor of food storage three," she said. "I was looking for some food for dinner and I noticed it. I didn't try to open it. But... what's under there?"

Tom frowned. He didn't remember seeing a trap door in the deck there—but then he hadn't been looking for one. There was a lot about this submarine he didn't know yet.

"Show me," he said.

He followed her down the ladder. She was getting to

be a real sailor, and she slid down the metal banisters like a seasoned pro. He followed the slow way, trying not to bang his head on the sides of the hatch.

Two more ladders and then they were on the level where the galleys and storage were found. She led the way along a narrow corridor and into storage three. At the back, on the deck between high metal shelves crowded with canned goods and boxes of freeze-dried food, was the trap door. It was closed, flush with the deck, and looked to be some kind of maintenance hatch, maybe for electrical connections.

"Doubt there's much under there but wires."

"Can we look?"

"If I can get it open..."

He knelt down, flipped up the latch. There was a little keyboard there, for punching in an access code. According to Umbrella's manual, that was 758666. He typed it in, a green light flicked on, and a click sounded inside the trap door.

Tom lifted the latch and the door swung back, lifted on its own servos. Below were a ladder and a narrow shaft, dropping just about seven feet down to what looked like a glass floor which emanated a mild light.

"Ooh, look Tom!" Dori said.

"Yeah. I didn't see this mentioned in the manual. There was something about a sub-storage unit, but it was marked "No Entry." I assumed it was nuclear fuel or something..."

Suddenly a chill went through him. Could this be, in fact, some kind of plutonium storage hold? He looked around, saw none of the usual radiation warning signs he'd expect to see if there was radioactive material down there.

"Well, this is a risk," he said, "but we need to know as much as we can about this damned Rusky tub. I'm going down!"

"What about me?"

"You want your JudyTech to kick my ass five ways from Sunday? No way you're going down there, not till I find out it's safe, and maybe not even then. Don't you move from that spot."

Grunting as he maneuvered his large, aging frame down the shaft, he descended, working his way down the ladder, barely fitting in the passage. As he did, he felt a deep, icy cold reaching up from below. When he reached the bottom he turned, looked at the glass floor under his feet—and swore blackly to himself.

Under the glass he could see several heads, and the upper bodies of six figures. What had been men, but were Las Plagas Undead. Not the powerful kind like that one he'd seen on the sea floor—these were the regular soldier types that Umbrella had been experimenting with.

They looked inert. Their eyes were cracked open and a sullen red glow seeped out from between the eyelids. He could see frost on the inside of the glass, around the edges, and on the eyelashes of the Undead. Could be they were in some kind of suspended animation—as neatly laid out as frozen chicken legs in a supermarket package.

Zombies under glass, he thought.

They looked for all the world like they'd been stored, like you'd store meat in a freezer. If Umbrella had put them there, then they were being kept to be weapons. Maybe part of a plan to bio-infect rival corporations... sneaking them into a rival base via submarine.

He had to be sure he didn't let them loose. Suppose he hit the controls on the computer, somewhere, and accidentally released them? Tom shook his head, baffled about what to do.

"What is it?" Dori called down impatiently. He almost told her that it was nothing she need concern herself with. But he didn't want to lie to her. She *did* need to be concerned about it. If anything happened, she should know what was going on.

"Come on down and see," he said. "But don't touch anything."

She climbed down the ladder, and looked at the faces under glass.

"Oh!"

"Yeah, oh! Las Plagas zombies, that's what they are. I'm thinking of sealing this up so they can't get out... I mean, if anything wakes them up."

"They're asleep?"

"The cold seems to keep them in some kind of what-you-call-it, suspended animation. Come on, that's enough. Let's get out of here."

Tom watched her climb up the ladder, then climbed up after her, closed and locked the trap door. But he had a strong feeling that wasn't the end of it. Once you opened Pandora's box...

Jack and Uncle Chung were standing on the pier of Avalon's marina, shivering a little in the early morning chill as they gazed out over the channel between the island of Catalina and Los Angeles. There was a boat coming and the sight of it—the possibilities—made his heart thump with excitement.

To their right rocked eight abandoned boats of varying sizes, tied up to the marina's floating slips. To their left was the harbor. Sea gulls gave their eerie cries, flying under the hazy, lowering clouds, and a pelican swam lazily by. Both Jack and Chung had their M1s on straps, over their shoulders.

"Maybe that's what you saw in your dream," Jack said. "Maybe it wasn't a submarine at all."

"Perhaps," Chung said. "These things are not always literal. It could be a symbol... but..." He shook his head. "It was a submarine. When I woke I had the taste for truth in my mouth."

"What's the taste for truth?"

"Something you have to learn, over time. So anyway, it looks like someone is driving that boat. The Undead can drive nothing. Except—on one of the radio transmissions I heard rumors of something, another kind. But I've never seen one capable of driving anything. Or doing anything but clawing and biting."

"So they're not Undead—then we should welcome them!"

"We shall see how happy we are to see them... when we meet them. There are many kinds of men, many kinds of women."

It was a cabin cruiser, throwing a white, bifurcated wake that was a novelty these days. There were so few boats being piloted on the seas anymore, and Jack could just make out a tall gangly man, with a small automatic weapon in hand, at the prow of the boat. Next to him was a woman with wide hips and shoulders, wearing skintight leopard-print pants and a jean-jacket top, a pump shotgun in her hands. Her hair was a blousy bleached corona waving in the wind of their approach.

"Rough customers?" Bim asked, walking up the pier behind them.

"Can't tell," Jack said. "I'm just glad to see anybody."

"Let's move onto the boat, over here," Uncle Chung said, nodding toward the sailboat to their right. It had a superstructure that would offer some cover if they needed it, but Jack didn't see why they should. Why would anyone, really, want to attack you, except for the Undead? That was one thing he'd always figured must be true—survivors must be united in having to fight the Undead. Everybody alive was on the same side now, he figured.

But he didn't know for sure. These were the first new people he'd seen since the last boats had left the island. So he followed Bim and Uncle Chung onto the boat.

"Doesn't it look kind of, I don't know, hostile or something," he said, "if we take up a firing position over here?"

"All in how it's done," Uncle Chung said calmly. He was always calm, no matter what happened. Though he'd wept when he had to shoot the walking corpse of his sister, he had done the shooting calmly.

They stood side by side on the slightly rocking deck of the sailboat, the cabin's superstructure poking up enough to give them cover from the neck down. Silently, fascinated, they watched the battered white and red cabin cruiser chug up to the pier. The lanky guy climbed out and tied up loosely. He was a grimy man, with a bunch of tattoos, in a grimy T-shirt and military trousers tucked into his boots. His gray-brown hair fell greasily to his shoulders. Over one shoulder was a submachine gun on a leather strap.

The woman grinned at them. She had sunken eyes and looked to be missing most of her teeth. Only a couple showed up in that grin. She had tattoos on her neck that seem to have been crossed out. A big man stepped out of the pilot house of the cabin cruiser. He looked Hispanic, was heavyset, almost obese.

How does anyone find enough fattening food to get obese anymore? Jack wondered. *They must've found an old junk-food warehouse.*

The Hispanic man had the number *3* tattooed on his cheek. He had big jug ears, and dangling earrings made of bullet cartridges. He wore a grimy silver-colored track suit and only when he stepped onto the pier did Jack see his weapon—the biggest pistol Jack had ever seen.

"That pistol's a Desert Eagle," Bim muttered. "Where's he get ammo for that thing?"

The three strangers were about thirty feet away, on the other side of the pier, staring. Finally the woman spoke.

"They got a young adult teeny boy, there." She chortled, at that.

"Hey there!" the Hispanic guy said, stepping forward, waving, smiling big. He had gold coating all his teeth, and it glinted in the morning light. "Good to see some real people around! Don't see many!" He had a slight Mexican accent.

"We feel the same way about that!" Uncle Chung said, at once both friendly and noncommittal. Jack noticed that Uncle Chung had taken his M1 off his shoulder, and was holding it in his hands. Reflexively, Jack did the same.

For all the world like a neighbor strolling over to talk to the fellow next door, the big man with the gold teeth started toward them. He had the Desert Eagle dangling in one hand.

"Best wait there, please!" Uncle Chung said, smiling—and he tucked the rifle to his shoulder. He pointed it at the stranger. The big man came to a halt, raising his eyebrows, as if surprised.

"Hey, *que pasa*, Chinese bro!"

"Yeah!" the woman piped up. "We come in peace to your new world and shit!"

The lanky man laughed at that. He slowly but deliberately brought the submachine up so it pointed in the general direction of Uncle Chung—but wasn't threatening enough to spur anyone to open fire.

"You are welcome here!" Uncle Chung said.

"Well, chrissakes I fuckin' hope so!" the lanky, greasy-haired guy said. "We got to stand against the Undead!"

"You are welcome," Uncle Chung said, "as long as you leave your guns on the boat! Just toss them onto the deck. We will escort you in, give you dinner, tell stories, learn much from each other! We can trade supplies."

"Suppose we want to stay on this island?" the big man asked, his voice lower, flat, and dangerous for some reason Jack couldn't quite fathom.

"If the others here agree," Chung said, "you can stay—but only after we get to know you. Starts with dropping weapons!"

"How about if we start by introducin' ourselves?"

the big Hispanic man said. "I'm Paco. This guy here is Roper. The lady there is his woman, Sandra!"

"Ya'll got any speed?" Sandra asked suddenly, licking her lips.

Paco turned and must've given her a dirty look. She scowled at the pier.

"One thing at a goddamn time, *puta*!" he told her. Then he turned back to them. "Sandra, she pick up bad habits, sometime. So—who are you?"

"I am Chung—this is Jack, this fellow here is Bim."

"Any more?" Paco asked, his eyes roaming over the island.

"Perhaps," Chung said. "Where do you come from?"

"Us?" Paco shrugged. "San Diego. Cabo. Lots of places. We can't stay in one place long. The Undead smell us and come...." He sighed. "So, we stay on the boat, mostly. Go in here, go in there. Was six of us but—we had to shoot three. They got bitten."

Chung nodded at that.

"Perfectly understandable. We had to kill many on this island, too."

"Any left? Is this island really free of the Undead?"

Chung hesitated.

"Not that I am aware of," he said.

"Got a lot of ammo here?"

Chung answered noncommittally once more.

"Some."

"They ain't trustin' us, Paco!" the woman said, and she chortled.

"Drop guns, that will add a kilogram to the trust side of the scales," Chung responded.

Paco just chewed his lips and looked at them. The wheels were turning in his head—so it seemed to Jack.

"How about we toss our guns down," Roper said. "All at the same time? You 'n us? We all just put our guns down! I mean—why you got to greet us this way, anyhow?"

"This is our island," Bim said. "We defend it. There are a lot of people took advantage of the chaos, got crazy out there. I heard a lot of reports about that on the short wave." He hesitated. "Back when there were reports on the short wave, anyhow. It's been a while."

"We don't put down our guns," Uncle Chung said with finality—but his voice was calm, reasonable. "Not at all. Not till we learn to trust you. That starts with tossing your weapons down."

"Well, sir," Paco said, "we got no more reason to trust you than you do us. And it doesn't seem right you should hog this island to yourself. It seems like a shame. We could all help each other, *comprende*? But no, huh? Okay. Okay. Come on, Roper. You too, woman. We'll get in the boat and go."

"What?" Sandra said, looking cross-eyed with confusion. "We going to go just like..."

"He said get in the fucking boat, bitch!" Roper said, back-handing her.

She blinked, hardly registering the blow, and muttered something to herself Jack couldn't hear.

They all piled onto the boat, Paco last as he cast off. He murmured to the others, and they moved around the pilot house as he went inside. The engine started up, and he swung the vessel around in a wide circle, as if heading back out to sea.

Jack hadn't had a lot of experience with people, but he knew they weren't leaving that easily. There was too much useful stuff here. And no sign of the

Undead. The island was a great prize...

Paco's boat picked up speed and was quickly out of the harbor, headed out to sea—ostensibly toward Los Angeles.

27

"Jack," Uncle Chung said. "You see those binoculars, hanging on the nail there? On the mast? Yes? Take them up to the masthead. Can you climb up there?"

"Sure..." Jack fetched the binoculars and slung them over his neck. He climbed the mast, using the small rungs, and when he got to the top—surprised at how queasy he felt up here—he held on with one hand and put the binoculars to his eyes with the other.

"Look to see where they're going!" Uncle Chung called. But Jack was way ahead of him. The boat was a pretty good distance off, and it was hard for him to get a clear image in the binoculars, at first. But there they were—

Dammit! The boat swayed as the waves picked up in the rising wind, and the top of the mast yawed sickeningly. His stomach lurched, but he held on, waiting for it to settle... and finally caught the cabin cruiser, almost lost in the haze. It took him a moment to be sure—yes, it was turning.

"It's heading north!" he called.

"Come on down, Jack! And be careful! The wind's picking up."

"I noticed!"

In a minute he was down, stepping gratefully onto the deck.

"You may as well keep those binoculars, if no one objects," Chung said.

"Where you think they're going?"

Bim snorted.

"Those sons of bitches? Seems pretty obvious to me..."

Chung nodded.

"They're going to head north, till we can't see them, then west. They'll wait till dark, cut their lights, and come in from the north to flank us. They'll probably see that beach over there, on that side of the island, and the path going up. They'll work out about where we're likely to be. Could be they've been observing us before now..."

Chung led the way back to the bunker, on the north side. It was on the rocky hillside below the palm-lined, run-down estate of Lony's father, where they made their home. They'd fixed up the bunker in case they had to live in it—if some fresh incursion of the Undead came to the island somehow. It hadn't happened yet. But they were ready.

Lony was waiting for them on the concrete steps leading up to the mouldering old imitation-Frank-Lloyd-Wright estate. He was still muscular, but he was also developing a sag around the middle. He had long blond hair with graying streaks, a weathered face graced by small blue eyes, and a tan—except for the perpetual sunburn on the end of his nose. He had his rifle over his shoulders, and a pair of binoculars in his hand.

"I saw the boat," he said. "And I saw you guys take a defensive post. We in trouble?"

"Maybe," Bim said. "They didn't want to disarm, so we sent them away. We think they're going to circle around and hit us tonight."

"They seem like rough characters?" Lony asked. "You know, even before the Big Mess, I never would've trusted a one of them." Now, of course, no one trusted anyone they didn't know like a blood brother.

The day wore on. Lony went hunting, and the rest of them stood watches. Chung and Jack played chess. Chung pretended to lose. They ate a light lunch of pickled fish and turtle's eggs. Jack kept scanning the sea with his binoculars, but didn't see the cabin cruiser, or a submarine. He was looking for both.

He helped Chung repair the wall around the lower part of the bunker, and Chung read to him, after, from the *Dhammapada*.

They ate dinner, though Jack had a flutter in his stomach that wouldn't let him eat much of the duck that Lony had shot, or the fish, or the spinach from Chung's garden. Soon as he could, just after sunset, he went out on the deck of the blocky, angular mansion, and sat out there on a folding aluminum chair, watching...

So it was that he was the first to see the dark shape against the glimmering water. Just as predicted, the cabin cruiser was coming in without its running lights. Coming slow and quiet.

They'd already worked out what their positions would be. Chung and Jack would be in the concrete bunker, with their guns pointing out through the half-crumbled old observation slits. Lony and Bim were positioned behind the rocks on either side of the path.

They'd left the solar-powered lights burning on the mansion, above the bunker, to draw the pirates' attention away from the bunker, where they waited in darkness.

Pirates. That's what Chung called them. He spoke of having to defend his father's fishing boat from Malaysian pirates, off Shanghai, decades before.

They sat in chairs, near the slits, smelling the sea air, watching and waiting...

"I hope Bim doesn't do anything dumb," Jack whispered.

"Yes." Uncle Chung knew what he meant. Bim was known for reckless acts of bravery. He liked to be the lion defending his mate... Lony. Although really, Lony was stronger and faster and a better shot.

The pirates used the predicted entry to the island, coming up the zigzag path, hunched low, but visible in the waning moonlight.

"I only see two of them," Jack whispered.

"Yes. We must be vigilant. Perhaps that is his strategy..."

The woman came first, walking with birdlike steps, almost hopping sometimes, while Roper seemed to weave along like a snake, curving this way and that on the path as he looked around. The submachine gun in his hands caught the moonlight—the woman still had the shotgun.

Then the shout came.

"Drop your weapons. You're covered!" Clearly Bim's voice.

"Drop your weapons and you can go in peace!" Lony shouted.

"Hee, fuck you!" Sandra shouted, and she fired the shotgun where she thought the shout was coming from. Shotgun pellets ricocheted from the rocks, striking sparks visible in the dimness.

Bim returned fire, *pop pop pop* with his rifle. The woman yelped. Roper fired that way with his submachine gun, a short spurt.

"Should we fire?" Jack asked. He'd never killed a *living* person before.

"Not yet—give them chance to be discouraged," Chung said. "Don't want to give away where we are. Watch for the third one…"

"One last chance! You can have peace in your lives!" That was so Lony, his saying that. "Get back down to your boat!"

"Where is that third one?" Chung wondered aloud. "Wait…"

He aimed his rifle carefully through the slit. Jack looked, trying to aim, to find the target…

Chung fired, twice, and someone yelled.

A big crack, that pistol of Paco's, Jack guessed, and Lony yelled, "Shit!"

"Out on the wall!" Chung hissed.

He and Jack emerged from the bunker's side door, ran to the wall they'd shored up that day, knelt behind it. Jack didn't wait for permission—bullets were humming by over his head, a spray of them from the submachine gun. He could see the muzzle flash as Roper backed down the hill, firing as he went.

Jack aimed and fired, his heart thudding louder than his rifle. He squeezed off three semi-auto rounds—and saw Roper stumble and go down.

A shotgun blast—and a bee-swarm of pellets buzzed over their head. Chung returned fire—and Sandra went down, crying and groaning.

"He's over here!" Lony yelled, firing his rifle—they couldn't see what he was shooting at.

"I can't shoot—I'll hit Lony!" Chung said.

Then they saw Bim running through the brush, shouting, "Lony! Lony!"

The tongue of flame from the Desert Eagle and Bim shouted in pain. They lost sight of him as he fell. Another tongue of flame from behind the Desert Eagle. Two more. Definitely an M1—Lony firing.

Then silence, except for muffled groaning...

"I think... I think Lony got him," Chung said. "You wait here."

Not a chance. Jack let Chung go on ahead, down the hill, then followed, a little ways back, a round chambered, ready to shoot to protect his uncle, if he had to.

But the woman was dying and Roper was dead. Shot through the chest, one bullet for each lung.

Paco, who'd used his friends to draw out the gunmen, had tried to flank Lony—and had succeeded, but he'd missed his shot, and gotten distracted by Bim. He'd shot Bim through the upper thigh—just missing the bone.

Lony had shot Paco...

The woman died before dawn, though Chung did try to save her.

Jack couldn't sleep. He stood watch for a while,

then came in and kept an eye on Bim while Lony rested. Chung came in just after the woman died.

At about dawn, Bim stopped groaning and slept for awhile. When he woke, he was a little feverish, but Chung felt sure he'd live. The bullet had missed the artery, but the round was so powerful, on the big pistol, that the shock of the impact had knocked him out, then kept him yawing between consciousness and waking. Finally, he sat up in his bedroom—ignoring Chung who told him to lie back down—and spoke raspily.

"I made up my mind about something," he said.

"What, babe?" Lony asked.

"We don't let anyone come anywhere near this island. We see them—we shoot at them before they get near. Anybody alive out there—what's the chances you can trust them? Most of them are going to be scum..."

Lony nodded. Chung said nothing.

Jack went outside, blinking blearily around in the first gray light. Chung joined him.

"Kind of scared?" Chung asked.

Jack shrugged. "More disappointed."

Chung nodded. "First people—bad people."

"And I killed one. Never killed a real person before."

"All this is a reminder," Chung said, "That there is more than one kind of living dead. There are those who are not infected. Who are not mad cannibals. But they, too, are soulless. They surrendered their soul—it was eaten by their selfishness. We try to have compassion for them, but we must preserve life—good human life. We must preserve those who have not abandoned their souls..." He shrugged. "You did the

right thing. It is not so Buddhist, to kill such men.
But it is what I believe we had to do. It's not always
possible to be perfectly compassionate." He said,
again, "There is more than one kind of living dead..."

Jack was staring out to sea. Was that another boat,
out there? Or some kind of big flotsam?

"What's that? Sticking up out there?" He raised
his binoculars to his eyes. "Oh, man! Chung—I think
that's a submarine!"

28

"We're on the ground again?" Alice asked, waking up. The quiet of the helicopter, the muting of its engines, had awakened her.

She had said it aloud, but Becky—sitting on the cot's edge—had watched her lips.

"More fuel," she signed.

"I hope it's safer than the last place..." Alice unstrapped herself from the cot and got up, not feeling as much pain as the last time. She stretched, and the girl handed her a can of chocolate-flavored nutritive fluid. She drank deeply, looking out the port.

They were up high—perhaps a rooftop. Curious, she went to the hatch, down the ramp, and they walked out into the cool morning. Wind blew across the ravaged buildings of a city. She heard a muted growling, the moaning of the Undead, far below.

They were on an aluminum-sheathed surface. A circle was painted there—a helipad, she suspected. Fuel tanks stood to one side. The guards in paramilitary togs stood near the tanks, and a technician was monitoring the refueling at the rear of the helicopter.

"This was an old Umbrella building," Jill said, smiling wryly as she walked around the back of the helicopter. "Wesker's helipad in this area..."

"We're in D.C.?

"Not yet. We're going to wait here a while, refuel, and then go to the LZ in Washington. This is Baltimore."

"Why the wait? It doesn't take that long to fuel."

"There have been developments, and they're trying to establish a safer LZ for us. We might be here an hour or two, even three, but we'll be heading over there today."

"Jill..." Alice stepped up close, and lowered her voice. "Look—do we really want to follow through on this?"

"Ada's up and about. Leon, too. You want to get into it with them? Especially her—she's a pretty tough chick. Not to mention..." She looked at the guards.

Alice shrugged.

"I like Ada. I don't want to fight her unless I have to. But if I have to..."

They were speaking in low tones, barely audible even to each other.

"She's determined to take us to Washington, D.C, Alice," Jill said. "I know how you feel. Wesker's there. But supposedly he wants to be an ally."

"Until he doesn't need us," she replied. "Then what? Jill, the guy tried to eat me. Tried to actually, physically, *consume* me."

"I know. I heard." Jill laughed softly. "Yeah, that'll put you off a person, alright. But think of it this way—what's left out there?" She gestured vaguely to include the whole world. "Where would we go? We'd be up against hell, wherever we went. At least there's some kind of base to work from in D.C. And maybe if Wesker's there, we'll find the opportunity to take him down for good. If we wait for the chance, you know?"

Alice thought about it. It was logical. But the revulsion she felt was strong.

Becky walked up to them then.

"What are you talking about?" she signed.

Alice smiled, and replied.

"Talking about where to go now."

"Did you decide?" she asked.

"I guess we'll go see... the White House."

Tom was up on the "sail," the submarine's conning tower, gazing almost rapturously at Santa Catalina. Dori and Judy climbed up the ladder to stand beside him.

"Ladies, look at that!" He waved with a flourish. "I think that's Catalina, right there! I don't see any Undead, and if it's clear of them... Oh, that'd be too much to hope for."

"I'd love to get off this—" Judy began. But she didn't finish saying it. She was interrupted by a bullet.

The shot cracked off one of the transmission fixtures on the conning tower. They heard the echoing bang of the shot a moment later.

"Get down!" Tom said, flattening.

They all dropped down, with the periscopes, pipes, and antennae providing good cover.

"Dori, get back inside," Judy whispered.

"If she tries, she might be too exposed," Tom said urgently.

"Someone shot at us?" Dori said. Her voice was quavering—that bullet had wounded her hopes.

"Yeah, kid, they did," Tom said. "That's the bad news. The good news is, most of the Undead can't shoot. Would there be Las Plagas on that island? Not hardly."

"So that means regular people..." Judy said.

"Got to be." Another bullet cracked by overhead. "And they're not even trying very hard to hit us. I got a feeling all this is to scare us off."

Someone yelled from shore. It was too far to hear what they were saying, but the tone wasn't friendly. Tom peeked over the edge with his binoculars. He could see something that looked like a weathered old concrete bunker, and solar power panels on a multilevel, modern-style house. He panned back and forth, looking at the beaches, what he could see of the harbor.

No movement, except birds.

"There really don't seem to be any Undead on that island," he said wonderingly. "They'd be attracted to the noise, and would be out here slaverin' after us on the beaches."

"We can't go to an island occupied by people who want to kill us," Judy said.

"I don't think they're serious," Tom said. "They really seem to be trying to scare us off. If they were scumbags, then they'd want us to come into the island so they could kill and rob us. Take all our stuff." He made up his mind. "I'm going to take a chance, here, Judy. I've got a feeling about this..."

"Tom—don't."

But he got up to a crouch, and rushed to the back of the sail. Climbed down a ladder to the Zodiac-style rubber boat that was tied up there, under a tarp. The conning tower protected him from being seen by whoever was shooting at them. His hands shaking, heart pounding, wondering if he were being a damned fool, he untied the black-rubber boat, and lowered it down into the water. Then he kept hold of it, and slipped down the side of the hull.

It was awkward climbing onto it—he nearly overturned it, but stabilized himself. The battery-powered engine had been provided by Umbrella, and he switched it on—it hummed. He put it in neutral, then unzipped his coveralls, and pulled off his T-shirt. The tee would have to do for a white flag. He put the coveralls back on, skin prickly with the chill wind off the sea.

Tom pulled in the line then took hold of the rudder, put the engine on drive, and took a deep breath. Was it the waves tossing the boat making him queasy—or fear?

"Tom! Wait!" Judy called to him.

"Got to go this alone!" he said. "Hold on…" Then he headed the boat out, over the choppy waves, toward the island, his T-shirt in his right hand.

He got a few yards past the forward end of the sub before they started shooting again. Two rifle shots cracked, the bullets kicking up the water just in front of him. He could see smoke drifting from a firing slit on the bunker. Another muddled yell of warning echoed across to him.

He licked his lips, took the white T-shirt in his right hand, raised it over his head and waved it. He raised his left hand to show it was empty.

"No weapons!" he yelled, loud as he could. "Got no gun here! Peace talk!"

* * *

"You shouldn't even be out of bed, Bim!" Lony said. "Shooting at people... you might have an infection, or you're gonna get one and we don't have but a few doses of antibiotics left."

Lony was sitting stiffly in a chair behind the firing slit of the bunker, his leg bandaged, rifle in hand, glaring out at the sea.

"They're a submarine," Jack said. He had come in with Lony. "Why are you shooting at a submarine? I mean, they might shoot a missile at us or something!"

"I saw 'em in the binoculars," Bim said through gritted teeth. "They're not military people!" There was sweat beading on his forehead. "Look what happened when those other losers, came to the island. We have to keep everyone away!"

Jack peered through another slit.

"One of them is coming in a boat!"

"Yeah," Bim growled. "I tried to warn him back. I'm gonna try to hit that boat..."

But then Jack saw someone else, below. It was Uncle Chung, walking across the beach, waving.

"Chung's down there!" Lony said, looking over Bim's shoulder. "Hold your damn fire!"

Jack grabbed up his rifle and ran outside, down the path toward the beach. He almost flew down the hillside. Puffing, he reached Chung's side. Saw that he wasn't armed. Uncle Chung looked at him disapprovingly.

"You should not be here," he said. "Not safe yet."

"You're the one came down without a gun."

"Safer, sometimes. It all depends. That man does not appear to be armed." He pointed at the man tooling slowly toward them in the black-rubber boat.

"He could have a gun down in that boat, somewhere you can't see."

"I don't think so. I would have..." He shrugged. "Anyway, don't point your gun at him. Is Bim still preparing to shoot?"

"I think Lony's got him in hand now. He was pretty freaked out by that bunch that came at us before"

"Yes. And wounded. A big wound."

They watched as the red-faced, middle-aged man with the broad, smiling mouth came toward them, his little boat bobbing in the surf. Every so often he raised both hands, waving the white flag—it looked like a yellowed T-shirt.

"Don't shoot!" he called.

"I'm going to cover him, Chung, but I won't fire unless... you know."

Chung looked at him, then nodded.

"Very well. It cannot hurt."

Jack raised the M1, sighted along it.

"Just keep your hands where we can see them and I won't shoot!" he called.

"No problem!" the man shouted back.

Three minutes more and he was dragging the rubber boat up onto the sand, then turning to face them, breathing hard and smiling.

"Look at you! You don't look like the criminals Judy was worried about!"

Chung chuckled.

"It's you we worry about," he said. "Who are you?"

"Oh, name's Tom. We stole that submarine! What do you think of that!"

Jack's mouth dropped open.

"You stole it? From who!"

"Umbrella Corporation. It's an old Soviet sub. I was barely able to get it moving the right way—but we got it here."

"How many are you?" Chung asked.

"Just three of us." Tom looked like he was thinking of adding something more, and then shut his mouth firmly.

"There's something you just decided not to say," Chung observed mildly. "Best tell us now."

Tom sighed.

"There's some frozen... things in that boat. Las Plagas. I think they're in some kind of dormant state. I haven't figured out how to do away with 'em safely like... They're locked away in a kind of... freezer thing. Under a deck."

Jack found those remarks hard to digest, but Chung didn't seem surprised by this.

"Ah. Well. I am convinced you are no danger to us. You may bring the other two over. No one must be armed, not at all. We will not harm you."

Tom looked at Chung closely, for a long moment. Finally he nodded.

"Okay. If they agree to come, I'll bring them. I'm going to push to take a chance, 'cause it seems to me... is it true?"

"Is what true?" Jack asked.

"That you have no Undead on this island? I mean, it just seems that way to me. I figure we'd have seen 'em by now."

"There are none," Chung said. "We put them all out of their misery."

Tom nodded, and looked pleased.

"Well, I'll be back soon as I can..."

"Um, can I come and help?" Jack asked.

"No," Chung said. "You wait here. With me."

They waited—Jack in a fever of impatience—and watched as the boat went back out to the submarine. They could see Tom arguing with someone on the big conning tower. Was that a woman up there? They talked for a long time, but at last the boat was on its way back—and with the man were two women.

Chung looked at his nephew and chuckled.

"Strange! You look very pale! Do women frighten you?"

"What? Pale? Fright... what?"

Chung just laughed.

The boat arrived, and Jack and Chung helped Tom pull it partly onto the beach. The two women clambered out, ankle deep in the surf. Impulsively, Jack stuck out his hand to help the younger one come up onto the beach. She stared at him, looked at the rifle over his shoulder, at his face, at his outstretched hand. She was a teenage girl, slender, with large brown eyes. Her lips looked soft and full. Both women, he saw, were wearing sailor suits that didn't fit them.

At last she took his hand and he helped her onto the beach. She quickly detached her hand from his, and turned to look at the woman. Tom was helping her out of the boat.

"My name's Jack—this is Chung," Jack said, looking at the girl. He felt like a hot wind was blowing through him.

She looked at him, and swallowed.

"I'm... Dori." She said in a small voice. "That's JudyTech."

"Judy... teck?"

"I'll explain that later, kid," Tom said. "Any more on the island we can meet?"

"Only two others," Jack said.

Chung frowned, probably not wanting to give Tom that much information. Chung seemed to want to trust these people—but he was being careful.

Jack simply didn't care.

"Come on," he said, smiling at Dori. "Come and meet them. And... welcome to Catalina."

29

"Two minutes to the LZ," the pilot said as they flew through the night to over what had been the nation's capital.

Alice was standing with Becky, just behind the cockpit of the helicopter, as they approached the heart of Washington, D.C. She went to a port and looked down, trying to see what kind of shape the city was in. The lights of the choppers swung over the Lincoln Memorial, and as they swung past, the monument looked quite intact. So did the Washington Monument. Fires from slowly burning gas lines illuminated portions of the city as they banked past the Capitol Building. That particular tourist attraction hadn't come through the apocalypse as well. The dome was cracked and burned; the windows were blackened, the glass shattered. Bodies lay scattered about, outside, mostly chewed down to the bone.

She saw a great many Undead surging about, but it was hard to see how many there were, in the darkness. Then they swung around over the Potomac

River—which was choked with floating bodies—and back toward the White House. A dark mass surged on Pennsylvania Avenue, but it was hard to make out what it was, with the glare of lights from the White House. The grounds were dotted with spotlights, all watching the skies, probing the clouds. Most of the eighteen acres around the White House were crowded with missile emplacements, helipads, tanks, and bunkers.

There were only a few trees left standing. The grass of the great lawn was overgrown in some places, trampled and crushed to the dirt in others. Flower beds were ground away under tank treads, and around the grounds enormous barricades had been erected, a new fortress, topped with razor wire and guard posts.

The White House itself seemed more or less intact but there were gun emplacements on the roof, and more spotlights that locked onto the helicopter as it descended toward the grounds.

The pilot was busily talking into the mike, getting permission to land, reciting code phrases. Then they were spiraling down, headed into a helipad.

Alice shook her head, looking at all the armed men, the weapons, around that helipad. She was getting into something it was going to be hard to get out of. Had she made a big mistake, bringing Becky here?

She'd had a choice—she could have risked both their lives to escape. Now she was stuck.

But Jill was right. *Wait and watch. Look for your chance...*

The helicopter settled on the helipad with a double thump of finality. The rotors whined, and slowed. Then a big man with flat-top hair, a scar down his cheek, and paramilitary togs stood outside the hatch of the chopper as it lowered to become a ramp. He had an assault rifle hung over his shoulder on a strap. Alice thought she remembered him.

"Grady?" she asked, as she came down the ramp.

"Yeah, Alice. It's Grady," he rumbled. He'd worked in the lower echelons of Umbrella Security at one time, under her authority.

"You still with Umbrella?" she asked, but she was pretty sure she knew the answer.

"Would I be working here?" he responded. "Nah. Come on—I got to get you and your little entourage into the big white place. We're gonna have some doctors look you over, see what needs to be patched up. Might even feed you. Then you're all going to see the Big Guy..."

The Big Guy?

Wesker.

Storage hold three seemed kind of spooky to Jack. He wasn't sure why. It was just a ship's hold, filled with shelves. Most of the stored goods were gone now— he, Lony, Tom, Judy, and Dori had spent most of the day unloading anything useful from the submarine. They were especially glad to get the medical supplies. By the time they were done, the only thing left on the shelves were a few big plastic bottles of engine-cleaning fluid.

Tom and Jack were alone now—Lony had gone back to the island, with Dori and Judy, to show them around, and to check on Bim.

"You think that fella that shot at us is ever going to

be... you know, friendly, at all?" Tom asked, as they walked between the shelves. Tom was carrying the Desert Eagle they'd taken off Paco, and it was fully loaded. They'd made up their minds to trust him.

Jack had his M1.

"Sure, he's a good guy. He was wounded and mad and not in the mood to trust anyone."

"Oh, I don't blame him, the shape the world's in now..."

"What are we looking for, here?"

Tom stopped, and hunkered over the floor.

"Right here—got to flip this back, punch in this code... And there she goes."

Jack felt a sick feeling of dread as the trap door lifted up, whirring on its servos, to show the eerie light below.

"That's what I was afraid of," Tom said.

"What?"

"I have to have a closer look to be sure..."

He climbed down the ladder, and Jack climbed after him. Both of them stared through the glass of the container, flush with the floor, containing the Las Plagas Undead.

"You see?" Tom said. "There's no ice. It's not as cold in here. See, just before we got here we had problems with the ship's power. It just failed—and I had to go to some emergency diesel back ups. And meanwhile, this thing... wasn't refrigerated."

Jack crouched down and looked closely.

"Aren't they dead?"

"I don't know—but I don't think so. When they got that glow in their eyes, the spark of life is still there. And there it is!" Jack could see the red glow seeping from between the eyelids of the recumbent Las Plagas, and jumped a little when he saw those eyelids twitch.

"Oh, shit. I think I saw one blink."

"Yeah. Well, I got that cabin cruiser tied up out back—we'll see if I can get this thing headed out to sea. You still willing to stand guard while I do that?"

"Yeah."

His mouth was dry. His hands were sweaty and cold. But Jack didn't want to seem like a coward. This man was Dori's friend. If he impressed Tom—maybe that would impress Dori.

And he'd do anything to impress Dori. It had been love at first sight. Maybe the only sight of a young woman he'd get for years... if ever.

"Okay. But you don't wait down here. Come on." He led the way back up the ladder, and they closed the trap door. "Let's shove some of these shelves down over the trap door," Tom suggested. "And whatever else we can find. Those fire extinguishers, that box of bolts there—just pile up the weight."

In twenty minutes they'd got it done. The room was a wreck, its shelves, and everything else they could find, piled up on the trap door.

"That should hold them," Jack said, though he wasn't sure. From what Tom had told him about those things...

"Alright, keep an eye on it. I'm gonna turn this thing around, and set it up to sink out to sea."

Jack nodded, and Tom left the hold.

Back in the attack center, Tom was dismayed to see he could only get a few of the systems online. The main batteries had been corroded, and he hadn't been able to recharge them. The reactors weren't pumping, and he couldn't figure out why. Luckily there was the diesel backup.

He directed the submarine to back up, then to swing slowly about till it was pointed west, out into the Pacific Ocean. He put it on top speed—wanted it to get as far from the island as possible before it went down—and tapped the controls to open up the valves for the ballast. Then he found the override on the hatches, which would keep them open even as the ship was submerging.

SCUTTLE ENGAGED

The notice began blinking on the control panel. He'd set it to start sinking in about thirty minutes.

Now he just had to wait...

Jack leaned against the bulkhead, shifting uncomfortably as the minutes passed. He'd been there nearly half an hour, and could feel the sub moving. They must've left the island some distance behind by now.

There was no sound from the trap door so far, but the room felt as if it was waiting for something.

He told himself it was foolish to feel spooked. There was no way the Las Plagas, even if they woke completely up, could get out through a locked trap door and past all that debris.

He really had to pee. He couldn't quite bring himself to pee on the floor, even though he knew the submarine was going to be scuttled soon, if all went well. The men's head was down the corridor... he'd just make it quick.

He hurried out through the hatch to the corridor, down to the head, rushed in and found a urinal. He got through it as quick as he could, and zipped up, picked up his rifle, stepped into the corridor—and then heard the banging from storage three.

"Oh, shit!"

Jack ran back—and looked through the hatch just in time to see the blockage they'd amassed, exploding upward, shelves and boxes and other debris flying as if a bomb had gone off under them. A plastic jug of engine cleaner rolled to his feet...

The trap door was up, bent from its hinges—and a man was climbing out into view. Jack was amazed. Those things were way stronger than he'd thought.

The man stepped onto the deck, kicked debris aside, and turned toward Jack. Its eyes glowed red, its body was swollen—just a little too big for its soldier's clothing. Its face was veiny, its hands clawed...

Jack found himself unable to move; staring with fascination into those gleaming red eyes. Then the thing started toward him.

He raised the rifle, flicked off the safety, tucked the butt into his shoulder and fired. And fired again. And again...

With each bullet the Las Plagas rocked back... but it didn't stop.

And another one came climbing up into view. He fired, emptying his clip—not seeming to have much effect, though he hit one of them right in the head.

"Shit shit *shit*!"

Jack looked down at the big bottle of cleanser, picked it up, then slammed the hatch shut on the hold. He spun the wheel—but didn't know how to lock them in, if it could be done at all.

He ran down the corridor, to the ladder. Encumbered by his rifle and the bottle of fluid, which was a full two gallons, he went clumsily up to the next deck. He heard the creak of a door opening, down below, and moved all the faster.

When he got to the attack center, Tom was just coming out.

"We're on our way—whoa, what's wrong, kid?"

"They busted out," Jack said. "I shot two of them, but it didn't slow 'em down much."

"Yeah, you need a bigger caliber weapon than that to bring 'em down." He looked at what Jack was carrying. "What's with the jug there?"

"I don't know—it says 'danger flammable.' I just thought..."

"Bring it!"

They hurried to the ladder, climbed up, then up another, eventually emerging onto the deck below the conning tower.

"Good thinking, bringing that stuff, Jack," Tom said. "Open it up. I got a lighter, haven't used it in a year, hope it's still got some fluid in it." He tore a piece of cloth from his already-torn trouser leg, stuffed it into the opening of the plastic bottle.

They could hear the snarling Las Plagas coming up the ladder, from below.

And the submarine, heading west, was beginning to go under. Water was washing around their ankles.

Tom fumbled at the lighter.

"Dammit!"

He stumbled, and dropped it into the water.

Frantically, Jack felt around under the surging, rising waters, hoping the lighter hadn't already been washed overboad. His hand closed over it, and he gave it to Tom, who wiped it off. At that moment a Las Plagas reached the top of the ladder, moving into the entrance chamber just inside the hatch.

Tom snapped the lighter, again, again—and *finally* it lit. He held the blue flame to the chemical-soaked cloth, and it caught instantly.

"Ha!"

He tossed the big plastic jug through the hatch— and it exploded, inside, almost instantly. The Las Plagas was covered in burning fluid, shrieking, falling back down the ladder onto his fellow. The fire dripped and spread...

"Come on, Jack!" Tom splashed along the submerging deck, back to a line that was fixed to a cleat over the rudder. The submarine was going down faster now, and they untied the line. Tom took hold of it and Jack jumped into the water, swimming the few yards to the drifting cabin cruiser. He climbed up the rope ladder that hung over its side, and went forward, pulling the line in, helping Tom get aboard.

"We got to get this thing out of here, so we don't get sucked down with the sub!" Tom shouted.

But Jack was already starting the engine, and he turned it back toward Catalina, tearing full throttle toward the island. He only looked back once, to see the submarine still heading out to sea, just the top of its conning tower showing.

And then it vanished under the waves...

* * *

That evening, the island of Catalina witnessed a small party. They used the old mansion's solar power supply to rev up the sound system. Chung danced to an old Blue Oyster Cult song, "Dancing in the Ruins," and Dori and Jack watched him, Jack a little embarrassed at the old man's creaky dancing.

"I like Chung," Dori whispered. "He's... the most gentle person I've ever met." After a moment she added, "But then, I haven't met that many people. I'm a... I should tell you about it, I guess..." She seemed uncomfortable, and he didn't quite know what to do.

"You want to take a walk with me—on the beach? You can tell me what you want, and leave out what you want. I'm just glad you're here."

"Okay," she said shyly.

They went out the door. As they did, Jack noticed that Judy and Tom were dancing, now, too, Tom with his arms around her. Bim was on the deck, lying on a lounge chair, with Lony sitting beside him. They waved as Jack and Dori went out.

They took a long, long walk, under the moonlight on the beach... and when they came back they were holding hands.

30

Alice, Ada, Becky, Jill Valentine, and Leon were led by Grady and two other guards, through the war torn White House. At times they heard explosions, some distant, others too close for comfort. The floor rocked, and the lights flickered. They walked past portraits of presidents and beautiful old furniture, their feet quiet on the carpet.

Grady stopped at a door flanked by soldiers, knocked, listened, then opened it. Alice went in, but the guards kept the rest from following.

She knew the room—the Oval Office. And sitting at the president's desk, dressed in black leather from head to toe, hair slicked back, dark shades covering his eyes... was Albert Wesker.

"Wesker," Alice said, nodding once. "Making yourself at home?"

Wesker rose from behind the presidential desk and came casually around toward her.

"I must say, it does have a certain ease to it..."

Then he struck.

Lightning-fast, he stabbed Alice in the neck with a syringe. The high-tech device instantly injected her with a red fluid. Alice screamed in fury and frustration—she knocked his hand away, but it was too late. The infected fluid was traveling like a blinding flash of electricity through her nervous system, making her arch her back with agony.

She trembled, and as the trembling became shaking, she fell to her knees, rocking back and forth as waves of pain and heat alternated when they swept through her.

"What... was in there?" she demanded through gritted teeth.

Wesker smiled down at her.

"You were the only one to successfully bond with the T-virus. To fully realize your powers." He gestured with a magisterial flourish. "Well, now I have need of you. The *old* you. You are the weapon...

"Come with me," he continued.

He led the way to a stairs, and up. They climbed, floor after floor—Wesker, Alice, Becky, Ada, Leon, and Jill—until they reached a hallway just under the roof. They followed the hall to a door at the end, where they saw a sign.

SECURITY / OBSERVATION

Wesker nodded to the guard there, and they all went through, then up another set of steps, through a small structure on the roof of the building. Finally they were standing atop the White House roof, behind the barricades and razor wire, near gun emplacements and watchful guards.

He led the way to the edge of the roof, where they commanded a good view of what had been the front lawn, and Pennsylvania Avenue.

"A lot has changed in the past weeks," Wesker said. "This is the last that remains of us... of the human race itself."

Alice could have argued with that. The world was a big place. There would be other survivors. But still— he wasn't far wrong.

"It seems we are bonded against a common foe," Wesker continued. "This is why we needed you back. The ultimate weapon..."

Alice stared at him.

I'm the ultimate weapon? It was an impossible concept to grasp. *He's insane.* But still she said nothing.

At Wesker's signal, the spotlights swung down to illuminate the streets. He gestured out toward the Avenue, and as Alice looked that way, her eyes adjusted. She felt a sick shock ripple through her...

"This," Wesker said, "is humanity's last stand."

Thousands of them out there. No... there were *hundreds* of thousands of them.

The Undead. Surging against the walls of the makeshift fortress around the White House. Troops on the barriers by the Avenue were using flamethrowers to try to keep them back. The creatures fell, burning and thrashing—but others clambered over their charred bodies and charged at the walls.

Rocket launchers coughed, and shells exploded amongst the Undead. Their bodies flew to pieces, and yet more came to replace them, surging from the inky darkness that lay out past the lights. As if the darkness itself were spawning the endless horde.

"...the final conflict..." Wesker said.

A burst of lights came stabbing down from the circling choppers, and in it Alice saw that she'd been wrong in thinking that there were hundreds of thousands of Undead out there.

There were *millions* of them.

And there was every kind of Undead in the horde; every perversely transfigured mutation. There were Lickers, mutated dogs, Executioners, Giant Spiders, all the creatures of the apocalypse, joined together in a vast mindless army. It was an army without a commander—unless its commander was hunger itself, the mad rapacious furious unstoppable hunger to kill and consume that burned within each of the monsters.

The millions of Undead surrounded the White House. The last bastion of civilization, under siege...

"...the beginning of the end..." Wesker continued softly.

And then, as a helicopter flew overhead, using a prow-mounted turret gun to strafe the mobs, to keep them back from the barricades, things Alice had never seen before began to rise up, flapping on leather wings from the shadowy corners of the restless crowd of zombies...

Dark, winged creatures, they were, a cloud of them, rising up from the horde. A storm of fangs and claws, they swarmed over the helicopter, clustering on it, screeching in fury, tearing at its mechanisms... and the helicopter came tumbling down to crash in a ball of fire.

Alice shuddered. But she also felt the new strength in her. She felt the promise of that strength, and the promise of battle. An epic battle to end this dark journey at last.

It was coming, and she would be its spear point.

It was all down to her...

Alice.

ACKNOWLEDGMENTS

With thanks to Steve Saffel, Cath Trechman, Nick Landau, Vivian Cheung, Tim Whale, Natalie Laverick and Elizabeth Bennett at Titan Books, and Johannes Schlichting, Franz Trosthammer and Kat Kleiner at Constantin Film Development.

ABOUT THE AUTHOR

John Shirley's novels include *Everything is Broken,* the *A Song Called Youth* cyberpunk trilogy (omnibus released in 2012), *Bleak History, Demons, City Come A-Walkin'* and *The Other End.* His short story collection *Black Butterflies* won the Bram Stoker Award, and was chosen by *Publishers Weekly* as one of the best books of the year. His new story collection is *In Extremis: The Most Extreme Short Stories of John Shirley.* His stories have been included in three *Year's Best* anthologies.

For more fantastic fiction from Titan Books in the
areas of sci-fi, fantasy, steampunk, alternate history,
mystery and crime, as well as tie-ins to hit movies,
TV shows and videogames:

VISIT OUR WEBSITE
TITANBOOKS.COM

FOLLOW US ON TWITTER
@TITANBOOKS